THE
BURGLAR
IN THE
LIBRARY

The Bernie Rhodenbarr Mysteries

Burglars Can't Be Choosers
The Burglar in the Closet
The Burglar Who Liked to Quote Kipling
The Burglar Who Studied Spinoza
The Burglar Who Painted Like Mondrian
The Burglar Who Traded Ted Williams
The Burglar Who Thought He Was Bogart
The Burglar in the Library

THE
BURGLAR
IN THE
LIBRARY

A BERNIE RHODENBARR MYSTERY

LAWRENCE BLOCK

NO EXIT PRESS

June 2002

This edition published by No Exit Press,
18 Coleswood Road, Harpenden, Herts, AL5 1EQ

www.noexit.co.uk

Copyright © Lawrence Block 1997

First No Exit publication 1998

A CIP catalogue record for this book is available from the British Library.

ISBN 1-84243-052-1 The Burglar In The Library

2 4 6 8 10 9 7 5 3 1

Printed by Bookmarque

For PETER STRAUB

The author is pleased to acknowledge the contribution of the Ragdale Foundation, of Lake Forest, Illinois, where this book was begun, and of John B. Keane's public house in Listowel, County Kerry, where it was exhaustively contemplated.

ONE

At three in the afternoon on the first Thursday in March, I got Barnegat Books settled in for the weekend. I dragged my table of bargain books inside, closed the door, and turned the cardboard sign in the window from OPEN to CLOSED. I ran the cash-register tape—the work of a moment, alas—and took the checks to my desk in the back room, where I filled out a deposit slip and prepared a mail deposit. I returned with a box a little over a foot in length. It was shaped like a little house in a child's drawing, peaked roof and all, with a handle where the chimney ought to be. I opened the hinged top, set it on the floor, and looked around for Raffles.

He was in the window, treating himself to a few rays. I called his name, which might have worked if he'd been a dog, but he's not and it didn't. Raffles is a cat, a declawed unmanned tailless gray tabby, and if he even knows his name he's not letting on. True to form, he didn't stir at the sound of my voice, but lay motionless in what little sunlight there was.

So I crumpled a sheet of paper, and that worked. We have a training ritual that involves my hurling paper balls for him to run down and kill. It probably looks like a game to the casual observer, but it's serious business, designed to sharpen his mousing skills. I guess it's working; I stopped finding gnawed book spines and suspicious organic matter on my shelves the day he moved in.

I threw the ball of paper and he was off and running. He had it before it stopped rolling, sank the memory of his claws deep into it, took it in his mouth, shook it fiercely to and fro, and left it for dead.

A dog would have brought it back so I could throw it again. A cat wouldn't dream of it. "Good job," I said, and crumpled a fresh sheet, and he made another clean kill. I congratulated him again, prepared a third paper ball, and tossed it gently into the open cat carrier.

He looked at it. Then he looked at me, and then he looked at the floor.

A few minutes later there was a knock on my door. "We're closed," I called out without looking. My eyes were on Raffles, who had removed himself to an open spot in the Philosophy & Religion section, on the same high shelf with the bust of Immanuel Kant.

The knock was repeated, and so was my response. "Closed for the weekend!" I sang out. "Sorry!"

"Bernie, open the door."

So I looked, and of course it was Carolyn, looking larger than life in a down-filled parka. There was a suitcase at her feet and a frown on her brow. I let her in and she blew on her hands and rubbed them together. "I thought you'd be ready by now," she said. "We've got a train to catch, remember?"

"It's Raffles," I said.

"What about him?"

"He won't get in the cat carrier."

She looked at me, then at the cat carrier, then bent over to retrieve two paper balls from it.

"I thought maybe I could get him to jump in after them," I said.

"You thought that, huh?"

"Well, it was just an idea," I said.

"You've had better ones, Bern. Where'd he go?"

"He's sitting up there with the father of the categorical imperative," I said. "Which figures, because it's imperative that he get in the cat carrier, and he's categorically opposed to it. I don't know, Carolyn, maybe it's a mistake to take him. We're only going to be gone three nights. If I put out plenty of food and water for him, and leave the radio on to keep him company . . ."

She gave me a look, shook her head, sighed, and clapped her hands fiercely together, calling the cat's name in a loud voice. Raffles sprang down from his perch and flattened himself against the floor. If he'd lowered his center of gravity one more inch he'd have been in the basement.

She bent over, picked him up, and put him in the carrier. "Now you stay there," she told him, in a tone that brooked no argument, and snapped the lid shut to give him no choice in the matter. "You can't con them into it," she explained. "You have to get physical. Ready, Bern?"

"I guess so."

"I hope that coat's warm enough. The temperature must have dropped twenty degrees since lunch. And the forecast's calling for snow north of the city."

"It'll warm up," I said.

"You think so?"

"It's March already. I know the groundhog saw his shadow, but the extra six weeks of winter are almost up. Even if we do get a little snow, it won't stick around long." I took my suitcase in one hand and Raffles's carrier in the other and let Carolyn hold the door for me. Outside, I went through what you have to go through to close up a store in New York, hauling the steel gate across, fastening innumerable padlocks. These chores are best performed barehanded, and by the time I was done my fingers were numb.

"It's cold, all right," I admitted. "But we'll be cozy at Cuttleford House. Snow on the roof, a fire on the hearth—"

"Kippers for breakfast. Afternoon tea with cream and clotted scones." She frowned. "Is that right, Bern? Or should it be the other way around?"

"No, it's right. Kippers for breakfast, scones for tea."

"I know that part's right," she said. "It's just a question of which is supposed to be clotted, the cream or the scones, and I'm pretty sure it's the cream. 'Scones and clotted cream.' Yeah, that sounds better."

"Either one sounds good about now."

"And all those other great English dishes. Bangers and mash, bubble and squeak, toad-in-the-hole. What exactly *is* toad-in-the-hole, Bern, do you happen to know?"

"Not exactly."

"It always makes me think of *The Wind in the Willows*. I bet it's good, though, and it makes you feel all safe and secure and cozy when you eat it. How about bubble and squeak, Bern? Any idea what that is?"

"Maybe it's the sound the toad makes," I suggested, "when you yank him out of the hole."

"And sherry trifle," she said. "That's a dessert. I know that much."

"It sounds like a frivolous girl," I said. " 'Sherry Trifle —she'll boost your blood sugar while she breaks your heart.' "

"Reminds me of a little cupcake I met a couple of weeks ago at Pandora's."

"Really?" I said. "It reminds me of Lettice."

That was a conversation stopper, all right, and for the next hour or so neither of us said very much. We caught a cab to Grand Central and a train to Whitham Junction, where we'd transfer to a spur line leading north and east to Pattaskinnick, a hamlet nestled at the juncture of New York, Connecticut, and Massachusetts. There we could hire a taxi to carry us the last three or four miles to Cuttleford House.

On the way up to Whitham Junction we sat on the left-hand side of the train so that we could look out the window at the Hudson. Two of our three pieces of luggage rode in the rack overhead. The third rested on the floor between my feet, emitting an occasional meow.

"You're going to love this, Raffles," Carolyn assured him. "A genuine English country house just three hours from New York."

"It may be a little more than three hours," I said. "And it may be a little less than genuine."

"It'll be close enough, Bern. Raffles, there might even be some genuine English mice for you."

"There's a charming thought," I said. "I hope they haven't spent the past fifty years grazing on the library."

"If it's a real English country house," she said, "they've got cats of their own."

"I'm sure they'll be thrilled to see Raffles." I nudged his case with my foot. "I don't see why we had to bring him. He was perfectly comfortable at the store."

"It's too long to leave him, Bern."

"You left your cats."

"Ubi and Archie have each other for company. Besides, Fred from across the hall is going to pop in once a day to feed and water them. I'd have done the same for Raffles, but since you invited me along—"

"I know."

She patted my hand. "Incidentally," she said, "I really appreciate it, Bern. It's great of you to bring me."

"Well, I didn't want to go by myself."

"I guess that wouldn't be much fun."

"I'd go nuts," I said. "Just sitting around twiddling my thumbs, waiting for the scones to clot."

"I'm pretty sure it's the cream, Bern."

"Whatever. You're my best friend, Carolyn. There's nobody I'd rather be taking to Cuttleford House."

"That's a sweet thing to say, Bernie. Even if it's not exactly true."

"What do you mean?"

"Bern," she said, "let's have a quick reality check here, okay? A romantic weekend at an English country house in the dead of winter—"

"Some dead of winter. It's March already. It's almost spring."

"Forget the calendar, Bern. It's too cold to go for a walk in the woods. There'll be a fire on the hearth and frost on the counterpane."

"A counterpane's like a bedspread," I said, "and I hope there won't be any frost on ours."

"Well, you know what I mean. Now go ahead and tell me you wouldn't rather be spending the weekend with a beautiful woman."

"You're a beautiful woman, Carolyn."

"I'm reasonably attractive," she allowed, "but I think beautiful is stretching it. Anyway, that's beside the point. You don't want a woman who's apt to lose her head over some sweet young thing like Sherry Trifle. You want a woman who'll lose her head over you."

"Some other time," I said. "Right now all I want is a friend."

The conductor came through. "Next stop Whitham Junction," he announced. "Change here for . . ." and he named a string of places no one ever heard of, Pattaskinnick among them. Carolyn nudged me and pointed out the window. Snow was falling.

"Well, they said it would snow north of the city," I said. "And here we are, north of the city, and that's what it's doing."

"I think it's beautiful," she said, "and I hope it doesn't stop. I hope it snows all weekend."

I might have bridled at that if I'd been paying attention. But my mind was otherwise engaged, so much so that I missed what she said next. When I'd let a couple of lines pass without comment, she said, "Bernie?"

"Sorry. I guess I was lost in space."

"She's been on your mind a lot, hasn't she?"

"Who, Lettice?"

"Uh-huh. It's okay, Bern. It's only natural. You took a real shot to the heart, and now you're on this trip with me instead of her, and it stands to reason you're going to spend a certain amount of time mooning over the woman."

"Mooning," I said. "Is that what I was doing?"

"Well—"

"I don't think I was mooning," I said. "As a matter of fact I wasn't thinking of Miss Lettice Runcible at all."

"You weren't?"

I stood up, got our bags down from the overhead rack. "As it happens," I said, "I was thinking of Raymond Chandler."

TWO

I should start at the beginning.

Well, near the beginning, anyway. At my apartment, say, some ten days before Carolyn and Raffles and I caught a train to Pattaskinnick by way of Whitham Junction. It was around eleven o'clock, and my Mel Tormé tape was about to reverse itself automatically once again, and I was trying to decide what to do about it.

"Would you like to hear it again?" I asked Lettice. "Or should I put on something else?"

"It doesn't matter, Bernie."

I reached out a hand, rested it on her flank, and let my fingers do the walking. "We could try silence," I suggested, "interrupted only by our own heavy breathing, and occasional cries of passion."

"I'm afraid you'll have to do all the heavy breathing yourself," she said. "It's time I got on home."

"You could stay."

"Oh, not tonight, Bernie." She sat up in bed and extended her arms overhead, stretching like a cat. "I have an early day tomorrow, I'd best be off. I don't suppose you've seen my panties, have you?"

"Not since you took them off. At that point I lost interest in them."

She hopped out of bed and looked for them, and I looked at her. This was an agreeable task, because she looked absolutely splendid. She was about five-six or -seven, and quite slender, but by no means angular. Curves everywhere, but they were all gentle curves with no hairpin turns; if she'd been a road, you wouldn't have to downshift or, God forbid, hit the brake pedal. Her hair was the color of tupelo honey, and her skin was the color of cream, and her eyes were the color of an Alpine lake. The first time I laid eyes on her I'd been struck by her beauty, and she looked a hundred times better now. Because she'd had clothes on then, and now she didn't, and I'll tell you, it makes a difference.

She put a dainty hand on a gorgeous hip and studied the painting on the wall opposite the bed. "I'll miss this," she said idly. "It's really quite a good copy, isn't it?"

It's a canvas some eighteen inches square, with black vertical and horizontal lines on a white field. Some of the squares are filled in with primary colors. I asked her how she could tell it was a copy.

She raised an eyebrow. "Well, its location's a dead giveaway, wouldn't you say? You'd hardly be apt to find an original Mondrian here."

"Here" was a one-bedroom apartment at Seventy-first and West End, and it's actually a pretty decent place to live, even if you wouldn't be likely to mistake it for the Museum of Modern Art.

"Besides," she said, "you can just tell an original, can't

you? I spent two hours at the Mondrian show at MOMA. You must have gone."

"Twice. Once when it opened and again just before it closed the end of January."

"Then surely you know what I mean. When you've seen the actual originals, not just reproductions of them in books, you wouldn't be taken in by a copy like this." She smiled. "Not that it's not very good for what it is, Bernie."

"Well, we can't all be originals," I said. "What did you mean when you said you'd miss it?"

"Did I say that? I was talking to myself, really. Bernie, where *are* my panties?"

"I swear I'm not wearing them."

"Oh, here they are. Now how do you suppose they got all the way over here?"

"They flew on wings of love," I said. I got out of bed myself and turned off Mel Tormé. "There's something I keep forgetting to ask you. Are you free a week from Thursday?"

"A week from Thursday. Not this Thursday but the following Thursday."

"Right."

"Thursday week, the English would say."

"They probably would," I said, "and that actually ties in with what I'm about to suggest. See, I thought—"

"Actually, I'm not."

"You're not what?"

"Free. On Thursday week."

"Oh," I said. "Is it something you can get out of?"

"Not really."

"Because if you could postpone it, we could—"

"I'm afraid I can't."

"Oh," I said. "Well, Thursday would have been best, but I suppose we could let it go until Friday."

"That's Friday week."

"Right. A week from this coming Friday. We could—"

"We can't."

"I beg your pardon?"

"Actually," she said, "I'm afraid I'll be tied up the whole weekend, Bernie, from Thursday evening on."

"Oh," I said.

"Sorry."

"I was sort of planning on us spending the weekend together, but—"

"I'm afraid it's not on. Could you hook this for me, Bernie?"

"Uh, sure. Oh, sorry. My hand slipped."

"Oh, I'll just bet it did."

"Well, an irresistible impulse drew it here. But if you don't like the way it feels—"

"I didn't say that."

"Or if you want me to stop—"

"I didn't say that, either."

So we made do without Mel Tormé, and I can't say his absence was much noticed. Afterward I collapsed like a blown tire, and the next thing I knew she had all her clothes on and one hand on the doorknob.

"Wait," I said. "I can at least see you downstairs and put you into a cab."

"No need for you to get dressed, Bernie. And I am in rather a hurry."

"At least let me tell you what I had planned for the weekend."

"All right."

"Because we could always do it the following week, if I

can manage to get reservations. Or, once you hear what I've got planned for us, you might want to cancel your own plans."

"Well, tell me."

"Cuttleford House," I said.

"Cuttleford House." She frowned in thought. "Isn't that—"

"The English country house in the Berkshires," I said. "Exclusive, expensive, and authentic. A coal fire on every hearth. Serving girls dropping curtsies. Serving boys dropping aitches. Tea brought to your room at daybreak. Guests who still haven't recovered from having lost India. No television in the whole house, no automobiles anywhere on the property."

"It sounds heavenly."

"Well, I know what a passion you have for everything English," I said, "and I saw how much you enjoyed tea at the Stanhope, and I thought this would be the perfect weekend for us. I was planning on telling you on Valentine's Day, but it had come and gone by the time I managed to get through to them and make the reservation."

"What a sweet man you are, Bernie."

"That's me," I agreed. "What do you say, Lettice? If you're positive you can't shift your plans, I'll try to switch our reservations to the following weekend."

"I only wish I could."

"You wish you could which?"

"Either." She sighed, let go of the doorknob, and came back into the room, leaning against a bookcase. "I was hoping to avoid this," she said. "I thought it would be so much nicer for both of us to just make love and leave it at that."

"Leave what at what? You lost me."

"In a manner of speaking," she said, "that's precisely it.

Oh, Bernie, I wish I could go with you Thursday week, but it's just not on."

"What else are you doing," I heard myself say, "that's so important?"

"Oh, Bernie."

"Well?"

"You'll hate me."

"I won't hate you."

"But you will, and I won't blame you. I mean, it's so ridiculous."

"What is?"

"Oh, Bernie," she said yet again. "Bernie, I'm getting married."

" 'Oh, by the way, Bernie, I'm getting married Thursday,' " I said. "And my jaw dropped, and by the time I'd picked it up she was out the door and on her way. Can you believe it?"

"I'm beginning to, Bern."

I suppose she must have been, since she was hearing it for the third time. I'd told her that night, calling her minutes after Lettice crossed my threshold and closed the door gently but firmly behind her. I told her again the following day at lunch. Carolyn's dog-grooming salon is on East Eleventh Street between University Place and Broadway, just two doors down the street from Barnegat Books, and in the ordinary course of things we lunch together, one of us picking up sandwiches at one of the neighborhood delis and conveying them to the other's place of business. On this particular day I had bought the sandwiches and we ate them at the Poodle Factory, and between bites I told her the same sad story I'd told her over the phone.

Then, around six, I closed the bookstore and went back to the Poodle Factory, where she was putting the finishing touches on a bichon frise while its owners watched, beaming. "She's such a darling," one of them said, while the other wrote out a check. "And you bring out the best in her, Carolyn. I swear you're a genius."

They left, darling in tow, and the genius closed up for the night. We walked over to the Bum Rap on Broadway, as we generally do, and Carolyn started to order Scotch, as she generally does, and then she paused. "If you want," she said, "I'll order something else."

"Why?"

"Well, if you want to get good and drunk," she said, "I could make a point of staying relatively sober."

"We don't have a car," I said. "What do we need with a designated driver? Anyway, why would I want to get drunk?"

"You mean you don't?"

"Not particularly."

"Oh. Hey, this isn't going to be a Perrier night for you, is it?"

Perrier is my drug of choice when my plans for an evening include illegal entry. "No," I said. "It's not." And I proved it by asking Maxine to bring me a bottle of Tuborg.

"Well, thank God," Carolyn said. "In that case I'll have Scotch, Max, and you might as well make it a double. They said I'm a genius, Bernie. Isn't that something?"

"It's great."

"If I had my choice," she said, "I'd just as soon be a genius at something else. Nobody ever got a MacArthur Award for washing dogs. But it's better than nothing, don't you think?"

"Absolutely. You could be like me."

"A genius at picking locks?"

"A genius at picking women."

"I'm already a genius at picking women."

"Can you believe it?" I demanded, and launched into my third recital of Lettice's revelation. "What I want to know," I said, "is when she would have gotten around to telling me if I hadn't pressed her about the weekend. I mean, it's not like she had a date to go to the movies with some other guy. She's getting *married*."

"Did you know she was seeing somebody else?"

"I more or less assumed it. We weren't in a committed relationship. Actually we'd only recently started sleeping together."

"How was it?"

"You mean the sex?"

"Yeah."

"It was wonderful."

"Oh."

"Really special."

"Sorry to hear it, Bern."

"But it wasn't a major love affair. I had hopes that it might turn out to be, but deep down inside I think I knew it wouldn't. We didn't have that much in common. I figured it would run its course and resolve itself with some sort of bittersweet ending, and years from now she'd be one more tender memory for me to warm myself with as I slid off into senility. So I was fully prepared for it to come to nothing, but I didn't think it would happen so soon, or so abruptly."

"So you're essentially okay about it, Bern?"

"I'd say so."

"You're stunned but not devastated. Is that about it?"

"Pretty much. I feel stupid for having misread the situation so completely. I thought the woman was crazy about me, and all the while she was getting ready to tie the knot with somebody else."

"He's the guy to feel sorry for, Bern."

"Who, the bridegroom?"

"Uh-huh. A week and a half before the wedding, and his wife's rehearsing with somebody else? If you ask me, you're lucky to be rid of her."

"I know."

"Lettice. What kind of name is that, anyway?"

"I guess it's English."

"I suppose so. You know, ever since you started seeing her I've been good about resisting the obvious jokes. Like, what kind of a name is that for a tomato? Or, has she got a sister named Parsley? Or, I hope she's not the original Iceberg Lettice."

"She's not."

"I don't know, Bern. She was cool as a cucumber the other day. Who's the lucky guy, anyway? Did she tell you anything about him?"

"Not a word."

"Or where she met him, or anything like that?"

I shook my head. "Maybe she just walked into his store," I said. "That's how she met me. She picked out half a dozen books by Martha Grimes and Elizabeth George, and we got to talking."

"What's she do, Bern?"

"All sorts of things," I said, remembering. "Oh, you mean for a living? She does something in Wall Street. I think she's a stock analyst."

"So she's not just a bimbo."

"Not in the traditional sense of the term."

"And she's English?"

"No."

"I thought she was homesick for England. I thought that was why you took her for English tea at the Stanhope, and why you were planning on taking her to Cuttleford House."

"She's homesick for England," I said, "in a manner of speaking, but she's not English. In fact she's never even been there."

"Oh."

"But she has a faint English accent, and she uses some British constructions in her speech, and she's very clear on the notion that England is her spiritual home. And of course she's read a whole lot of English mysteries."

"Oh, right. Martha Grimes and Elizabeth George. They're both English, aren't they?"

"Actually," I said, "they're not, but they set their books over there, and she can't get enough of them. And she's read all the classics, too—Agatha Christie, Dorothy Sayers. Anyway, I thought Cuttleford House would be just her line of country."

" 'Just her line of country'?"

"See? Now I'm doing it. I thought she'd be nuts about it."

"And it's a lot cheaper than going to England."

"It's not cheap," I said. "But I had a very good evening around the end of January, and for a change money's not a problem."

"One of those Perrier nights."

"I'm afraid so," I said. "I know it's morally reprehensible, but I did it anyway, and I wanted to invest some of the proceeds in high living before I piss it all away on food and shelter."

"Makes sense."

"So I actually thought about hopping on the Concorde and whisking her off for a whirlwind weekend in England. But I wasn't sure I could find the right England."

"There's more than one?"

I nodded. "To get to the one she's mad for," I said, "you'd need a time machine, and even then you might have trouble finding it. Her England's some sort of cross between *Upstairs, Downstairs* and *The Body in the Library*. If I got off the plane at Heathrow I wouldn't know where to look for that England. But you can find it three hours from here at Cuttleford House."

"And it's some kind of hotel? I never heard of it, Bern."

"Neither did I," I said, "until fairly recently. And yes, it's a hotel of sorts, but it didn't start out that way. Ferdinand Cathcart built it just about a hundred years ago."

"That's a familiar name."

"He was one of the robber barons, and he made his money the old-fashioned way."

"By grinding the faces of the poor?"

"How else? After he'd made his pile, and after he'd already treated himself to a limestone mansion on Fifth Avenue and a summer place at Newport, Ferdie decided he wanted a country house. So he built Cuttleford."

"And lived there happily ever after?"

"I gather he hardly spent any time there at all," I said, "and he may have lived happily, but not ever after, because within five years of the completion of Cuttleford he had taken up residence in that great English country house in the sky. His heirs fought over the estate, and the one who wound up with it lost all his money in 1929 and the state took the place for back taxes. It passed through various hands over the years. After the Second World War it was a fancy drying-out farm for alcoholics, and I believe some monastic order had it for a while. Eventually it was abandoned, and then eight or ten years ago the Eglantines got hold of it and set about restoring it."

"The Eglantines. They're a religious order, too, aren't they?"

I shook my head. "They're Mr. and Mrs. Eglantine," I said. "I forget their first names, but they're on the brochure. I think he's English and she's American, or maybe it's the other way around. They met when they were both working for a big American hotel chain, and they quit and opened an English-style bed-and-breakfast in Bucks County, Pennsylvania. Then they had a chance to buy Cuttleford House, so they sold the place in Bucks County and took a shot at it."

I told her about the place, parroting back the better part of what I'd read in the brochure.

"It sounds great," she said.

"It does, doesn't it?"

"It really does, Bern. It's a shame Lettice couldn't have postponed the wedding a week or two. She would have loved it."

"I'd have enjoyed it myself."

"Well, sure. Who wouldn't?"

I sipped my beer, set the glass down, leaned forward. I said, "You know what?"

"What, Bern."

"Let's go."

"Just like that? Well, let me finish my drink first, okay?"

"Finish it and have another. I don't mean let's blow this pop stand. I mean let's go to Cuttleford House."

"Huh?"

"Well, why the hell not? I've got the reservations and I already sent them a deposit, which will probably turn out to be nonrefundable. Why don't the two of us make the trip? You're not planning on getting married a week from Thursday, are you?"

"Not that I remember, but I'd have to check my book."

"I hate the idea of canceling the trip," I said, "just because the person I was planning on taking happens to be marrying somebody else. But it's not the kind of place I'd want to go to alone."

"I know what you mean."

"So what do you say?"

"I don't know if I can afford it, Bern."

"Hey, c'mon. It's my treat."

"Are you sure?"

"Absolutely. I thought that went without saying."

"In that case," she said, "I can probably afford it."

"So is it a deal? Are we going?"

"Oh, what the hell," she said. "Why not?"

THREE

That was Tuesday night. The following day Carolyn bought the sandwiches and we ate them at the bookstore. After she'd washed down the last bite of felafel with the last sip of celery tonic, she cocked her head and said, "About next weekend, Bern."

"What about it?"

"Well, I've been thinking."

"We're still on, aren't we?"

"I guess so, but—"

"But what?"

"Well, I'm a little unclear about something."

"What's to be unclear? We'll leave here Thursday afternoon and be back sometime Sunday night. If you're wondering what clothes to pack—"

"I've got that worked out."

"Then what's the problem?"

"I'd sort of like to know why we're going."

"Why we're going?"

"That's right, Bern. That's where it gets a little unclear for me."

"I know why I'm going," I said, "and I thought I'd told you. I'm going because I had it all planned, had my heart set on it, and I don't see any reason to let a perfidious anglophile leave me stranded. Another reason I'm going is because I need a vacation. I can't remember the last time I got out of the city, and I've been putting in long hours in the store, not to mention the occasional off-the-books enterprise at night."

"I know you've been working a lot."

"That's why I'm going. As for you, I figure you're going because you want to keep your best friend company in his hour of need. And you've been working hard yourself. How many dogs got a wash and set from you the week of the big Kennel Club show?"

"Don't remind me."

"So you can use a break, and how often do you get a chance to do a good deed for a friend and get a free vacation in the bargain?"

"Not too often."

"So now we know why I'm going, and why you're going, and if you put the two together, they add up to why *we*'re going."

She considered the matter. I crumpled up one of the sandwich wrappers and threw it for Raffles to chase, then gathered the rest of our luncheon detritus and put it in the trash. When I got back, Carolyn had the cat on her lap and a determined expression on her face.

"There's more," she said.

"More what? More lunch? More garbage? What are you talking about?"

"More to the story," she said. "You know that bit about the truth, the whole truth, and nothing but the truth? Well, I think you're telling the truth, and I think you're telling nothing but the truth, but I don't think you're telling the whole truth."

"You don't, huh?"

"No," she said, "I don't. Maybe I should just shut up and go along for the ride, because you know what they say about looking gift whores in the mouth."

"What do they say?"

"They say not to. But I can't help it, Bern. You picked out Cuttleford House as a special treat for Lettice. Once she took herself out of the picture, why would you want to go there?"

"I told you—"

"I know what you told me, but if you need a vacation why wouldn't you want to take it somewhere else? I just can't keep from feeling that you've got a hidden agenda."

"A hidden agenda," I said.

"If I'm wrong," she said, "just tell me once and for all, and I'll shut up about it, I promise."

"I wouldn't say hidden," I said. "I wouldn't call it an agenda."

"But there's something, isn't there, Bern?"

I sighed, nodded. "There's something."

"I knew it."

"Or maybe there's nothing, but there's the possibility of something. At least there *was* something. I'm fairly certain of that, but I don't know if there still is. Something, I mean."

"Bern—"

"Although there'd still be something, wouldn't there? But instead of being there, it could be somewhere. Somewhere else, I mean."

"Bernie, those are real words you're using, and you're making whole sentences out of them, but—"

"But you don't know what I'm talking about."

"Right."

I took a deep breath. I said, "What do you know about Raymond Chandler?"

"Raymond Chandler?"

"Right."

"The mystery writer? That Raymond Chandler?"

"That's the one."

"What do I know about him? Well, I read all his books years ago. I don't think he wrote very many of them, did he?"

"Seven novels," I said, "plus two dozen short stories and four or five articles."

"I probably missed some of the short stories," she said, "and I don't think I ever read any of the articles, but I'm pretty sure I read all of the books."

"I read everything at one time or another. The books, the short stories, the articles. And his collected correspondence, and two biographies, one by Philip Durham and one by Frank MacShane."

"That puts you way ahead of me, Bern." She shrugged. "I just read the guy because I liked the books. So I don't know a whole lot about him. Was he English or American? I don't even know."

"He was born here," I said, "in 1888. Conceived here, too, in Laramie, Wyoming, and born in Chicago. Spent his summers in Nebraska. When he was seven his parents split up and he and his mother moved to England. Then when he was twenty-three he borrowed five hundred pounds from his uncle and moved to America. He wound up in southern California, of course, and that's where he set his stories. He was in the oil business, until he drank his way out of it. Then he tried writing."

"Because you can't drink your way out of it?"

"He'd been interested in it before, but now he really worked at it. He sold his first short story to *Black Mask* in 1933, and published his first novel in 1939."

"*The Long Sleep.*"

"*The Big Sleep,*" I said. "You're mixing it up with the sixth novel, *The Long Goodbye*. It's a natural mistake. Both of the titles are euphemisms for death."

"Right."

"His last years weren't much fun," I went on. "His wife died in 1954 and he was never the same after that. He wrote a seventh novel, *Playback*, that wasn't very good, and the opening chapters of an eighth that would have been even worse if he'd finished it. But he didn't. In March of 1959 he said his own long goodbye and took his own big sleep."

"But his books live on."

"They certainly do. They're all in print, and his place in the crime fiction pantheon is unchallenged. You don't even have to be a mystery fan to like Chandler. 'I never read mysteries,' you'll hear people say, 'except for Raymond Chandler, of course. I adore Chandler.'" I crumpled a sheet of paper and threw it to Raffles. "Sometimes," I said, "they'll say that, and it turns out they're adoring him sight unseen, because they haven't really read him at all."

"I guess that's real literary success," she said. "When you've got devoted fans who haven't even read you."

"You can't beat it," I agreed. "Anyway, that's Raymond Chandler. There's another writer who gets mentioned in the same breath with him, and I know you've read his stuff. Hammett."

"Dashiell Hammett? Of course I've read him, Bern. He didn't write very much either, did he?"

"Five novels and around sixty short stories. He'd pretty much stopped writing by the time Chandler had his first story published. His health was never good, and his last years couldn't have been much more fun than Chandler's."

"When did he die?"

"In 1961. Like Chandler, his work lives on. They teach his books in college courses. You can probably buy Cliff's Notes for *The Maltese Falcon*. How's that for fame?"

"Not bad."

"Hammett and Chandler, Chandler and Hammett. The two of them are considered the founders of hardboiled crime fiction. There were other writers who got there first, like Carroll John Daly, but hardly anybody reads them anymore. Hammett and Chandler were the cream of the crop, and they're the ones who get the credit."

"Were they great friends, Bern?"

"They only met once," I said. "In 1936, if I remember it correctly. Ten *Black Mask* regulars got together for dinner in L.A. Chandler lived out there, and Hammett was working in Hollywood at the time. Norbert Davis and Horace McCoy were there, too, and Todhunter Ballard, and five other writers I don't know much about."

"I don't know anything about the ones you just mentioned."

"Well, Ballard wrote a lot of westerns, and I think he was distantly related to Rex Stout. Horace McCoy wrote *They Shoot Horses, Don't They?* I forget what Norbert Davis wrote. Stories for *Black Mask*, I guess."

"And that's the only time they met?"

"That's what everybody says."

"Oh?"

"Every biography of either of the two of them mentions that meeting. They had a photo taken of the group, to send to the editor of *Black Mask* back in New York." I went over to the Biography section and came back with *Shadow Man*, Richard Layman's life of Hammett, and flipped through it to the photos. "Here we go. That's Chandler with the pipe. And that's Hammett."

"It looks as though they're staring at each other."

"Maybe. It's hard to tell."

"Did they like each other, Bern?"

"That's also hard to tell. Years later Chandler wrote a letter in which he recalled the meeting. He remembered Hammett as nice-looking, tall, quiet, gray-haired, and with a fearful capacity for Scotch."

"Just like me."

"Well, you're nice-looking," I agreed. "I don't know about tall."

She glowered at me. Carolyn can stand six feet tall, but only if she happens to be wearing twelve-inch heels. "I'm not quiet or gray-haired, either," she said. "I was referring to the fearful capacity for Scotch."

"Oh."

"Is that all Chandler had to say about him?"

"He thought a lot of him as a writer." I flipped pages, found the part I was looking for. I read: " 'Hammett took murder out of the Venetian vase and dropped it into the alley; it doesn't have to stay there forever, but it looked like a good idea to get as far as possible from Emily Post's idea of how a well-bred debutante gnaws a chicken wing. Hammett wrote for people with a sharp, aggressive attitude to life. They were not afraid of the seamy side of things; they lived there. Violence did not dismay them; it was right down their street. Hammett gave murder back to the kind of people who commit it for reasons, not just to provide a corpse; and with the means at hand, not hand-wrought dueling pistols, curare, and tropical fish.' "

"Tropical fish?"

" 'He put these people down on paper as they were,' " I went on, " 'and he made them talk and think in the language they customarily used for these purposes.' Wait, there's more. 'He was spare, frugal, hardboiled, but he did over and over again what only the best writers can ever do at all. He wrote scenes that never seemed to have been written before.' " I closed the book. "He wrote that in 1944, in an essay for *The Atlantic*. I wonder if Hammett ever saw it. He was in the army at the time, stationed in Alaska during the Aleutians campaign."

"Wasn't he a little old for that?"

"He was born in 1894, so he would have been forty-eight in 1942 when he enlisted. On top of that his health wasn't good. He'd had TB, and his teeth were bad."

"And they took him anyway?"

"Not the first two times he tried to enlist. The third time around they weren't as finicky, and they took him after he had some teeth pulled. Then after the war they jailed him when he refused to tell a Congressional committee if he'd been a communist."

"Was he?"

"Probably, but who cares? He wasn't a candidate for president. He was just a writer who hadn't written much of anything in twenty years."

"What did Hammett think of Chandler?"

"As far as anybody knows, he never expressed an opinion." I shrugged. "You know, it's entirely possible he never read a thing Chandler wrote. But I think he had the opportunity."

"What do you mean?"

"I think the two of them met a second time, two years or so after Chandler's first novel was published. I think Chandler brought a copy of the book with him and presented it to Hammett."

"And?"

"And I think I know where the book is," I said. "I think it's at Cuttleford House."

FOUR

Chandler never mentioned a second meeting, I told Carolyn, and neither did Hammett. But nine or ten months ago I'd been browsing through some books I'd bought for store stock, and I wound up getting caught up in one I'd never seen before, a memoir called *A Penny a Word—and Worth It!* by an old pulp writer called Lester Harding Ross.

Carolyn had never heard of him.

"Neither had I," I told her. "Ross seems to have been a hack of all trades. He turned out thousands of words of fiction every day, none of it very good but all of it publishable. He wrote sports stories and western stories and detective stories and science fiction stories, and he did all of his work under pen names. He listed thirty pen names in his book, and admitted that there were others he'd forgotten. He really did spend his life writing for a cent a word, and never seems to have aspired to anything more. I hope he did a little better with his autobiography. It's pretty interesting stuff, and I'd hate to think he only got six or seven hundred dollars for it."

"He probably dashed it off in three days."

"Well, that's all the time Voltaire spent writing *Candide*. But all of that's beside the point. The thing is, Ross really enjoyed being a writer, whether or not he took much pride in the stuff he was writing. And he enjoyed the company of other writers. He was acquainted with most of the pulp writers of his era, directly or by correspondence."

"Including Hammett and Chandler?"

"Well, no, as a matter of fact. But including George Harmon Coxe."

"I know that name."

"I'm not surprised. He published a lot of books, good tough hardboiled stuff. And he was a friend of Chandler's. After *The Big Sleep* came out, Chandler wrote to Coxe, who had just built a house in Connecticut. Chandler was interested in moving there himself."

"It's hard to imagine Philip Marlowe in Connecticut. He's such an L.A. kind of guy."

"I know, but Chandler was looking for some place more affordable than California. He was also thinking about moving back to England. He wound up staying in California, but, according to Lester Harding Ross, he actually did visit Coxe at his home in Connecticut."

"When?"

"That's not clear, but it was probably sometime in the summer or fall of '41." I slipped behind the counter and found my copy of *A Penny a Word—and Worth It!* "Here's what Ross has to say. 'I wish I could find a letter Coxe wrote me around that time. It seems Chandler came east to confer with his people at Knopf, then stayed a day or two with the Coxes. One night they drove to visit some friends named Fortnoy or Fontenoy, and also visiting were Hammett and the Hellman woman. Evidently Fortnoy or Fontenoy or whatever his name was had a free hand with the liquor bottle, and all in attendance drank deeply. Chandler had brought along a copy of his book, and made a big show of presenting it to Hammett, writing a flowery inscription on the flyleaf. The rich thing is that he'd originally brought the book with him from California as a gift for Coxe, and now had no copy to give him! Coxe's words on the subject were wonderfully wry, but, alas, his letter must have been a casualty of one of our many moves.' "

" 'The Hellman woman.' Lillian Hellman?"

"Uh-huh. She'd bought Hardscrabble Farm in 1939, and Hammett spent a good deal of time there. The farm wasn't exactly a hop-skip-and-jump from Cuttleford House, but it wouldn't have been more than a two-hour drive."

"I must have missed something, Bern. When did Ross say anything about Cuttleford House?"

"He didn't. But he said something about a man named Fontenoy."

"And?"

"And I looked for references to Fortnoy or Fontenoy in the biographies of Hammett and Chandler, but I couldn't find anything close. I also looked for any indication that a presentation copy of *The Big Sleep* had been part of Dashiell Hammett's estate, or Lillian Hellman's. I checked auction records, and I called people in the book trade who would be likely to know about that sort of thing. I checked the letters of George Harmon Coxe, to see if he reported the incident to any of the other people he corresponded with."

"Did he?"

"He may have, but I couldn't turn up anything. They have some of his papers at Columbia, and I spent a few hours going through them with a very helpful librarian, and I found plenty of references to Chandler *and* Hammett, but nothing to confirm Chandler's trip east, let alone his second meeting with Hammett."

"I don't suppose he mentioned Fontenoy, either."

" 'Fraid not."

"Maybe Ross dreamed the whole thing up."

"That occurred to me," I admitted. "It also struck me that I was searching in a coal mine for a black cat that wasn't there. I gave up, finally, and months later I started seeing a woman with a mad passion for the England of tea cozies and corpses in the gazebo, and I heard something about Cuttleford House, so I called them up and asked them to send me a brochure."

"And they did."

"And they did," I agreed, "and it was pretty impressive. I was going to show it to you earlier, but I can't remember what I did with it."

"That's okay, Bern. I'm going anyway, so what do I need with the brochure?"

"I almost took the same position. After a quick glance I knew it was the perfect place to take Lettice, so why bother reading the history of the place? But it was interestingly written, and business was slow that day."

"For a change."

"Right. So I started reading, and they mentioned the various hands the property had passed through, and it turned out that a man named Forrest Fontenoy had owned it for a couple of years. The chronology's a little uncertain, but he definitely would have been the owner from the time *The Big Sleep* was published until the time Hammett was accepted into the United States Army."

"That does a lot for Ross's credibility, doesn't it, Bern?"

"I'd say so. I checked the *Times* Index and found out a little more about Fontenoy. He was married to one of the Mellon heirs, and he had some family money of his own. He backed a few Broadway shows, and was a fairly substantial supporter of leftist causes in the years immediately preceding the war."

"That would connect him to Hellman. The theater and the politics."

"It would certainly explain how they happened to know each other. But none of that matters. The real question is what happened to the book."

"*The Big Sleep*."

"Right. Here's what I think happened. Chandler, tight as a tick, whipped out the book, wrote something heartfelt, and presented it to Hammett. Hammett, whom everybody describes as an extremely polite man, took it as if it were the key to the Kingdom of Heaven. Then Chandler went home with the Coxes, and Hammett and Hellman went back to Hardscrabble Farm, or drove all the way home to New York."

"And the book stayed behind."

"That's my guess."

"Why, Bern? Wouldn't Hammett take it with him?"

"He might," I said, "if he thought of it. By the time he left Cuttleford House, he was probably too drunk to remember or too hungover to care." I held out my hands. "Look, I can't prove any of this. Maybe he took it home with him, read a couple of chapters, and tossed it in the trash. Maybe he lent it to somebody who passed it on to somebody else who gave it to the church rummage sale. Maybe it's rotting away in somebody's basement or attic even as we speak."

"But you don't think so."

"No, I don't. I think he left it on a table in Cuttleford House, accidentally or on purpose, and I think one of the maids stuck it on a shelf in the library. They've got a classic formal library—there's a photograph of it in the brochure. Shelves clear up to the twelve-foot ceiling."

"And that's where you think it is."

"I think it might be. Oh, a lot of people have been in that house since then. Monks, drunks, workmen, guests. Any one of them could have picked up *The Big Sleep* and walked off with it."

"Bernie, it's over fifty years."

"I know."

"I don't suppose any of them are still alive, are they? I know Hammett and Chandler aren't, or Lillian Hellman. What about Coxe and Ross?"

"Gone."

"And Fontenoy and his wife?"

"Long gone, and I don't know what became of their children."

"Over fifty years. How could the book still be there?"

"The house is still there. And so's the library. I saw the photo in the brochure, and those shelves are chock-full of books, and I don't think the Eglantines trucked them in by the pound to make a decorating statement. I think they've been there forever."

"And somewhere, tucked away on some high shelf—"

"*The Big Sleep*," I said. "Signed by Raymond Chandler, and inscribed to Dashiell Hammett. Sitting there, just waiting to be found."

"I've been thinking," she said, a few hours later at the Bum Rap. "About that book."

"I can understand that. I've been thinking about it myself for months now."

"Suppose it's actually there," she said, "and suppose you actually find it, which would take another miracle all by itself."

"So?"

"So is it worth it? Aside from the fact that you're obsessed, and it's hard to put a dollar value on an obsession. But in terms of actual dollars and cents—"

"What's it worth?"

"Right."

I didn't have to think. I'd worked it out often enough over the months.

"*The Big Sleep* is Chandler's scarcest book," I said. "A first-edition copy in very fine condition is legitimately rare. With a dust jacket, the jacket also in top condition, you've got something worth in the neighborhood of five thousand dollars."

"That much, huh?"

"But this one's signed," I said. "With most modern novels, an author's signature will boost the price by ten or twenty percent. But it's different with Chandler."

"It is?"

I nodded. "He didn't sign a lot of books. Actually, nobody did back then, not the way they do now. Nowadays just about everybody with a book out goes traipsing around the country, sitting in bookstores and signing copies for all comers."

"Ed McBain signed his new book for me," she said. "I told you about that, didn't I?"

"Repeatedly."

"Well, it was an exciting day for me, Bern. He's one of my favorite writers."

"One of mine, too."

"Whenever I read one of his Eighty-seventh Precinct books," she said, "I wind up looking at cops in a new light. I see them as real human beings, sensitive and vulnerable and, well, human."

"That's how he portrays them."

"Right. And then Ray Kirschmann walks in the door and drives me right straight back to reality. I'll tell you, I like Ed McBain's fantasy world a whole lot better, and it was a thrill to meet him in person. That book's one of my proudest possessions."

"I know that, but you're not the only person he signed a book for. He's signed thousands of books, and so have most of the writers around today. Back in Hammett and Chandler's time, authors just signed books for their friends. And Chandler didn't even do that."

"He didn't?"

"Not often. If you were a friend of his he might give you a book, but he wouldn't sign it unless you made a point of asking him. So a genuine Raymond Chandler signature is valuable in its own right. On one of the later, more common books, it might increase the value from a few hundred dollars to a couple of thousand. On *The Big Sleep*, it could double the value."

"So we're up to ten grand."

"And we're not done yet. If Ross is telling the truth, Chandler didn't just sign his name on Hammett's copy. He inscribed it personally to Hammett."

"That makes a difference?"

"It's a funny thing with inscriptions," I said. "If the person it's inscribed to is just Joe Schmo, the book tends to be a little less desirable than if it's just signed."

"Why's that, Bern?"

"Well, think about it," I said. "If you were a collector, would you want a book personally inscribed to somebody that nobody ever heard of? Or would you be happier with a simple signature?"

"I don't think I'd care one way or the other."

"You're not a collector. Collectors care." I thought of some of my more idiosyncratic customers. "About everything," I said. "Believe me."

"I believe you, Bern. How about a copy that's inscribed to Sid Schmo? That's Joe's famous brother."

"Now you're talking. As soon as the person named in the inscription is prominent, the book becomes an association copy."

"And that's good?"

"It's not bad," I said. "Just how good it is depends on who the person is, and the nature of his or her relationship to the author. A book inscribed by Raymond Chandler to Dashiell Hammett would have to be the ultimate association copy in American crime fiction."

"Bottom-line it for me, Bern."

"Assuming near-mint condition, for the book and dust jacket, and assuming the handwriting is verifiably Chandler's—"

"Assume everything, Bern. Let's hear a number."

"This is just a ballpark figure, remember. We're talking about a unique item, so who can say what it would bring?"

"Bernie—"

"Say twenty-five."

"Twenty-five?"

"That's ballpark."

"Twenty-five thousand."

I nodded.

"Dollars."

I nodded again.

"And what percentage of that could you fence it for?"

"You wouldn't need a fence," I said. "Because no one would have reported it stolen, because who even knows it exists? You could walk up to any of the top dealers and put it on the table."

"And when they asked where you got it?"

"You picked it up at a garage sale or found it on the two-for-a-quarter shelf at a thrift shop. Hell, I'm a book dealer. I could say it came in at the bottom of a carton of junk, and I assumed it was a book club reprint until I took a good look at it. You wouldn't even have to say how it came into your hands. You could just smile wisely and keep your mouth shut."

"So you could wind up with the whole twenty-five thousand."

"Or more, if you stuck it in a Sotheby's auction and two fanatics both decided they had to have it."

"Wow."

"But there's no guarantee it ever existed in the first place," I said, "and even if it did it probably disappeared long ago. Or it *is* still there, for all the good it does us, because it's hidden away and you could go through the house from top to bottom and never find it."

"We've got to look, Bern."

"That's what I figured."

"Twenty-five grand."

"It could be a lot less, you know. Maybe the dust jacket's gone. Maybe the spine is faded. Maybe the pages are dog-eared. Maybe there's insect damage."

"Maybe a kid came along and colored in all the O's," she said. "Maybe a mad botanist pressed leaves between the pages. The hell with all that. We've got to take a shot at it, Bern." She looked at me. "We'd never forgive ourselves if we didn't."

FIVE

We had a short wait on the platform at Whitham Junction. Then the local for Pattaskinnick came chugging into the station, and when it chugged out again we were on it. The little train's course ran north and east, and with each turn of its wheels the terrain grew more rugged and remote and the snowfall intensified.

By the time we got to Pattaskinnick it was dark out and the snow was several inches deep. Carolyn scooped up a handful and made a snowball, then looked around for something to throw it at. The only car in sight was a Jeep Cherokee with *Buck's Taxi Service* inexpertly lettered on its side. You couldn't peg a snowball at a cab and then expect the driver to make you welcome, so she shrugged and tossed the snowball over her shoulder.

"Hey!"

"Sorry, Bern. I didn't know you were there."

"Well, I've never been here before. Welcome to Pattaskinnick."

"It's like a village in the Cotswolds, isn't it? Chipping Camden or one of those."

"Sodding Boardham," I suggested.

"Miss Jane Marple could be living in one of those cozy little cottages, Bernie. Knitting things and poking around in the garden and solving murders left and right."

"Cottages? I don't see any cottages."

"Not with all this snow. But I'm sure they're there. So's our cab. Wouldn't you think he'd hop out and help us with our bags?"

He did, finally, after we'd walked over and tapped on his windshield. I told him our destination and he clambered out from behind the wheel, a squat, broad-shouldered fellow with less than the traditional amount of space between his eyes. He wore one of those weird hunting jackets in orange camouflage, which makes it hard for deer to see you and hard for human beings to look at you, and he lifted our suitcases effortlessly into the Cherokee's luggage compartment, then looked warily down at Raffles's cat carrier.

"You got an animal in there," he said.

"It's a cat," I agreed.

"I don't pick up no animals."

"But that's ridiculous," I said. "He's not going to damage your car."

"Ain't a car. 'T'sa Jeep."

"Even if it's a brand-new John Deere tractor," I said, "there's no way on earth he's going to hurt it. He's locked up in there, he can't get out, he couldn't even fit a paw through the wire mesh, so—"

"I got nothing against transporting 'em," he said. "Where I draw the line is picking 'em up."

"Picking them up?"

"Oh, for God's sake," Carolyn said. She lifted the cat carrier and placed it on the floor of the Jeep, between the two suitcases. The driver closed the rear door, then went up front and got behind the wheel. Carolyn and I got into the passenger compartment.

"Could be it strikes you as peculiar," he said, "but a man has to draw the line. People want you to haul all manner of livestock. If it's a cat today it'll be a horse tomorrow."

I snuck a peek at Raffles. He was a cat today, and somehow I couldn't make myself believe he'd be a horse tomorrow.

"Snowing to beat the band," our driver said, starting the engine and pulling away from the curb. "Good thing for you you're in a four-wheeled vehicle."

"As opposed to a bicycle?"

Carolyn treated me to an elbow. "Four-wheel *drive*," she said, and leaned forward. "You think we're in for a lot of snow?"

"Wouldn't be the first time, and she's coming down right heavy. I'll get you to Cuttleford, though. This here'll get through most anything. Can't take you over the bridge, though."

"The bridge?"

"There's a parking lot," I explained, "where you have to leave your car, and then you walk across a bridge, and then it's a few steps to the house itself."

"Quarter mile," the driver said. "Be a wagon there for your bags. I suppose you could put your animal into it."

"We'll manage," Carolyn told him.

The roads to Cuttleford were something out of a Judy Garland song. They kept getting rougher, and lonelier and tougher. The snow fell steadily, and the Jeep proved equal to the challenge, going where no vehicle had gone before. I wouldn't have dreamed of calling it a car.

"Cuttleford Road," the driver announced, braking and turning to the left, where a one-lane road made its way through thick woods. "Been plowed within the hour. The young 'un's doing."

"The young 'un?"

"Orris," he said. "Works for them, don't he?" He tapped his head significantly with his forefinger. "The least bit slow, Orris. Does his work, though. Have to give him that. I never credited those stories, anyway."

"Stories?"

"You can't believe half of what you hear," he said. "Better to have the boy plowing driveways than locked away for his whole life."

"Why would they lock him up?" Carolyn wanted to know. "What did he do, anyway?"

"Not my place to say. Never been a believer in carrying tales."

Carolyn started to press the issue, then broke off when we braked to a stop alongside a clearing where eight or ten cars were parked, as well as a half-ton panel truck and a Jeep with a snowplow attached to its front.

"If you brought your own car," he said, "that's where you'd have to leave it. Except you'd likely be stuck somewhere, 'less you had four wheels."

I'd been planning on suggesting that quaintness could yield to expediency for once, and that he drive us across the bridge and drop us at the door. One look at the bridge made it clear that was out of the question. It was narrower than the Jeep, narrower indeed than any four-wheeled vehicle larger than a shopping cart, and it was suspended by rope cables across a deep gorge.

The driver cut the Jeep's engine, and I got out and

walked to the edge, or as close as I cared to get to it. I couldn't see anything below, and I couldn't hear anything, either.

"Quiet," I said.

"Cuttlebone Creek. She's iced over. Be frozen clear to the bottom by daybreak, if she's not already."

"Is the bridge safe?" Carolyn wanted to know.

"What a question," I said. "Of course it's safe."

" 'S good strong rope," he said.

"Good strong rope," I echoed.

"Thing about rope," he said, "is it rains, don't it? And the damp soaks into it, and then it turns cold and freezes. And then it's brittle, innit?"

"It is?"

"Snap like a twig," he said.

"Er."

"But it ain't yet," he said with satisfaction. "Best cross before it does. See the wagons? Put your luggage in 'em. And your animal."

"Look," Carolyn said. "This is a Jeep, right? Not a car but a Jeep."

He looked at her.

"Well, he's a cat," she said. "Not an animal. So don't call him an animal. Show a little respect."

He didn't call him an animal again, but neither did he call him anything else, or say another word. I think Carolyn left him dumbstruck, and I only wish she'd spoken up earlier. He opened the back of the Jeep, lifted out our suitcases, and stepped back in silence. Cat, animal, or four-wheeled mammal, the rules weren't about to change. Whatever he was, we had to tote him ourselves.

We picked out a pair of little red wagons, loaded Raffles and the luggage, and made our way across the bridge and along a winding path to Cuttleford House. Crossing the bridge was actually a lot less perilous than some of the things I've been called upon to do in my career as a burglar, but there's something about walking upon a surface that moves beneath your feet that can put one, well, off-stride.

Carolyn wanted to know how deep the gorge was. I asked her what difference it made. "Either way," I said, "it's the same rickety bridge. Either way we have to cross it."

"I guess I just want to know how far we're gonna fall, Bern."

"We're not going to fall."

"I know," she said. "But if we do, are we looking at bruises or broken bones or a grease spot? When you can't see, you wind up picturing a bottomless abyss, but maybe it's more like five or six feet."

I didn't say anything.

"Bern?"

"I'm trying to picture a bottomless abyss," I said. "What would it look like?"

"Bern—"

I don't think Raffles was crazy about the bridge, either, although he didn't seem that much happier when we were back on solid ground. Plaintive noises issued from his cat carrier. I wondered if he could see his breath. I could see mine.

The path to the house had been recently cleared, and I wondered how Orris had managed it with the plow parked on the other side of the bridge. Then we rounded a bend and the house came into view, a light glowing in every window, a plume of smoke rising from the chimney. Near the front entrance, just to the side of one of a pair of pillars, stood a snow blower, its own top surface already covered with an inch of fresh snow.

"Orris can't be too slow," I said, "if he can figure out how to work one of those things." I lifted our bags onto the porch, set the cat carrier alongside them. "I pick up animals. I brake for yokels. What are we supposed to do with the wagons?"

She pointed, and I saw a whole herd of red wagons, a counterpart to the group on the other side of the bridge. I parked ours with the others. "Now they can catch up on all the gossip," I told Carolyn. "What stories they'll have to tell."

She rolled her eyes. I rang the doorbell, and I was just about to ring it again when the heavy door opened inward, held by a hulking youth with a shock of dark blond hair. He had the look in his eyes that the average person gets by being smacked in the forehead with a two-by-four. He motioned us inside, then reached for the suitcases and dropped them at the front desk, even as a tall gentleman with a well-bred smile was emerging from behind it.

"Welcome, welcome," he said. "Wretched weather, isn't it? And I'm afraid we're in for rather a good deal of it, if the chap on the radio is to be believed. Did you have a horrid time getting here?"

"It wasn't so bad."

"Ah, that's the spirit." You'd have thought I'd kept a stiff upper lip through the Blitz. "But let me welcome you formally to Cuttleford House. I'm your host, actually. Nigel Eglantine. And you would be—?"

"Bernard Rhodenbarr."

"I rather thought you would be Mr. Rhodenbarr, although you might have been Mr. Littlefield. We're not really expecting the Littlefields for another hour, and they may be even later the way it's snowing." He frowned at the prospect, then brightened and beamed at Carolyn. "And this would be Miss Lettice Runcible," he said.

"Uh, no," I said. "This would be Miss Carolyn Kaiser."

"Quite," he said. "Of course it would. Ah, Mr. Rhodenbarr, Miss Kaiser, let me just see where we've put you." He checked the register, snatched up a pencil, used one end of it to rub out Lettice's name and the other to jot down Carolyn's, and managed all this while telling us that we must be famished, that dinner had already been served, actually, but that there'd be something for us in the dining room as soon as we'd had a chance to get to our room and freshen up.

"We've put you in Aunt Augusta's Room," he said. "I think you'll be quite comfortable there."

"I'm sure we will," Carolyn said. "But what about Aunt Augusta? Will she have to sleep in the hall?"

He laughed richly, as if Carolyn had said something wonderfully amusing. "Oh, that's just our way," he said. "I'm afraid we've named all the sleeping rooms for friends and relatives, and of course we'd be delighted to put Aunt Augusta into her room if she were ever to come visit, but it's not terribly likely. She's in a nursing home in Harpenden, poor thing."

"That's too bad."

"But I do think she'd like the room if she ever saw it, and I hope you'll be happy there yourselves. It's Cissy's particular favorite."

"Cissy?"

"My wife. Christened Cecilia, but there's nothing quite

so enduring as a childhood nickname, is there? Your room's up that staircase and along to the left, and you just keep going until you get to it. Will you want a hand with your luggage?"

"We can manage."

"If you're quite certain. I'd send Orris with you, but he seems to have slipped off somewhere." His eyes narrowed. "I say, is that a cat in there?"

It would have been difficult to deny, the animal in question having just announced himself with a meow like chalk on a blackboard. "He's a Manx," I said. "His name is Raffles."

"Of course it is," he said. "And of course he's a perfect gentleman about, ah, bathroom habits and that sort of thing."

"Of course."

"Then I'm sure he'll be quite at home here," he said smoothly, "and I'm sure we'll be glad of his company."

"It's nice that the rooms all have names," Carolyn said. "It's so much cozier than having a room with a number."

I was at the window, watching it snow. It seemed pretty serious about it.

"More challenging, too," she went on. "If they'd put us in Room 28, we'd have known to look for it between Room 27 and Room 29. But how would anybody know to look for Aunt Augusta between Uncle Roger and Cousin Beatrice?"

"And directly across the hall from Vicar Andrews."

"That sounds a little scandalous, if you ask me. Maybe there's rhyme and reason to it, but you'd need a copy of the family tree to sort it all out. This is a great room, though, Bern. Nice, huh? Beamed ceiling, fireplace, big window looking out at—what does it look out at, Bern?"

"Snow," I said. "Whatever happened to global warming?"

"You only get that in the summer. Anyway, I don't care how much it snows now that we're inside. I'd rather look at snow than a fire escape and a row of garbage cans, which is all you can see from my window on Arbor Court. You know, Bern, all this room needs is one more thing and it would be perfect."

"What's that?"

"A second bed."

"Oh."

"I mean, this is a real beauty, a four-poster with a chintz canopy and all, and it looks really comfy." She hopped onto it, kicked her shoes off, stretched out. "It's even better than it looks," she reported, "and if you were a beautiful woman I'd like nothing better than to share it with you. They made a mistake, huh? You told them twin beds, didn't you?"

"I must have."

" 'I must have.' That's a *no*, right?"

"I meant to, Carolyn."

"You meant to."

I sighed. "When I made the reservation," I said, "it was for me and Lettice, and I specified a double bed. As a matter of fact, I made a special point of specifying a double bed."

"I bet you did."

"And when I sent them a deposit, I put that in the note I enclosed along with the check."

"And then Lettice decided to get married instead."

"Right."

"And you brought me in off the bench."

"To save the game," I said. "And I realized we would be happier with twin beds, and I started to make the call, and I felt like an idiot. 'Hi, this is Bernie Rhodenbarr, that's R-H-O, right, and I'll be arriving as scheduled a week from Thursday, but I want twin beds instead of a double. Oh, and by the way, Ms. Runcible won't be coming with me. But Ms. Kaiser will.'"

"I see what you mean."

"I figured I'd wait until I could think of a graceful way to do it, and I'm still waiting. Look, we've been friends a long time, Carolyn. Neither of us is going to turn into a sex maniac in the middle of the night. We can share a bed platonically."

"I just wonder if we'll get any sleep. This bed's comfy, but it sags in the middle. We may keep rolling into each other."

"We'll manage," I insisted. "Anyway, we'll probably be sleeping in shifts."

"I brought pajamas."

"I mean we'll take turns. The middle of the night's the best time for me to check out the library shelves."

"Won't that be suspicious, Bern?"

"Why? What else do you do when you have insomnia? You look for a good book to read."

"Preferably a signed first edition. So you figure you'll be up nights?"

"Most likely."

"So I'll be all alone in a haunted house."

"What makes you think it's haunted?"

"If you were a ghost, Bern, would you pass up a place like this? The walls tilt, the floorboards creak, the window-panes rattle every time the wind blows. You might as well hang out a sign—'Ghost wanted—ideal working conditions.' "

"Well, I didn't see any sign like that."

"Of course not. The position's been filled. I'll be lying here awake and you'll be downstairs looking for *The Big Sleep*. Bern, look at Raffles, he's pacing back and forth like an expectant father. Open the bathroom door for him, will you?"

I opened the door and looked straight at a batch of coat hangers.

"Bern, don't tell me."

"It's an old-fashioned authentic country house," I said.

"Does that mean they don't have bathrooms?"

"Of course they have bathrooms."

"Where?"

"In the hall."

"Gee," she said, "I sure am glad we're not in some impersonal modern resort, with numbered rooms and separate beds and level floors and rattle-free windows and private baths. I'm glad we don't have to put up with that kind of soul-deadening experience."

I opened the hall door and followed Raffles through it. I came back to report that the bathroom was just down the hall, between Uncle Edmund and Aunt Petra. "And Raffles doesn't seem to mind that it's a communal john," I added. "He found it perfectly suitable."

"How's he going to get in there by himself, Bern? If the door's closed, he won't be able to turn the knob."

"If the door's closed," I said, "that means somebody else is in there, and he'll have to wait his turn. If the john's not occupied, you leave the door ajar. That's how it works with communal bathrooms."

"What about this door?"

"Huh?"

"How's he going to get out in the middle of the night," she said, "if our door's closed?"

"Hell," I said. "We should have brought a cat box."

"He's trained to use the toilet, just like a person. You can't go and untrain him."

"You're right. I guess we'll just have to leave the door open a crack."

"That's great," she said. "You'll be downstairs, and ghosts'll be dragging chains through the halls, and I'll be lying in here in the dark with the door open, waiting for the young 'un to murder me in my bed. This gets better every minute."

" 'The young 'un.' Orris? Why would he murder you in your bed?"

"Because that's where I'll be," she said, "unless I'm hiding under it."

"But what makes you think he—"

" 'Better to have him plowing driveways than locked away his whole life.' What do you figure he did that made them lock him away?"

"But that's the point, Carolyn. They *didn't* lock him away."

"It evidently crossed their minds," she said, "and they decided against it. What do you figure gave them the notion?"

"He's evidently a little slow," I said. "Maybe there was some sentiment in favor of institutionalizing him for that reason, but instead it was determined that he could lead a productive life outside."

"Plowing driveways, for instance."

"And being a general handyman."

"And lurking," she said. "And drooling. And slipping into Aunt Augusta's Room with an ax."

"Sometimes," I said, "when people are cranky, it's because they're hungry."

"And sometimes it's because they need a drink, and sometimes it's both." She got out of bed, combed her hair with her fingertips, brushed some imaginary lint off her blazer. "C'mon," she said. "What are we waiting for?"

After all that, I was expecting dinner to be a disaster—translucent roast beef, say, and vegetables boiled into submission. The outlook improved, though, when we got to the bottom of the stairs and met a woman with feathery blond hair, plump chipmunk cheeks, and an air of radiant well-being. "The Rhodenbarrs," she said, beaming, and who could presume to correct her? "I'm Cissy Eglantine, and I do hope you're happy in Aunt Augusta's Room. I think it's quite the coziest, myself."

We assured her it was charming.

"Oh, I'm so glad you like it," she said. "Now we're getting a late supper laid for you in the dining room, but I wonder if you might want to stop in the bar first? Nigel's especially proud of his selection of single-malt Scotches, if you have any interest at all in that sort of thing."

We admitted to a sort of academic interest and hurried off to the bar. "The trouble with trying to compare different whiskies," Carolyn said when we finally moved on to the dining room, "is that by the time you're sipping the fourth one, it's impossible to remember what the first one tasted like. So you have to go back and start over."

"And before long," I said, "you have trouble remembering other things. Like your name."

"Well, nobody else remembers my name, so why should

I? I just got here an hour ago and already I've been Ms. Runcible and Mrs. Rhodenbarr. I can't wait to see what the future holds. What's the matter?"

"Nothing's the matter," I said. "Something smells terrific."

And so it was. A rich and savory soup, a salad of romaine and Boston lettuce with walnuts and dill, and a thick slab of prime rib flanked with crisp little roasted potatoes. The waitress, a skittish country girl who might have been Orris's sister (or his wife, or both), brought us mugs of brown ale without asking, and filled them up when we emptied them.

Dessert was some sort of fruit cobbler, topped with what Carolyn said had to be clotted cream. "Look at this," she said. "You could float a scone on it. You could float the Stone of Scone on it. Bern, forget everything I said."

"Starting when?"

"Starting when we got here. You want to know something? I don't give a rat's ass if the place is haunted. If the ghost's got any sense he won't come anywhere near our room, anyway. He'll hang out in the kitchen. Bern, this is one of the best meals I've ever had in my life."

"You know what they say. Hunger's the best sauce."

"I was hungry enough to eat my shoes," she said, "I'll admit it, but it was still an incredible meal. Can you believe it? The coffee's good. I meant to order tea, because everybody knows the English can't make a decent cup of coffee. But this is great. How do you explain that, Bern?"

"Maybe they didn't come straight here from England," I suggested. "Maybe they stopped off in Seattle."

"That must be it," she said, and wiped her mouth with her napkin. "Look at me, Bern. A couple of pops and a decent meal and I think I died and went to heaven. I'll tell you something. I like it here. I'm glad we came."

SIX

After dinner we drifted from room to room, getting our bearings on the first floor of Cuttleford House. There was, God knows, an awful lot of it, and one room just sort of led to another. We started out in a sort of sitting room called the East Parlour, and I might have taken it for the library if I hadn't already seen the Great Library in the brochure. The parlor had floor-to-ceiling bookshelves on either side of the fireplace. The other walls sported memorabilia—crossed spears, West African ceremonial masks, and the stuffed head of one of those crossword-puzzle animals. An oryx, say.

There were more books on a breakfront, braced by a pair of bronze Abraham-Lincoln-seated-and-looking-pensive bookends, and there were revolving bookcases flanking the floral-patterned sofa.

"There are books all over the place," Carolyn murmured. "You saw the bookcase in our room, didn't you?"

"Uh-huh. It reminded me of my bargain table."

"No *Big Sleep*, huh?"

"Just a large yawn. Mostly late-model paperbacks. Last

year's best-sellers. The kind of book you take along to a resort and leave behind when you go home."

"If you managed to finish it."

"Or even if you didn't," I said.

We broke off to get into conversation with Colonel Edward Blount-Buller, a florid-faced gentleman in moleskin trousers and a tweed Norfolk jacket. We'd been introduced to him in the bar before dinner, and he'd evidently lingered there amidst the single-malt Scotches. Now he was moved to discourse upon the inherent nobility of the hunting trophy on the opposite wall.

"It's the horns, don't you know." We must have looked puzzled. "The horns, the horns," he said. "The long graceful tapering horns. What would he be without them, eh?" He held up a finger, its knuckle knobby with arthritis. "I'll tell you," he said. "Be a bloody nanny goat."

"I'd rather be a live nanny goat," Carolyn said, "than have some jerk shoot me and stick my head on his wall."

"Ah," he said. "Well, you're a woman, eh?"

"What's that supposed to mean?"

"No slight intended, I assure you. But the gentler sex has a more practical nature, takes short views. Better to munch grass and give milk than to take a bullet, eh?"

"If those are the choices," she said, "I wouldn't have to spend a long time thinking it over."

"Without his horns," the colonel said, "our springbok would have gone on grazing until age made him easy prey to a lion or a dog pack. He'd have left his bones bleaching in the hot African sun. The world would have long since forgotten him." He gestured at the mounted head. "Instead he lives on," he announced, "countless years past his ordinary lifespan. It's immortality of a sort, wot? Not quite the sort you or I might choose, but quite the best available to him."

"A springbok," I said.

"And a fine one, sir, wouldn't you say?"

"You're sure it's not an oryx?"

"Hardly that."

"Or an ibex," I suggested. "Or an okapi, or even a gnu."

"Fine beasts, all of them," he said. "But our friend here is a springbok. You have my assurance of that."

In the Sitting Room, the walls were given over to framed Ape and Spy caricatures from the old *Vanity Fair*, with not a single stuffed head to be seen. There were books, though, filling a three-tiered set of glassed-in shelves and propped between a pair of sailing-ship bookends.

I had a quick look at the books while Carolyn leafed through a year-old copy of *Town & Country*. When I dropped into the chair next to hers she closed the magazine and looked at me.

"Better books," I said. "Hardcover fiction, most of it between fifty and eighty years old. Some mysteries, all by authors that nobody reads nowadays. A lot of general fiction. James T. Farrell, one of the books in his Danny O'Neill tetralogy. And *Mammonart*, by Upton Sinclair."

"Are they valuable, Bern?"

"They're both important writers," I said, "but they're not very actively collected. And of course the dust jackets are long gone."

"What do you mean, 'long gone'? For all you know they were there until five minutes ago."

"You're right," I said. "I jumped to a conclusion, based

on the fact that all but two or three of the books in the case are missing their jackets."

"Then it's a good thing they're inside, Bern. In this weather, they'd freeze their flyleaves off." She pointed at the window. "Still coming down," she said.

"So it is."

"You hardly looked at those books, Bernie. You just scanned each shelf for a couple of seconds, and you knew what was there and what wasn't."

"Well, I'm in the business," I said. "When you look at books day in and day out, you develop a knack."

"Makes sense, Bern. I'm the same way with dogs."

"And it's easier," I said, "when you know what you're looking for. There's just one book I'm looking for, so I don't have to take a careful inventory of everything else. As soon as I know I'm not looking at Raymond Chandler, I can go on and look at something else."

"Like a springbok," she said. "If that's what it was."

"What else could it be?"

"You named a whole lot of other things, Bern. You didn't want it to be a springbok. How'd you learn so much about African antelopes?"

"All I know about them I learned from crossword puzzles," I said, "and that's why I didn't think it was a springbok. It's nine letters long, for God's sake. When's the last time you saw a springbok in a crossword puzzle?"

"You should have pointed that out to the colonel. Don't you love the way he talks? I guess that's what you call a pukka sahib accent."

"I guess so."

"If he were any more English," she said, "he couldn't talk at all. This is great, Bern. It's not just that Cuttleford

House is something straight out of an English mystery. The guests could have stepped right out of the pages themselves. The colonel's perfect in that respect. He could be Jane Marple's neighbor, recently retired to St. Mary Mead after a career shooting people in India."

"People and springboks," I said.

"And those two women we met in the Sewing Room. Miss Dinmont and Miss Hardesty. The frail Miss Dinmont and the outgoing Miss Hardesty."

"If you say so," I said. "I couldn't keep them straight."

"Neither could God, Bern."

"Huh?"

"Keep them straight."

"Oh. You figure they're gay?"

"If this were an English mystery," she said, "instead of life itself, I'd go along with the pretense that Miss Dinmont is a wealthy invalid and Miss Hardesty is her companion, and that's all there is to the relationship." She frowned. "Of course, in the last chapter it would turn out that the wheelchair's just a prop, and Miss Dinmont would be capable of leaping around like a gazelle, or one of those other animals you got from the crossword puzzle. That's because in the books things are never quite what they appear to be. In real life, things tend to be *exactly* what they appear to be."

"And they appear to be lesbians?"

"Well, it doesn't take x-ray vision, does it? Hardesty's your typical backslapping butch, and Dinmont's one of those passive-aggressive femme numbers. If you want to remember which is which, incidentally, try alliteration. Dim little Miss Dinmont and hearty horsey Miss Hardesty. As a matter of fact—"

She broke off the sentence when a small force of nature burst into the room. We'd encountered her before in another room—don't ask me which one—but then she'd been accompanied by her parents. Now she was all by herself.

"Hello," she said. "Have we met? I saw you both before, but I don't believe we've been introduced. I'm Millicent Savage."

"I'm Bernie Rhodenbarr," I said. "And this is Carolyn Kaiser."

"It's ever so nice to meet you. Are you married?"

"No," Carolyn said. "Are you?"

"Of course not," Millicent said. "I'm just a little girl. That's why I can get away with asking impertinent questions. Guess how old I am."

"Thirty-two," Carolyn said.

"Seriously," the child said.

"I hate guessing games," Carolyn said. "You're really going to make me guess? Oh, all right. Ten."

"That's your guess? Ten?" She turned to me. "How about you, Bernie?"

"Ten," I said.

"She already guessed ten."

"Well, it's my guess, too. How old *are* you, Millicent?"

"Ten," she said.

"Then we got it right," Carolyn said.

"*You* got it right. He just tagged along."

"You're disappointed that we guessed your age, aren't you?"

"Most people think I'm older."

"That's because you're precocious. That probably makes them guess you're twelve or thirteen, but if you were you wouldn't be precocious, and you obviously are. So that would make you about ten, and that's what I guessed, and I was right."

She looked at Carolyn. She was a pretty child, with straight blond hair and Delft-blue eyes and a crescent-shaped half-inch scar on her chin. "Is that what you do?" she wanted to know. "Do you work in a carnival guessing people's age?"

"It'd be a good sideline," Carolyn said, "but it's a tough business to break into. I'm a canine stylist."

"What's that?"

"I have a dog-grooming salon."

"That sounds super. What's your favorite breed of dog?"

"I suppose Yorkies."

"Why? Appearance or disposition?"

"Size," she said. "There's less to wash."

"I never thought of that." She turned to me. "What about you?"

"What about me?"

"What do you do? Are you a canine stylist too?"

I shook my head. "I'm a burglar."

That got her giggling. "A burglar," she said. "What kind of a burglar? A cat burglar?"

"That's the best kind."

"Well, there's a cat here," she said, "just waiting for somebody to burgle him. But I'm afraid his tail has already been stolen."

"It's our cat," I said.

"Is it really? Is he a Manx?" I nodded. "I've never actually seen a Manx before," she said. "Did you get him on the Isle of Man?"

"Close. The Isle of Manhattan."

"And they let you bring him here? I didn't know you were allowed to bring pets."

"He's not a pet," Carolyn said. "He's an employee."

"At Carolyn's salon," I said quickly. "Burglars don't have employees, human or feline. But there are a lot of supplies at the salon, and the mice were getting into all sorts of things. It's Raffles's job to put a stop to that."

If Raffles was a working cat, she demanded, then why wasn't he on the job now, guarding the stock from rodent damage? I told her I'd wondered about that myself.

"He needs company," Carolyn said. "We won't get back until late Sunday, or possibly not until Monday. How would you like it if your parents left you home alone that long?"

"I wouldn't mind."

"Well, you're not a cat," Carolyn said. Millicent agreed that she wasn't, and I asked her what she did for a living.

This elicited another burst of giggles. "I don't do anything," she said. "I'm a little girl."

"Are you English?"

"No, I'm American. We live in Boston."

"You sound English."

"Do I?" She beamed. "It's an affection."

"You mean an affectation."

"Yes, of course that's what I meant. But I have an affection for England, too. I must have been English in a past life. Do you know who I think I was?"

"Not a scullery maid, I'll bet."

"Lady Jane Grey," she said. "Or possibly Anne Boleyn. They were both queens, you know." She leaned forward, eyes narrowed. "And they were both put to death," she said.

"Well, I certainly don't think—"

"Oh, that was then and this is now," she said airily.

"But I love to watch *Masterpiece Theatre*, and all the other English programs on PBS, and I get yelled at in school all the time for spelling words like 'colour' and 'harbour' with a U, and 'programme' with two M's and an E. I think it looks ever so much nicer that way, don't you?"

"I don't think there's any question about it," Carolyn said.

"And I love coming here," Millicent went on. "This is our third time at Cuttleford House. I have my own room this time. I'm in Uncle Roger's Room. That's right near you, because you're in Aunt Augusta's."

"How did you happen to know that?"

"Oh, I know everything," she said. "People tell me things. I know you're a burglar, Bernie, and I bet nobody else here knows that."

"Maybe it could be our little secret," Carolyn suggested.

She mimed locking her lips with a key. "My lips are sealed," she said, "and only Bernie can pick the lock. And if I'm locked out of Uncle Roger's Room, you can let me in. Except I shan't be." She lifted a string encircling her neck to show a key dangling from it. "I've never stayed in Aunt Augusta's Room. The first time I came here all three of us were in the Vicar's Upstairs Parlour. It's the largest sleeping room of all, the one with three beds. How many beds do you have?"

"One at the most," Carolyn said.

"The last time we came the Vicar's was taken, and they were going to put us in Poor Miss McTavish's, but it was too small. My father said he drew the line at that, and my mother said perhaps it was time I had my own room. Do you know what I said?"

"You probably said that was jolly good."

"How did you know? Anyway, Nigel put Mummy and Daddy in Lucinda's Room, and I had Poor Miss McTavish's all to myself."

"Why do they call it that?" Carolyn wanted to know. "Is it the room that's poor, or Miss McTavish?"

"I think it must be Miss McTavish," the child said, "because it's a perfectly lovely room. The walls are bright yellow and it's very cheery. Miss McTavish must be the governess, don't you think? Someone must have broken her heart."

"The butler," Carolyn suggested.

"He's a bounder," Millicent agreed. "Or a cad. Is there a difference between a bounder and a cad?" Neither of us knew. "Well, whichever he is," she said, "he's certainly a bad hat. And Poor Miss McTavish—"

She broke off when a woman darted into the room, looking a little harried. "There you are," she said. "Millicent, I've been looking all over for you. It's time you were off to bed."

"I'm not tired, Mummy."

"You're never tired," Mrs. Savage said, aggrieved. One sensed she was often tired herself, and that it was largely Millicent's fault. She sighed, and became aware of our existence. "I hope she hasn't been driving the two of you nuts," she said. "She's really a pretty good little kid, except when she decides she's Mary, Queen of Scots."

"Oh, Mummy. *Not* Mary, Queen of Scots." She rolled her eyes. "Mummy, this is Bernie and Carolyn. They have Aunt Augusta's Room."

"That's a nice room, isn't it? It's nice to meet you both. I'm Leona Savage. My husband Greg's here somewhere, but don't ask me where."

We said we were pleased to meet her. "They're very nice," Millicent announced. "Carolyn's a canine stylist. And you'll never guess what Bernie does."

"I'll never guess what a canine stylist is, either, I'm afraid."

"She grooms dogs, Mummy. Especially Yorkies, because there's less to wash. And Bernie's a burglar."

"That was going to be our little secret," I reminded her.

"Oh, Mummy wouldn't tell anyone. Would you, Mummy?"

SEVEN

Our next stop was the library. I'd already seen a picture of it in the brochure, but you know what they say about the Grand Canyon. Nothing prepares you for it.

It was an enormous room, with built-in floor-to-ceiling bookshelves running the length of it and a wall of windows opposite. There was a fireplace at one end, with various savage-looking tribal weapons mounted above it and a bookcase on either side. At the room's other end, a carved Jacobean table held magazines and newspapers; above it, a Mercator-projection map was mounted on the wall. It showed all of Britain's crown colonies and dominions and protectorates in pink, and it dated from a time when the sun never set thereon.

A lectern displayed an opened copy of the *Oxford Universal Dictionary*, while another showed a National Geographic atlas some fifty years more recent than the map. A two-tiered bookcase on casters held an eleventh edition of the *Britannica*. Other tables and chairs and sofas were strategically positioned around the room, with good reading light wherever you might happen to sit. A vast oriental covered most of the wide-board pine floor, with area rugs and runners helping out where needed.

I just stood there and stared. I have been in a lot of magnificent rooms, including more than a few fine private libraries. Sometimes I have been present by invitation, and other times I have turned up on my own, without the owner's permission and much to his chagrin. I have found it difficult to leave some of those rooms, wanting to extend my stay as long as I possibly could, but this was different.

I wanted to steal the whole room. I wanted to wrap it up in a magic carpet—perhaps the very one beneath my feet; it looked entirely capable of having magical properties—and whisk it back to New York, where I could install it with a snap of my fingers on the top floor, say, of an Art Deco apartment building on Central Park South. Drop-dead views of the park through that wall of windows, and a gentle north light that wouldn't fade the carpet or the spines of the books . . .

I wouldn't need anything else. No bedroom. I'd sleep sitting up in one of the chairs, nodding off over a leatherbound Victorian novel. No kitchen, either. I'd pick up something at the deli around the corner. A bathroom would be handy, though I could make do with one down the hall if I had to, even as we were doing this weekend.

Give me that room, though, and I could be perfectly happy

I said as much to Carolyn, said it in a whisper to avoid disturbing the older woman reading Trollope on the green velvet sofa or the intense dark-haired gentleman scribbling away at the leather-topped writing desk. She was not surprised.

"Of course you could," she said. "This room's gotta be twice the size of your whole apartment. Forget my little rathole. You could just about lose my apartment in that fireplace."

"It's not just the size."

"It's pretty nice," she agreed. "And look at all those books. You think one of them's the one you're looking for?"

"One at the most."

"That was my line, Bern. When Millie asked how many beds we've got in Aunt Augusta's Room."

"You figure she likes being called Millie?"

"She probably hates it," she said, "but she's not here, and anyway I'm whispering. Bernie, don't look now, but that man is staring at me. See?"

"How can I see? You just said not to look."

"Well, you can look now. He's not doing it anymore."

"Then why look if there's nothing to see?" I looked anyway, at the fellow at the writing desk. He looked as though he'd stepped out of a Brontë novel and might at any moment step out of Cuttleford House as well, flinging his scarf around his neck and striding across the moors. Except that he wasn't wearing a scarf, and there weren't any moors in the neighborhood.

"I think he was just staring off into space," I said. "Trying to think of *le mot juste*, and you happened to be where his eyes landed."

"I suppose so. Incidentally, are you out of your mind?"

"Probably. What makes you ask?"

"I was just wondering what possessed you to tell little Princess Margaret that you're a burglar."

"Not Princess Margaret."

"Bern—"

"Lady Jane Grey," I said. "Or Anne Boleyn."

"Who cares? The point is—"

"I get the point."

"So?"

"I almost slipped," I said. "I almost let out what I really am."

"What you really . . ."

"I almost said I was a bookseller."

"But fortunately you caught yourself at the last minute and told her you were a burglar."

"Right."

"Am I missing something here?"

"Think about it," I said.

She did, and after a long moment light dawned. "Oh," she said.

"Right."

"There's a million books in the damn house," she said, "and most of them are old, and some of them are sure to be rare. And if they knew there was a bookseller in their midst—"

"They'd be on guard," I said. "At the very least."

"Whereas knowing they've got a burglar on the premises gives them a nice cozy warm feeling."

"I didn't want to say 'bookseller'," I said, "and I had to do something quick, and I wanted to stay with the same initial."

"Why? Monogrammed luggage?"

"My lips were already forming a B."

" 'A butcher, a baker, a bindlestaff maker.' All of them start with B, Bernie, and they all sound more innocent than 'burglar.' "

"I know."

"It's a good thing her lips are sealed."

"Yeah, right. She already told Mummy. But you don't think Mummy believed it, do you?"

"She thought you were joking with the kid."

"And so will anyone else she happens to tell. As far as that goes, do you really think Millicent thought I'd come here to steal the spoons? She assumed it was a gag and she was happy to go along with it. When anyone presses the point, I'll let it be known that you and I work together at the Poodle Factory. What's the matter?"

"Bern, don't take this the wrong way, but I never had a partner and I never will."

"It's just a story to let out, Carolyn."

"I mean it's not much, the Poodle Factory, but it's mine, you know?"

"So I'm your employee. Is that better?"

"A little bit. The thing is, what do you know about washing dogs? I'm the last person to compare it to rocket science, but it's like any other trade. There's a lot of information involved, and if you should happen to come up against a pet owner who's familiar with what goes on at a dog-grooming salon, it might blow your cover."

"I'm just helping out," I said. "I lost my job, and now I'm helping you at the salon while I wait for something to open up in my own field."

"And what's that, Bern?"

"I'll think of something, okay?"

"Hey, don't bite my head off, Bernie."

"Sorry."

"You know what's funny?"

"Hardly anything."

"Bern—"

"What's funny?"

"Well," she said, "remember when you bought Barnegat Books from Mr. Litzauer? You were a big reader, and you always liked books, and you figured owning a bookstore would be a good front. You could pretend to be a bookseller while you went on breaking into houses."

"So?"

"So now you're pretending to be a burglar," she said, "while you chase around after old books. Don't you think that's funny?"

"Sure," I said. "It's a riot."

From the library we went through another parlor, winding up in something called the Morning Room. Maybe it was situated to catch the morning sun, or maybe it was where you took your second cup of coffee after breakfast. (It wasn't where you had breakfast. That's what the Breakfast Room was for.)

In the Morning Room we met Gordon Wolpert, a fiftyish fellow dressed all in brown. He was a widower, we learned, and he was on the seventh day of a ten-day stay. "But I might extend it," he said. "It's a spectacular house, and the kitchen is really quite remarkable. Did you arrive in time for dinner? Well, then you know what I mean. I'm putting on weight, and I can't honestly say I give a damn. Maybe I'll have my clothes let out and become a permanent resident, like the colonel."

"Colonel Buller-Blount? He lives here all the time?"

"Blount-Buller, actually. And I guess it's not accurate to call him a permanent guest. He stays here half the year."

"And spends the other half in England? I suppose it must have something to do with taxes."

"It has everything to do with taxes, but he doesn't spend

a minute in England. He told me he hasn't been there in years. Hates the place."

"Really? He's the most English person I ever met in my life."

Wolpert grinned. "With the possible exception of young Millicent," he said. "As a matter of fact, it's his Englishness that makes him stay away. He can't stand what's become of the country. He says they've ruined it."

"They?"

"A sort of generic 'they,' from the sound of it. He wants the England he remembers from boyhood, and he has to come here to Cuttleford House for it."

Carolyn wanted to know where he spent the other six months.

"Six months and a day, actually. In Florida. That way he doesn't have to pay any state income tax, and I think there are other tax savings as well."

"Oh, sure," she said. "A lot of New Yorkers do the same thing. Hey, wait a minute. Hasn't he got it backwards?" She waved a hand at the window, on the other side of which the snow continued to fall. "It's winter. What's he doing up here?"

"The colonel reverses the usual order of things," Wolpert said. "He comes north during the fall foliage season and heads south in April. That way the old boy is always paying the low off-season rates."

"That's the good news," I said. "The bad news is he never gets decent weather."

"That's the whole point."

"It is?"

"Remember, he's looking to recapture the rapture. Winter here reminds him of happy boyhood hours on the moors, chasing the wily grouse or whatever you do on the moors. And Florida in the summer puts him in mind of his years in Her Majesty's Service, most of which seem to have been spent in one tropical hellhole or another."

"That's perverse," Carolyn said.

"The English word for it is 'eccentric,' " Wolpert said. "He's got the worst of both worlds, but evidently it works for him. I suppose you could say that he's like the proverbial fellow with one foot in a bucket of boiling water and the other in a bucket of ice water. On the average, he's perfectly comfortable."

I wondered what kind of work Gordon Wolpert did that gave him the option of extending his stay. I might have asked, but that would only have invited the same question in return, and I hadn't yet decided how to respond.

So we talked about some of the other guests instead, and about Cuttleford House and its staff. Wolpert had met the Misses Dinmont and Hardesty, but he hadn't had much chance to size them up. "The one looks as though she'd be trying to get everybody out on the Great Lawn for field hockey if it weren't for the snow," he said. "And the other has a *Magic Mountain* air about her, doesn't she?"

"Magic Mountain?" Carolyn said. "You mean the theme park?"

"The Thomas Mann novel," I said gently. "The one set at the sanitarium. Do you think Miss Dinmont has TB?"

"I don't know what's wrong with her," he said. "Not TB, I wouldn't think, but most likely something else with initials. She just seems to me to have the air of somebody who came here to die."

I had that sentence echoing in my mind for a while, so I

missed most of what he had to say about the Eglantines and the handful of people who worked for them—Orris, a pair of chambermaids, and the cook. We'd met Orris, for all that was worth, and hadn't yet set eyes on the others, although the cook had made her wondrous presence known.

"Nigel and Cissy Eglantine have made a good thing of this sprawling old pile," he said. "I don't know what he did before this, but he certainly has the knack for playing hotelier. I suppose you've seen his array of single-malt whiskies."

"He has quite a collection."

"I don't know that you can label a Scotch 'rare,' but I gather some of them are the product of distilleries with extremely limited production. There are more varieties than you might imagine. I'd have thought it a confined area of expertise." His eyes sought mine. "A small field indeed," he said deliberately. "Nigel has developed quite a palate for them."

"Oh?"

"Late in the evening," he said carefully, "or at times of stress, there's something about him that will remind you of Basil Fawlty. But most of the time he's the perfect host." He cocked his head. "Of course, he's not the first person to make a show of appearing sober when he's three sheets to the wind. Everybody does it. But it's a sham, isn't it?"

"I suppose you could call it that," I agreed.

"And a petty sham at that," he said, his eyes on mine. "You could call it that, couldn't you? A petty sham?"

I gave a noncommittal nod, and it seemed to me that he looked just the slightest bit disappointed.

There were books in the Morning Room, too, and after Gordon Wolpert had left us I picked up one of them and turned its pages. "Frances and Richard Lockridge," Carolyn read over my shoulder. "Writing about Pam and Jerry North. Maybe we'll be like Mr. and Mrs. North, Bernie. Isn't there a book where they go on a vacation?"

"It wouldn't surprise me."

"And while they're off somewhere, there's a murder. And they solve it."

"I should hope so," I said, "or otherwise there's no book."

"So maybe that'll happen to us."

"Maybe what'll happen to us?"

"Maybe somebody'll get killed, and we'll solve it."

"No one will get killed," I said. "There won't be anything to solve."

"Why's that, Bern?"

"Because we're on vacation."

"So were Mr. and Mrs. North, and then murder took a holiday."

"Well, this time around murder better take a siesta. I want to kick back and relax, and I want to eat three great meals a day and sleep eight hours a night, and then I want to go home with Raymond Chandler. I don't want cops poring through my luggage, and that's exactly what I'll get if we wind up in the middle of a murder investigation. And why should that happen in the first place? We're in a perfectly peaceful place with perfectly charming people."

"That's how it starts, Bern."

"What are you talking about?"

"Perfectly nice people, some of them slightly wacky, but all of them well-bred and well-spoken. Some of them may not be what they seem, and a couple of them have a dark secret in their past, and they're isolated somewhere, and somebody gets killed. And then somebody says, 'Oh, it must have been some passing tramp who did it, because otherwise it would have to have been one of us, and that's plainly impossible because we're all such nice people.' But guess what, Bern?"

"It's really one of them?"

"Every last time. And it's not the butler, either."

"Well, that part's right," I said, "because that's where Cuttleford's imitation of an English country house begins to break down. There's no butler."

"That doesn't mean there won't be a murder."

"Sure it does," I said. I closed the Mr. and Mrs. North mystery—hardcover, no dust jacket, spine shaky, some pages dog-eared—and put it back where I'd found it. "I haven't got time for a murder, not to commit and not to solve. I'm tired. I want to turn in soon and sleep until the snow melts."

"You can't sleep, Bern."

"Want to bet?"

"Even if you want to," she said. "Remember? You're going to be up all night. You've got a book to find."

"That's what you think."

"You're giving up? Well, I'm disappointed, but I can't honestly say I blame you. It'd be like looking for a needle in a haystack, except it wouldn't."

"I see what you mean."

"You do?"

"No."

"Well, it's the opposite of a needle in a haystack, isn't it? It's more like a needle in a needle stack. Not just any needle, but one particular needle in the midst of all the others."

"A needlestack," I said thoughtfully. "I don't think I've ever come across one."

"So? When's the last time you saw a haystack?"

"I'm sure I wrote it down," I said, "but I don't have my notebook with me. What's the point?"

"The point is every room is crawling with books, and the library alone has more volumes than you've got in your store, including the back room. So it may be an easy place to find something to read, but it's an impossible place to find something specific, even if it's there to start with, which it probably isn't." She took a deep breath. "So I can understand why you're abandoning the hunt."

"Is that what I'm doing?"

"What else? I said you've got a book to find, and you said, 'That's what you think.' "

"Right."

"Meaning you're not going to bother looking."

"Meaning I don't have to look."

She looked at me.

"Meaning I already found it," I said. "So why shouldn't I treat myself to a good night's sleep?"

"The top shelf," I said. "You see the section closest to the wall?"

"Uh-huh."

"Well, it's the section immediately to the right of it. See the one I mean?"

"I think so," she whispered. "I don't want to look directly at it."

"Why not?"

"I don't want to arouse suspicion, Bern."

"We're in a library," I said, as indeed we were, having gone there directly from the Morning Room. "Looking at books is a natural occupation in a room like this. And it's a lot less suspicious to stare right at them than it is to glance furtively."

"Is that what I was doing? Glancing furtively?"

"Well, it looked furtive to me. I don't think it made any impression on anybody else because nobody else noticed."

Not that we were alone. The two guests we'd seen earlier were gone. The intense man with long dark hair who'd been writing letters (or ransom notes, or working out the square root of minus two, for all I knew) was nowhere to be seen, and the older woman (whom Gordon Wolpert had identified as a Mrs. Colibri, a widow of undetermined origin) had gone off as well, leaving *The Eustace Diamonds* on the table next to the couch. But two others had taken their place. Leona Savage, Millicent's mother, was reading a Bruce Chatwin travel book and periodically consulting the globe, and a very fat man who'd been introduced to us earlier as Rufus Quilp was dozing in an armchair, with a book open on his ample lap.

"All right," Carolyn said. "The top row of shelves, the second section in from the fireplace wall. I'm looking right at it, Bern."

"What do you see?"

"Books."

"Four or five books in from the left-hand edge of that section," I said, "there's an oversize volume, *The Conrad Argosy*. See it?"

"I see a thick book that's a lot taller than the others. I can't read the title from here. Can you?"

"No, but I recognize the book. I've had copies in the store. Now to the right of it there are three dark books, and then one with a sort of yellow cover, and next to *that* one—"

"Next to the one with the yellow cover?"

"Right. Just to the right of the yellow book is one in a dust jacket, and you probably can't read that title from here, and neither can I. But it's *The Big Sleep*."

"By Raymond Chandler."

"That's the guy."

"And you can't read the words on the spine, but you can recognize it anyway?"

"Uh-huh."

"Is it a first edition, Bern? Is it inscribed? Can you tell that from here, too?"

"I don't have magical powers," I said. "What I do have is eyes that look at books all day long. I can identify hundreds of books, maybe thousands, on the basis of a quick glimpse from the other side of the room. I probably haven't read it and I may not know the first thing about the contents, but I can tell you the title and author and who published it."

"Who published *The Big Sleep*?"

"Knopf in the U.S. and Hamish Hamilton in England. That's the Knopf edition over there. Otherwise I wouldn't have spotted it, because I don't know what the British edition looks like. And it most likely would have been a copy of the American edition that Chandler brought east to give to Hammett."

"He brought it for George Harmon Coxe, Bern. Remember? He gave it to Hammett on a whim."

"At the time it was on a whim," I said. "Now it's on a shelf. We're looking at it."

" 'Here's looking at you, Chandler.' "

"It's a genuine piece of American literary history," I said. "And we tracked it down, and there it is."

"Assuming that's the right copy."

"A first of *The Big Sleep*'s a rare book to begin with. If they've got any copy at all, it's pretty sure to be the one Chandler gave to Hammett. It's not like *Anthony Adverse*, with at least one copy in any old collection of books." I drew a breath. "That's the Hammett copy on the shelf. The Hammett association copy. When they write about it—no, that's ridiculous."

"What is?"

"I was thinking it might go down in bibliographic literature as 'the Rhodenbarr copy.' Silly, huh?"

"I don't think it's silly."

"You don't? Well, it won't happen. Be nice, though." I got to my feet. "Come on," I said. "I'll buy you a drink, and then I'm about ready to turn in. What's the matter?"

"You're just gonna leave it there?"

"I'm not going to wheel the library steps over there and climb up them in the middle of the night. Not with other people in the room."

"Why not? You told me it was okay to look at the book. It's a library, you said. It's natural to look at books in a library. Well, it's every bit as natural to take them off the shelf and start reading. Where does it say look but don't touch?"

I shook my head. "Later. It's not going anywhere."

EIGHT

Let's say you had this old tweed jacket.

It's a fine old jacket, woven of wool from the thick fleeces of Highland sheep, crafted in a croft or crofted in a craft, something like that. If you look closely enough you'll find threads of every color of the rainbow, with more hues and shades and tints and tones than in the biggest box of crayons Crayola ever made.

You bought it years ago, and even when it was new it looked old. Now it has leather patches on the elbows and leather piping on the cuffs, and by this time the leather itself is worn. And the pockets bulge from all the things you've stuffed into them over the years. And you've worn that jacket for long moonlit walks on the moors and spirited rambles in the fells. You've worn it on horseback, and your high-spirited dog has marked it with his muddy paws. It's been rained on, and dampened by the mist. It's soaked up the smoke from campfires in the open and peat fires in thatched cottages. And there's sweat in it, too, honest human sweat. And human joy and human grief—and, if you look closely enough, you'll be able to distinguish more hues and shades and tints and tones of emotion than there are crayons in the biggest box Crayola ever made.

And it's soaked up music, too, the haunting screel of the bagpipes and the reedy piping of a tin flute, from glen to glen and o'er the mountainside. Toss in the lilt of an old ballad heard in a public house and stir in the murmur of a lullaby sung to a child. It's all there, all absorbed by osmosis into the very warp and woof of the tweed.

Now you take that jacket and transmute it by some subtle alchemy involving a copper kettle and a copper coil. You distill the very essence of that jacket into a cask of liquid, and you age that liquid in a charred oaken barrel for longer than the lifetimes of the Old and Young Pretenders combined.

Then you pour it into a glass, and what you've got is Glen Drumnadrochit.

"Glen Drumnadrochit," Carolyn said, echoing our host, Nigel Eglantine, who'd pronounced its name even as he poured it. "What do you think, Bernie?"

"Not bad," I said.

"You want to make a ceremony of it," Nigel said, "in order to get the full experience." He picked up his own glass, a small brandy snifter like the ones he'd filled for us, and held it to the light. "First the color," he said, and we copied his actions, holding our glasses to the light and dutifully noting the color. It was, I should report, generally Scotch-colored, though definitely on the dark side of the Scotch spectrum.

"Next is bouquet," he announced, and held the glass so that it was cupped in his palm, moving his hand in a little circle and roiling the strong waters within the glass. Then he breathed in its aroma, and soon we were doing the same.

"And now taste. While holding a sip in the mouth, draw in breath through the nose. It strengthens and deepens the flavor." Indeed it did. "And, finally, aftertaste," he said, and tipped up his glass, and drank deep of the precious nectar. Ever a quick study, I copied his every action.

"I might have a little more of this one," I said, setting down an empty glass. "Color, bouquet, taste, and aftertaste. I want to make sure I've got the drill down pat."

He beamed. "Rather special, wouldn't you say? The Drumnadrochit."

"It's remarkable," I said, and topped up my glass.

We'd found him in the bar, where his role was more that of host than bartender. The bar at Cuttleford House ran on the honor system; you poured your own drink and made a note of it in the leather-bound ledger kept for that purpose. There seemed to me to be an inherent danger in the system; as the evening wore on, wouldn't one become increasingly apt to forget to make an entry?

"Shocking weather," he said, as I nursed the second wee snifter of Glen Drumnadrochit. "It's still snowing, you know."

"I was watching out the window," Carolyn said. "It's really beautiful."

"Quite so. If all one has to do is look at it, it's rather an admirable display of nature's majesty and all that." Color, bouquet, and flavor—and down the hatch, even as he reached for the bottle to top up his glass. He was putting it away at a good clip, was Nigel Eglantine, for all the ritual he made of appreciating it. There is, I suppose, a thin line between the connoisseur and the common drunk, even as there is a similarly fine distinction to be drawn between the gourmet and the glutton. Nigel wasn't slurring his words or tripping over his shoelaces, nor was he telling the same story over and over. He seemed perfectly fine to me.

Still, the night was young.

"I couldn't say how many times Orris has been out already," he said. "Clearing the path with the snowblower, then shoveling snow from the footbridge and plowing the drive clear out to the road. I told him not to bother again until morning. No point." He looked up. "Ah, good evening, Colonel."

"Evening," said Colonel Blount-Buller, who had just joined us. He made himself a drink and noted the act in the leather-bound ledger, a ritual he went through daily for half the year. "A long winter, eh? Snow's got some depth to it, Eglantine. Good job you've got Orris. Had another couple due, didn't you? Did they ever get here?"

"Mr. and Mrs. Littlefield." Color, bouquet, flavor. "I rather doubt we'll be seeing them, Colonel. I just hope they're not stuck in a snowbank somewhere. Much better if they've had the good sense to turn around and go home." He turned to me. "They're New Yorkers as well, Mr. Rhodenbarr. Don't suppose you know them?"

"It's a big city," I said.

"Too big for my taste," the colonel said. "Bad as London. That the bell, Eglantine?"

"I don't think . . . *there*, I heard it just then." He set his glass on the bar and hurried off to answer the doorbell.

"Good chap," the colonel said. "They run a tight ship, Eglantine and his wife. Not an easy thing, making a go of a place like this."

"It must be a lot of work," Carolyn said.

"You're working all the time," Colonel Blount-Buller said. "Man thinks he's done for the day, relaxes with a drink, and the bloody doorbell rings. Far cry from a soldier's life, where you're either fighting off wogs or fighting off boredom. Hard to say which is worse, yet when you add it all up there's no better life for a man."

Carolyn asked a question that drew him out a little bit, and he waxed eloquent in his reply. Then Eglantine returned with two new people, still wrapped in their overcoats and alternately rubbing their hands together and stamping their boots to get the last of the snow off.

"Mr. and Mrs. Dakin Littlefield," Nigel announced. "Of whom we'd quite despaired, and in whose safe arrival we rejoice. And these are the Rhodenbarrs, Mr. and Mrs. Rhodenbarr, and this is Colonel Blount-Buller. And before anything else I'm going to insist that you both have a drink. That's our first order of business, getting the chill out of your bones."

While he was at it, Nigel set about filling everyone else's glass as well. He was pouring yet another unblended malt whisky, and he announced its name and pedigree, but I didn't pay close attention, nor did I let him add any to my glass. I still had a little of the Drumnadrochit left, and felt it might as well stay unblended. Anyway, I'd had enough to drink, so I reached out a hand and covered my glass.

"Mrs. Rhodenbarr?"

"Well . . ."

"You know what they say," Dakin Littlefield put in. "A bird can't fly on one wing."

Mrs. Rhodenbarr indeed. One wing indeed. I thought of alternative analogies that might better fit the circumstances. A dog can't walk on three legs, or an ant on five, or a spider on seven. But I kept my mouth shut and took a good look at the Littlefields as they got out of their heavy coats and into the spirit of things.

She was a honey blonde, medium height, with a pretty face and a pleasing figure, and in the ordinary course of things I would have done most of my looking at her, but instead he got the lion's share of my attention. He was tall, with wavy dark hair worn long; he looked as though he might at any moment sit down at the piano and play something mournful. Prominent brows shaded his dark eyes. He had a hawk nose and an aggressive chin, and he had a cruel mouth. I'd seen that phrase in books and always wondered what a cruel mouth looked like, and now I knew. His narrow lips seemed poised somewhere between a pout and a sneer. You took one look at his mouth and you wanted to give him a smack in it, because you somehow knew you were dealing with a real son of a bitch.

"Past my bedtime," I said abruptly, just as the colonel had paused for dramatic effect in a reminiscence of the old days in Peshawar. "Carolyn?"

She took a moment to knock back the rest of her drink, then said good night all around. We found the staircase and climbed it, and at the top she paused for breath, then asked if I remembered the way to Aunt Agatha's Room. "Aunt Augusta," I said.

"What did I say, Bern?"

"Agatha."

"I did? I meant Augusta. Though it's not hard to figure out where I got Agatha from, is it?"

"The misty Miss Christie?"

"Uh-huh. Snow falling, and nobody here but us chickens? This could turn out to be a cross between *The Mouse-*

trap and *Ten Little Indians*. All that's missing is a body in the library."

"There's going to be something else missing in the library," I said. "Something by Raymond Chandler."

Her eyes widened. "You think somebody's going to swipe it?"

"Uh-huh. In an hour or so, when the house settles down and most of the people in it are asleep."

"You're the one who's gonna swipe it."

"Good thinking, Carolyn."

"But I thought you wanted to leave it for the time being, Bern. You explained it all on the way to the bar, how it would be safer to leave it where it was until the last minute. What changed your mind?"

"Nothing."

"Huh?"

"This is the last minute," I said, "or at least you could call it the penultimate minute. Or the eleventh hour, anyway."

"What are you talking about, Bern?"

"In the morning," I said, "the faithful Orris will blow the snow off the path and shovel the snow off the bridge and plow the snow out of the driveway, and, just as soon as he's done all that, you and I are going to get the hell out of here."

"We are?"

"If there's a God in heaven."

We had reached Aunt Augusta's Room, and not a moment too soon. Carolyn put her hands on her hips, cocked her head, and stared at me. I pushed the door open—we'd left it ajar, for the cat's benefit—and motioned her inside, then followed her in and drew the door shut.

She said, "Why, Bern? Hey, was it something I did?"

"What did you do?"

"I had that last drink, and I saw the look you gave me when I let him fill my glass again. I'm a little bit snockered, I admit it, but—"

"But a centipede can't walk on ninety-nine legs," I said. "No, that's not it, and if I gave you a nasty look it was unintentional. The nasty look wasn't for you."

"Who was it for?"

"That asshole."

"Nigel? I thought you liked him."

"I like him fine."

"I mean he's sort of pompous about the Glen Drumna-whatsit, but—"

"That's not pomposity," I said. "That's reverence, and the Drumnadrochit deserves it. He's not the asshole."

"The colonel's the asshole? What did he say that was assholeish? I must have missed it."

"The colonel's good company. I miss a word here and there because certain consonants get stuck in his clenched teeth, but I can usually get the gist of what he's saying. No, I like the colonel. Dakin Littlefield's the asshole."

"He is?"

"You said it."

"Actually, you said it, Bern. But what did he do? He just got here. He hardly opened his mouth."

"It's a cruel mouth, Carolyn. Open or shut."

"It is? I didn't notice. Bern, we don't know a thing about him except that he's from New York. Is that it? Do you know him from the city?"

"No."

"I never even heard of him myself. I'd remember the

name, it's distinctive enough. Dakin Littlefield. Hey, Dakin, what's shakin'? Dakin, Dakin, where's the bacon?"

"He ought to get a haircut," I said.

"Are you serious, Bern? His hair's a little shaggy, but it's not even shoulder length. I think it's attractive like that."

"Fine," I said. "Go share a bed with him."

"I'd rather share a bed with her," she said. "That's why I hardly noticed him, because I was busy noticing her. She's stunning, don't you think?"

"She's all right."

"Great face, fantastic shape when she took off her coat. Damn shame she's straight."

"What makes you so sure she's straight?"

"Are you kidding, Bern? She's here with her husband."

"How do you know he's her husband?"

"Huh? They're Mr. and Mrs. Littlefield, Bern. Remember?"

"So? We're Mr. and Mrs. Rhodenbarr, according to everybody here at Cuttlefish House."

"Cuttleford House, Bern."

"Whatever. Everybody thinks we're the Rhodenbarrs, that nice couple, she's a canine stylist and he's a burglar. Does that make us married? Does it make you straight?"

"It makes me confused," she said. "Are you telling me they're not married?"

"No," I said. "They're married, all right."

"Well, that's a relief. I'll sleep a lot easier knowing they're not living in sin. But what makes you so sure?"

"They're newlyweds," I said. "It sticks out all over them."

"It does? I didn't even notice."

"I did. They got married today."

She looked at me. "Did they say something that I missed?"

"No."

"Then how can you tell?. Has she got rice in her hair?"

"Not that I noticed. What was that?"

"What was what?"

"That pathetic scratching noise."

"It's the best he can do," she said, "without claws." She opened the door and Raffles walked in, looking as confused as everybody else. He walked over to a chair, hopped up on it, turned around in a slow circle, hopped down again, and left the room.

"I wonder what's on his mind," I said.

"Don't change the subject, Bern. Why don't you like Dakin, and how come you're so sure he's married to her, and—"

"Don't say 'her,'" I said. "It's impolite."

"It is?"

"Of course it is. She's got a name."

"Most people do, Bern, but I didn't happen to catch it."

"Neither did I."

There was a pause. "Bernie," she said slowly, "I know it tasted great and everything, but I think maybe there's something in that Drums-Along-the-Drocket that doesn't agree with you."

"It's called alcohol," I said, "and it couldn't agree with me more. Here's what I'll do, Carolyn. I'll tell you Mrs. Littlefield's first name, and all at once everything will be clear to you."

"It will?"

"Absolutely."

"What difference does it make what her name is?"

"Believe me, it makes a difference."

"But you just said you didn't catch her name either."

"True."

"Then how can you tell it to me?"

"Because I know it."

"How can you possibly . . . oh, God, don't *tell* me."

"Well, all right, if you're sure, but—"

"No!"

"No?"

"Tell me her name, Bernie. No, wait a minute, *don't* tell me! Is it what I think it is?"

"That depends on what you think it is."

"I don't want to say," she said, "because if it isn't, and even if it is, and . . . Bernie, I don't know how we got into this conversation, but we have to get out of it fast. Tell me her name. Just blurt it out, will you?"

"I'll give you a hint," I said. "It's not Romaine."

"Oh, God, Bern. I bet it's not Curly Endive either."

"It's not."

"Bern, spit it out, huh?"

"Lettice," I said.

"Oh, shit. You're kidding, right? You're not kidding. Ohmigod."

NINE

The bookshelves in the Great Library of Cuttleford House extended all the way to the twelve-foot ceiling. One couldn't be expected to reach the uppermost shelves without standing on the shoulders of giants; in their absence, one of the several owners of the property had thoughtfully provided a set of library steps.

This article of furniture was made of mahogany and fitted with casters so it could be rolled to where it was needed. It consisted of a freestanding (and freewheeling) staircase of five steps. It had been the designer's conceit to give it the form of a spiral staircase, and the steps were accordingly triangular, tapering from a width of four or five inches at their outer edge to no width at all at the center.

I was poised on the fourth step, one hand clutching a shelf for balance, the other hand reaching out for *The Big Sleep*, when I heard my name called.

"Bernie!"

It was Lettice, of course, Lettice Runcible Littlefield. I didn't have to turn around and look at her to establish as much, but I did anyway, and there she was.

I should have waited. My plan, if you want to dignify it with that name, was simplicity itself. Step One—get the book. Step Two—go home. As long as I performed those two tasks in that particular order, things ought to work out. I wanted to undertake Step Two as soon after breakfast as was decently possible, which gave me something like eight hours to execute Step One and scoop up Chandler.

I thought of sleeping first and going after Chandler at the last minute, virtually on the way out the door. I thought of napping for a few hours, giving the rest of the house time to settle in for a good night's sleep, and then paying a visit to the library in the hour of the wolf. But I didn't want to rush, nor did I want to risk appearing furtive to a fellow insomniac. Best to get the book now, I'd thought, and tuck it under my pillow for the night, and make off with it first thing in the morning.

There were guests in the library when I got there. Rufus Quilp, the very stout gentleman who'd been reading and dozing earlier, was still at it, breathing heavily if not quite snoring. A copy of *Dombey and Son*, part of a broken half-leather set of Dickens whose volumes I'd spotted here and there around the house, lay open on his lap. Greg Savage, unaccompanied by wife or child, looked up at my approach to flash the apologetic smile frequently found on the lips of the parents of precocious children, then returned to his book, a Philip Friedman courtroom novel. It was the author's latest, and, from the looks of it, his longest; if I'd borrowed Savage's copy and stood on top of it I might not have needed the library steps.

I did a little reading myself, hoping Quilp and Savage would decide to call it a night, and before long Savage did, slipping away quietly so as not to disturb us. Quilp's eyes were closed, and what did it matter if he saw me climb the steps and reach for a book? That's what the steps were there for, and what the books were there for. And, by God, it was what I was there for.

Then Lettice called my name.

"What the hell are you doing here, Bernie?"

I was already on my way down the steps. I touched a finger to my lips, then pointed across the room to the chair where Rufus Quilp sat in a Dickensian doze.

"All right, then," she said. "Let's go where we can talk." She spun on her heel and stalked out of the library, and I followed in her wake.

We wound up in the East Parlour, beneath the gaze of the putative springbok. I turned on a lamp. Lettice told me not to bother, we wouldn't be here that long. I said we might as well be comfortable. "Besides," I said, "how will it look if somebody sees us sitting together in the dark?"

"If it's dark," she said, "how will they see us?"

"Sit down," I said. "You're looking well. Marriage agrees with you."

"What are you *doing* here, Bernie?"

"What am *I* doing here? I'm spending a traditional weekend in a traditional English country house, with more than the traditional amount of snow. I don't know where you get off being surprised to see me. I told you I had a reservation here."

"You also told me you were going to take me."

"Well, you had a prior engagement."

"So you brought your wife." She treated me to a sidelong glance. "You never told me you were married, Bernie."

"I'm not."

"Oh, really? Is little Mrs. Rhodenbarr your mother?"

"Her name is Carolyn Kaiser," I said, "and she's not Mrs. Rhodenbarr. That seems to be an honorary designation a woman receives here when she arrives in the company of a man."

"So you're just good friends."

"That's exactly what we are, as a matter of fact. Not that it's any of your business. Now it's my turn to ask a question. What the hell are *you* doing here? I thought you were getting married today."

"Dakin and I were married this afternoon."

"What a coincidence. He surprised you by taking you to the same place I'd picked."

"No, of course not."

"I didn't think so."

"I suggested it," she said. "You made it sound so wonderful I couldn't think of anything else. We had reservations in Aruba, but I managed to convince Dakin that we'd have ever so much more fun coming here. And luckily they had a room available."

"Not with twin beds, by any chance?"

"With a double bed, of course. Dakin's in it now, sleeping like a lamb."

"I'm surprised you're not with him."

"I was," she said, lowering her eyes. "You know what they say about lovemaking, that it puts men to sleep and wakes women up."

"As opposed to the *idea* of lovemaking," I said, "which wakes men up and gives women a headache."

"I couldn't sleep," she went on, "and I knew I had to find you and talk to you. You can't imagine what a shock it was to run into you."

"Oh, yes I can."

"You know, I rather assumed it was your room they'd given us, that you'd canceled your reservation after our conversation. I never dreamed you'd come after all."

"Well, I never figured you'd show up. I thought this was the last place on earth I'd run into you."

"You seemed so devastated the last time we were together. I was afraid of what you might do."

"Like what? Stick my head in the oven? Take holy orders?"

"Nothing that extreme. But I thought you might be in something of a funk for a while. I certainly didn't think you'd appear all coupled up with another woman. How do I know you haven't been married all along?"

"At this point," I said, "why on earth would you care?"

"Because I never date married men, for one thing."

"Neither do I," I said, "or married women, either, so maybe you ought to scoot back upstairs where you belong."

"Why, Bernie!"

"I'm serious, Lettice. You're a married woman now. We shouldn't be sitting here in the dark together."

"If it were any brighter in here," she said, "I'd need to put on sunscreen. Bernie, you're furious with me, aren't you?"

"What makes you say that?"

"For one thing, you're glaring at me. You and that animal."

Had Raffles joined us? I looked around for him.

"On the wall," she said. "That poor creature that someone shot and stuffed."

"He's immortal," I said. "He's supposed to be a springbok, but he sure looks like an oryx to me. You can't really blame him for looking disgruntled. Someone shot him. But why should I be furious?"

"Because you really cared for me, and you truly *were* devastated when I told you I was getting married. And of course you're furious, you're positively seething. Bernie, that's so sweet!"

"It is?"

She nodded. "And you came here this weekend to prove to yourself that you don't care, but of course it proves just the opposite, doesn't it?"

"It does?"

"You know it does." She leaned toward me and laid her cool hand against my cheek. "Bernie," she said earnestly, "I'm not saying that we can never ever be together again. But this weekend is out of the question. You must understand that."

"Huh?"

"I've been married for less than twelve hours," she said. "I'm on my honeymoon. For God's sake, I just left my husband's bed. You can't expect me to—"

"To what?"

"Oh, Bernie," she said. "When we're both back in the city, when some of these powerful emotions become a little easier to deal with, who knows what might happen?"

"Not me," I said. "I don't know anything."

"But while we're here," she went on, "we'll have to be on our best behavior. We'll be friendly but distant, reserved. As far as anyone else has to know, we met for the first time this evening in the bar. We never knew each other before."

"Whatever you say."

"And we never slipped into the East Parlour together,

and had this conversation." She perched on the arm of my chair, her face inches from mine, and treated me to a whiff of her perfume. "Oh, Bernie," she said. "I wish it didn't have to be like this."

"You do?"

She leaned in and kissed me, and without thinking about it I kissed back. She was always a good kisser, and she hadn't lost a step in the week and a half since I'd seen her. I put my arms around her, and she put a hand on my knee for balance.

I guess it didn't work, though, because the next thing I knew she was in my lap.

"My goodness," she said, squirming around, and sort of rubbing her body against me like a cat. It was, though, a good deal more interesting than it is when a cat does it.

She moved her hand, then gasped in mock alarm. "Oh, my! Bernie, what have we here?"

"Uh . . ."

"I should speak sternly to you," she said, "and tell you to take that upstairs to your wifey. Are you absolutely certain you're not married, Bernie?"

"You've been to my apartment," I reminded her.

"And made love beneath the fake Mondrian. I'll never forget that, Bernie."

"Did it seem like the home of a married man?"

"Hardly. But whether you're married or not, it's clear you and your little friend are more than just friends." Her hand did something artful. "You're planning on sharing a bed with her this weekend, aren't you?"

"Well, technically, yes. But—"

"And she's waiting for you, and you're down here with me." She was purring with excitement and delight. "She's lying awake, and Dakin's sound asleep, and we're together, aren't we?" She sort of flowed from my lap to the floor, as if she were a liquid drawn there by gravity. And she put her hands in my lap, and she put her head in my lap.

I reached to switch off the lamp.

"Poor Dakin," she said a while later, getting to her feet. "I swore I'd be a faithful wife, and in less than half a day I've gone and committed adultery. Or have I?"

"Can't you remember?"

She ran the tip of her tongue across her upper lip. "I shouldn't think I'm in great danger of forgetting the act," she said. "I was just wondering if it qualifies. In terms of adultery, that is. Does what we just did count?"

"Well, what's adultery? Extramarital sex, right? This was certainly extramarital, and it seems to me it was sexual."

"Quite," she said.

"So I guess that makes it adultery."

"Sitting in your lap was sexual," she said. "Kissing you was definitely sexual. Rubbing up against you was deliciously sexual. You wouldn't label any of those acts adulterous, would you?"

"No."

"It seems to me," she said, "that anything short of the main event, so to speak, is not *exactly* adultery."

"I see, Lettice. In other words, you figure you ought to get off on a technicality."

"Is it a technicality? Perhaps it is." She grinned. "In any event," she said, "you're the one who got off. I just hope your sweet little nonwife won't be too disappointed."

"She'll get over it," I said.

"Oh, I do hope so," she said, and flashed a wicked grin, and blew me a kiss, and left.

TEN

I stayed where I was, under the watchful gaze of the presumptive oryx, and I sat and mused. Was this the sort of thing that went on in English country houses? I swear nothing like it had ever happened in any Agatha Christie novel I ever read. Iris Murdoch, maybe, but not Agatha Christie.

Mine had seemed like such a clear and simple program —or programme, as young Millicent Savage would no doubt prefer it. Step One, get the book. Step Two, go home. But now, with an encounter in the Great Library having led to an interlude in the East Parlour, some sort of reappraisal of the agenda seemed called for.

First off, did we really have to cut out of Cuttleford House first thing in the morning? I'd wanted to avoid an unpleasant confrontation with Lettice, but I'd had that confrontation in spite of myself, and, while any number of adjectives could be pressed into service to describe it, "unpleasant" seemed an unlikely choice. It had been unanticipated, certainly. It had been unsettling, to say the least. But unpleasant?

Hardly that.

My role in the incident was one I would normally have found uncomfortable. There are those who hold that adultery is to adults as infancy is to infants, but I've always felt that a wedding ring on her finger places a woman off-limits. I haven't always walked the walk, and sometimes I have in fact found myself grazing on the wrong side of a Keep Off the Grass sign, but by and large I've limited myself to single women.

Otherwise I tend to feel guilty and uneasy, and even if something gets started it doesn't last long. But now, as I matched the glassy-eyed stare of the oryx with one of my own, an examination of conscience revealed neither guilt nor unease.

I felt terrific.

It certainly didn't hurt that I'd taken an instant dislike to Dakin Littlefield. I'd loathed him at a glance, and I felt sure that a deeper acquaintance would see the feeling blossom into genuine hatred. One look at him was enough to determine he was no good. He was a cad, a bounder, and a bad hat, and he had a cruel mouth.

I didn't really feel that I was poaching on posted land. After all, I'd been there first, enjoying a perfectly pleasant affair with Lettice before the son of a bitch came along and married her. Technically, though, I had to admit I was cuckolding him, and I can't say it bothered me a bit. If anything, it gave me a special satisfaction to fit him with a pair of horns that would have been the envy of the oryx, the ibex, the zebu, and every other four-letter ruminant quadruped that ever stumbled out of a Scrabble dictionary.

If a run-in with Lettice was no longer something I had

to take pains to avoid, what was the rush to get out of Cuttleford House? I'd gone to a lot of trouble and expense to get us here, and now that we were here we might as well stick around and enjoy it. There was a lot to enjoy—the food, the company, and the grand house itself, not to mention the odd wee dram of Glen Drumnadrochit. Why miss out on it?

First, though, I had to do something about that book.

In some of the country-house mysteries I've read, the houses come equipped with mazes. Characters wander outside and wind up getting lost in the maze. I don't know if there are many real English houses with mazes, and I don't know if anybody ever really gets lost in them, but there was no need for a maze on the grounds of Cuttleford House. The interior was a maze all by itself.

I don't know how many ways there were to get from the East Parlour to the Great Library. I was tracing one of them, or trying to, when a wheelchair rolled out of a hallway on my right and just missed a collision with my foot. I stepped back, startled, and Miss Dinmont, for whom a backward step was an impossibility, shrank against the back of her vehicle and looked quite alarmed.

"Oh, Mr. Rhodenbarr," she said. "You startled me."

"I'm sorry," I said. "I didn't mean to."

"But it's I who should be apologizing," she said. "Surely the pedestrian has the right of way in these matters."

"It's my fault," I insisted. "I keep looking the wrong way before I step off the curb. I'm American, you see, and I can't seem to remember that you lot drive on the wrong side of the road."

"Oh, now, Mr. Rhodenbarr," she said, and smiled a

weary smile, and laughed a weary laugh. She was, I noticed, a pretty woman, albeit an exhausted one. "I was pre-occupied," she said, "or I shouldn't have come so close to running you down. Have you seen my friend, Miss Hardesty?"

"Not since I saw her with you, and that was hours ago."

"I think she may have stepped outside," she said. "She's mad about the outdoors, you know. And she loves weather."

"There's a lot of it out there to love."

"I know. All that snow, getting deeper every hour. But that wouldn't bother her." She sighed. "I was in our room, waiting for her. We've a room on the ground floor. Miss Postlethwaite's Sewing Room, it's called." She thumped the arms of her wheelchair. "Because of this," she said. "It's not terribly handy on the stairs."

"I don't suppose it would be."

"I can climb stairs if I have to," she said, "but it takes me forever, and then someone has to bring the chair up-stairs, and it's heavy. It's awful, being a burden."

"I'm sure no one would call you that."

"Perhaps not to my face, but it's what I am, isn't it? Do you know what's the worst thing about my situation, Mr. Rhodenbarr?"

I didn't, but I had a feeling she would tell me.

"Self-pity," she said. "I am constantly beset by self-pity."

"That must be awful."

"You have no idea, Mr. Rhodenbarr. I am altogether powerless against it. I'm quite certain I'm afflicted with the most severe case of self-pity in the history of the human race. It saps my energy and wastes my spirit, leaving me with nothing to do but wallow in it."

"You poor thing, Miss Dinmont."

"Yes," she said solemnly. "I am a poor thing indeed, am I not? I do wish I could find Miss Hardesty. There's no one like her for jollying me out of a bad mood."

"I can imagine."

"But where can she have gotten to?" She gripped the arms of her chair. "Maybe she's back at our room. She could have returned by one route while I went off on another in search of her. The layout's confusing here, isn't it?"

"Especially now, with the lights turned down."

"And especially when one is in a wheelchair," she said. "That makes everything just that much more difficult." She managed a brave little smile. "But please don't feel sorry for me, Mr. Rhodenbarr. That's the one thing I'm quite capable of doing for myself."

Maybe the conversation with Miss Dinmont had disoriented me, or maybe I was sufficiently addled to begin with. Whatever the cause, I took a wrong turn and wound up in the kitchen. I got out of there as soon as I realized where I was, and I'd walked through a couple of other rooms before it occurred to me that I'd missed a golden opportunity to raid the refrigerator. I was seriously considering retracing my steps when a small person darted around the corner in front of me and I had my second near-collision of the evening.

"Oh, hi!" this one said brightly, and I blinked in the dimness and recognized Millicent Savage. "It's Bernie, isn't it? What are you doing up so late?" She gaped, and put her hand over her mouth. "Don't tell me," she said.

"I wouldn't dream of it."

"You're a burglar," she said, "and these are your working hours, aren't they? You're about to break into Cuttleford House."

"Why would I do that? I'm already inside."

"That's right, you're staying here, aren't you? I just met your cat again. He's prowling the halls the same as you."

"It's a family tradition," I said. "Isn't it past your bedtime, Millicent?"

"Way past it," she agreed. "I went to bed hours ago, and I was just falling asleep when I woke up, and after that I wasn't tired at all. That happens to me a lot here at Cuttleford House."

"Maybe it's jet lag," I suggested. "After all, England's five time zones away."

"You're silly, Bernie."

"Everybody tells me that."

"It's probably the ghost," she said. "Cuttleford House is haunted, you know."

"It is?"

She nodded. "The man who built it," she said. "His name was Frederick Cuttleford, and do you know what happened to him?"

"If he's a ghost now," I said, "then he must have died."

"He didn't just die. He was murdered!"

"He was not."

"Are you sure, Bernie?"

"Pretty sure," I said. "If I remember correctly, he had an apoplectic fit. And he was nowhere near Cuttleford House at the time. He had four or five other homes, and I guess he was at one of them when it happened, but I'm certain he wasn't here."

"Oh."

"And his name wasn't Frederick Cuttleford in the first place. His name was Ferdinand Cathcart."

"Then what happened to Mr. Cuttleford?"

"There never was a Mr. Cuttleford," I said. "The place was named after the creek. It's called Cuttlebone Creek, and the name 'Cuttleford' must come from a spot around here where you can wade across the creek. It's not where we came in, though, because you have to walk across a suspension bridge instead."

"I know. Don't you love the way it sways?"

"No," I said. "But there's still never been a Mr. Cuttleford, bridge or no bridge, and . . . what are you laughing about?"

"I made it all up!"

"You did?"

"Oh, not about the ghost," she said. "I know there's a ghost, but nobody knows who it is or what he's doing here. I made up all that part."

"You got the initials right. Frederick Cuttleford and Ferdinand Cathcart."

"I got that from Carolyn."

"Huh?"

"I met her in the hall earlier," she said, "and I guess she's scared of ghosts, so I told her the ghost at this house was a friendly ghost."

"I'm surprised you didn't say his name was Casper."

"I said his name was Colin," she said, "because I like the name, and it goes nicely with Cuttleford, don't you think? And she said she thought the man who built Cuttleford House was named Frederick, so when I told you the story—"

"You improved it."

"Just to make it a better story. Anyway, that's why I'm awake. How about you?"

"I was reading," I said, "and I lost track of the time."

"I bet you were looking for something to steal."

Time to nip this in the bud. "You know," I said, "it made a nice joke, Millicent, but it's beginning to get a little tiresome. I was just kidding about being a burglar."

"You were?"

"Uh-huh."

"What are you really?"

"Well, I'm out of work at the moment," I said. "I'm hoping something will turn up soon. In the meantime, I've sort of been helping Carolyn out at the Poodle Factory. What's so funny?"

She had both hands over her mouth, smothering a laugh. "The Poodle Factory," she sputtered. "A factory where they make poodles!"

"It's just the name of her salon."

"And you work there."

"That's right."

"Just to help her out."

Kids. Why on earth do people have them? "And to pass the time," I said.

"And you're not really a burglar."

"Of course not."

"And you don't break into houses and steal things."

"Gosh, no," I said. "I'd be scared, for one thing. And it wouldn't be right to take things that didn't belong to me."

She thought this over. Then she said, "You know how I made up the part about Frederick Cuttleford? Well, I think you made that up."

"About being a burglar."

"About *not* being a burglar," she said. "You know what? I don't believe you. I think you're a burglar after all, no matter what you say." And she flashed me a demonic smile and darted around the corner.

ELEVEN

The library, when I finally got to it, was dark. Someone had drawn the curtains and switched off the lights. I stood at the threshold, trying to determine the most natural way to go in there and get the book. I had packed a narrow-beam pocket flashlight, but I'd left it in my room (or our room, or Aunt Augusta's, as you prefer). I could have gone upstairs to fetch it, but I'd had enough trouble already trying to find my way back to the library. I didn't want to have to look for it again.

Besides, there was something impossibly furtive about skulking around with a flashlight. One transformed oneself into a bumbling burglar out of the Sunday comics, the sort always portrayed wearing a domino mask and carrying a burlap sack of swag over his shoulder.

Why bother? I was a paying guest at Cuttleford House, fully entitled to be there. In the absence of a posted curfew, I had every right to make use of the Great Library at any hour of the day. There was, in short, no need to skulk. I could stride manfully in, bold as any base metal, switch on

111

all the lamps I wanted, mount the library steps, fetch the book I wanted, and take it back to my room. Moreover, I could do all of that without committing the merest infraction of the house rules, let alone the criminal code. I wouldn't even risk arousing suspicion. I was a guest, I wanted something to read before going to sleep, and where better to find the book of my choice than the library?

I would have to be on my way back to New York with the book tucked away in my luggage before I'd have done anything that could provoke so much as a raised eyebrow.

Still, there were precautions to be taken. Somewhere down the line, when the book went under the hammer at Christie's or Sotheby's, say, the volume's provenance would best be established by citing the Lester Harding Ross memoir, and anyone else could do as I had done, walking back the cat (as the counterspies call it) all the way to Ferdinand Cathcart's little pleasure dome in the Berkshires. It would be just as well if no one was in a position to remember seeing one Bernard Rhodenbarr striding through the halls of Cuttleford House with *The Big Sleep* clutched to his bosom.

First things first. Get the book, in an unobtrusive fashion, and tuck it away for safekeeping. Then get it off the premises and get it home. Sit on it for a while, thrilling in its possession, and then figure out a good cover story—how it had been at the bottom of a sack of book club editions and Grosset reprints that someone walked in off the street with, how I'd grabbed it up along with a dozen other old books in a thrift shop in Staten Island, how it was part of a nondescript collection of volumes acquired at a garage sale somewhere in Nassau County. It wouldn't be hard to tailor a story to fit the circumstances.

First, get the book.

And I was on my way. I was all set to enter the room, had in fact already extended one foot across the threshold, when I heard somebody talking.

I leaned forward and turned my head to aim an ear in the direction the sound had come from. It was impossible to make out, but someone was saying something, speaking in a hushed whisper at the far corner of the library from where I was standing. The very corner, in point of fact, where Raymond Chandler's first novel reposed (or had when last I looked) on the uppermost shelf.

Rufus Quilp, muttering in his sleep? Not unless he'd moved from the site of his earlier slumber. I slipped a little deeper into the shadows and stopped trying to see in the darkness, which was plainly impossible. I closed my eyes entirely, with the thought that it might sharpen my hearing. It's supposed to work for blind newsdealers, but I guess it takes years, because it had no immediate effect as far as I could tell. Just silence and murmuring and more silence and more murmuring.

More than one person. I was suddenly sure of that, because it seemed to me that one hushed whisper was responding to another hushed whisper. It remained impossible, though, to identify either whisperer, or to make out a word of what was being whispered.

Who could it be? The missing Miss Hardesty, two-timing poor Miss Dinmont and cuddling on the sofa with the upstairs maid? That rotter Dakin Littlefield, out from under the goosedown coverlet of his marriage bed and getting some sauce for the gander? Were these two even lovers at all, or were they conspirators planning . . . planning what? The overthrow of a Balkan government? It seemed to me that was what conspirators used to plan in English-country-house mysteries, and, now that there are once again Balkan governments begging to be overthrown, perhaps those people are back to their old tricks.

But what difference did it make what was being said or who was saying it? I'd already decided that I didn't want to call attention to myself, and that meant I couldn't barge in on their hush-hush conversation, switching on lamps and dashing up ladders. In fact it probably meant I shouldn't be lurking in the doorway, just waiting to be found out and exposed for what I so obviously was, a despicable eavesdropper manqué.

I was frozen there, wanting to leave but wishing I could see who they were and hear what they were saying. Then, from out of nowhere, something came and brushed against my ankle.

The cops, I thought, because that's the first thought that pops into my mind when something takes me by surprise. It was not an enduring thought, however, because it has been my experience that, while cops are apt to do many unsettling and sometimes inexplicable things, brushing up against your ankle is rarely one of them.

A ghost. That was my next thought, prompted no doubt by Carolyn's fears and Millicent Savage's mischief. I wasn't sure that I believed in ghosts, but if such a thing existed, well, a ghost couldn't ask for a better house to haunt, or a better night to walk the earth. Did ghosts rub up against one's ankles?

While I was pondering the point, it did it again. And now I knew what it was, and it wasn't the cops and it wasn't a ghost. It made a sound, you see, and it wasn't the sort of sound a cop would make ("Put your hands on the wall!"), nor was it the clanking of chains or the wail of a banshee.

The sound was akin to that of a very expensive and well-bred motorcar, its powerful engine idling, waiting for the light to change. In a word, it was purring.

I bent down and scooped it up in my arms, hoping it would stick to purring and not switch to anything as attention-getting as a full-throated miaow. And then, while a pair of invisible Anatrurian provocateurs went on inaudibly plotting a coup, I played the perfect counterspy—I walked the cat back to my room.

I guess he was hungry. That's what it usually means when Raffles does his ankle-brushing number, although it's tempting to interpret it as a display of affection. (Maybe that's what any display of affection really means, regardless of the source—"Hi there! I want something from you!")

Back in Aunt Augusta's bedchamber, I found the red plastic bowl we'd brought along, and the box of Friskies, poured the latter into the former, and put it down where he could get at it. He stood there in the dark, eating, and I stood there and watched him, and then he walked over to the door, which I'd closed, and made pathetic declawed scratching noises until I opened it and let him out.

I closed it again, took off clothes and put on pajamas, then opened it and left it ajar. In the double bed provided for us, Carolyn rolled over and snarled softly in her sleep. She'd been sleeping on one side of the bed, but now she was smack in the middle.

Outside our window, the snow went right on falling. If it had ever stopped or even slowed its pace, you couldn't prove it by me; every time I'd looked out a window, there it was, great big flakes of it, falling in great profusion. From where I stood there was no way to gauge its depth, but I figured there had to be a foot of it out there at the very least.

I got into bed, trying to pick the side with the most room. I settled my head on the pillow and got an elbow in the ribs from Carolyn. I tried to make do with the space available to me, but that didn't work. I'd start to drift, and then Carolyn would move around enough to rouse me with a knee or an elbow, or I'd draw so close to the edge of the bed that I'd start to fall out of it.

After a little of this I decided I had to risk waking her, and I put one hand on her hip and the other on her shoulder and shoved her gently but firmly over toward her side of the bed. That seemed to work, but then she came rolling back, and her arm wrapped around me as her face wound up nestled against my chest.

I had to lie there and decide how I felt about this. Carolyn is certainly an attractive woman, but it's safe to say she's not my type, even as I am emphatically not hers. One of the ways in which women differ from men, it seems to me, is that the distinctions between gay and straight are a little more apt to blur for them. A lot of straight women seem inclined to experiment with a female lover now and then—Carolyn keeps getting involved with women of this sort, and keeps swearing it's a mistake she's made for the last time. And I've known lesbians with a similar inclination to try something different once in a blue moon.

Not Carolyn. She's no more interested in having sex with a man than I am. That was clear from the day I met her, and it made it easier for our friendship to develop. We were best friends, we were buddies, and one thing we were not destined to do was share a pillow.

But that was what we were doing. She may have had a pillow of her own, but her head was on my pillow now, and so was mine.

No problem. If I hadn't had that interlude with Lettice in the East Parlour, maybe my body would have had other ideas. But it was a tired and depleted old body by now, and all it wanted was a good night's sleep. Toward that end, huddling together for warmth like this was just what the doctor ordered. Snug in the arms of my best friend, basking in her body heat, I felt myself drifting.

See, I had the edge here. I was awake.

Carolyn was not. Sound asleep, though not in sleep's deepest stage, she had no idea the person she clung to was her good buddy Bernie, or indeed any man at all. She was probably dreaming, and I'm sure you know how a dream will change direction in order to accommodate to circumstance. If the phone on the nightstand rings, the sleeper instantly inserts a ringing telephone into the scenario of his dream. Carolyn's dream had to embrace not a ringing telephone but a warm body, and in her dream it became a female body, a lover's body.

In the dream, she began to make love to this body to which she was clinging.

And not just in the dream.

It was unendurably weird. There I was, on the verge of sleep, and my best friend in the world was nuzzling my neck and moving her hands on my body. I wanted to wake her up, but I couldn't think of a way to do so without making things worse. Wouldn't it be better to wait it out?

Hard to say. On the one hand, the dream could quickly run its course. (They're speedy little devils, always demanding far more time to recount than it takes to dream them in the first place.) On the other hand, there was always the chance that Carolyn's wandering hand would fasten on a part of me not entirely consistent with the fabric of her dream, and that might give new meaning to the term "rude awakening."

What to do? Suppose I just let out a scream and sprang out of bed. I could say I was having a nightmare, and by the time she'd calmed me down she would have lost all track of her own dream. Still, it wasn't a very nice thing to do, and how would either of us be able to get back to sleep after that?

She moved, burrowing still closer, fitting herself against me. Her thighs wrapped around my leg, and she sort of rocked against me in a fairly basic rhythm. It took me a minute to realize what was happening, and then I just lay there while it went on happening, with the pace picking up a little and growing a touch more urgent. Then her hands tightened their grip on my arms, and she gave a little terrier-like yelp and followed it with a sort of moan, and then she sighed and rolled away from me and was still.

You can never tell her about this, I told myself. In fact, I added, it would be best all around if you could manage to forget that it ever happened.

Fat chance, I thought. About as much chance as I had of getting to sleep, and I'd been so close to drifting off. . . .

The next thing I knew it was morning, and somebody somewhere was screaming bloody murder.

TWELVE

Any number of things can set a person screaming. A mouse, say, emerging suddenly from behind a piece of furniture, is apt to coax a cry from the lips of the right sort of woman. (In my experience, it's altogether useless to point out to such a woman that the mouse is more afraid of her than she is of it. Few women seem to find this information comforting, and I'm not even sure it's true. You rarely hear a mouse scream when a woman pops out from behind the sofa.)

By the same token, a scream might indicate that the screamer had just seen a ghost, or a potential assailant, or a winning number on his lottery ticket. "Scream bloody murder" is, after all, just an expression, and just because you've heard such a scream doesn't mean you're going to find a body in the library.

But we did.

I'd seen the dead man before, although we hadn't met. He'd been in the Great Library the first time we visited that magnificent room. He was the one who had given Carolyn a bad moment when his gaze fixed on her. At the time he'd been seated on a fruitwood fiddleback chair in front of the little leather-topped writing desk, and he'd been writing letters, I'd assumed, scribbling away furiously, then pausing to cap his pen and gaze off into the middle distance, then uncapping the pen and scribbling anew.

Now he lay a few yards from the fireplace, and no farther than that from the shelf where I'd spotted *The Big Sleep*—and where I could see it still, I was pleased to note. He was dressed as he'd been the previous evening, wearing a camel-hair blazer with leather buttons over a tattersall vest and dark brown corduroy slacks. His shoes were chukka boots, and one of the bootlaces had come untied.

He lay on his back, sprawled at the base of the library steps. His dark hair was still neatly combed, but blood had flowed from a scalp wound, staining the carpet beneath his head. His strong features were softened in death, and his dark eyes, which had gazed with such intensity in life, were as glassy as those in the stuffed oryx.

The oryx, of course, was nowhere to be seen, having remained on the wall of the East Parlour. This placed it in the minority, as almost every other resident of Cuttleford House had responded to the outcry the way automatic elevators respond to a fire in a high-rise office building. They rush right to it, mindless of the danger, and that was just what we had done.

The hour may have had something to do with it. It was the crack of dawn, and I don't suppose Carolyn and I were the only ones who'd been sound asleep until the cry awakened us. If we'd been reading Jane Austen, say, or playing gin rummy, we might have responded in a more gradual fashion, instead of leaping out of bed, throwing on clothes, and plunging headlong down the stairs toward the source of the disturbance.

There were five folks in the library when we got there, not counting the dead man, and there were quite a few more by the time we'd caught our breath. The screamer, I learned, was a pretty little blonde named Molly Cobbett. She was the downstairs maid, and had come in to open the drapes and tidy the room, and had responded in traditional fashion when she suddenly came face to face with the late Jonathan Rathburn.

That, Nigel Eglantine informed us, was the name of the deceased. Eglantine had been in the library when Carolyn and I burst in, as had Molly Cobbett, of course, along with Colonel Edward Blount-Buller and the redoubtable Orris, whose eyes seemed to be set even closer together than I remembered them. Others were quick to join us—Millicent Savage, her parents, Gordon Wolpert, Cissy Eglantine. The cook stood off to one side, fussing with her apron and looking quite distraught, while a red-haired young thing with a complexion that was just one big freckle gaped at the fallen guest, at once appalled and delighted that life could be so like the tabloids. (She was the upstairs maid, I later learned, and a cousin of Molly's, the daughter of Molly's father's brother Earl. Earlene Cobbett was her name.)

"Awful," Nigel Eglantine was saying. "Hideous tragedy. Dreadful luck."

"All of that," the colonel said. "But not terribly difficult to reconstruct, eh? Easy to see what happened." He cleared his throat. "Up late. Couldn't sleep. Came down here, wanted something to read. Saw just the book he wanted but couldn't reach it." He laid a hand on the set of library steps.

"Climbed these, didn't he? Lost his balance. Took a tumble." He pointed to the scalp wound. "Struck his head, didn't he? Bled like a stuck pig, if the ladies will excuse the expression."

The ladies looked as though they could handle it. One of them, the Hardesty woman, had entered the library during the colonel's speech, pushing her companion's wheelchair. Now she took up Blount-Buller's account.

"No wonder he fell," she said. "His shoelace had come undone. He must have tripped over it."

"He should have tied it," Miss Dinmont put in, "before climbing the steps. That was terribly careless of him."

Carolyn looked at me and rolled her eyes. "I bet he learned his lesson," she said dryly. "Bern—"

"A terrible accident," Nigel Eglantine said, taking up the reconstruction. "I suppose the fall rendered the poor man unconscious. Then he must have expired from loss of blood, or perhaps the skull fracture killed him. If another person had been in the room, the tragedy could very likely have been averted."

"Or if he'd tied his shoes," Miss Dinmont said. For someone who didn't walk much, she had a lot to say on the subject.

"They might not have been untied to start with," Greg Savage offered. Interestingly enough, he himself was wearing loafers. "He might have stepped on the end of one shoelace while he was adjusting his position on the steps," he explained, "and then when he raised the other foot it would have untied the lace and tripped him up, all at the same time."

"Exactly why I double-knot my own laces," Miss Hardesty said.

"It could still happen," Savage told her. "The lace wouldn't come untied, but you could still step on the end and trip yourself up."

Hardesty wasn't having any. "When you double-knot the laces," she said, "it shortens them. So the end's not long enough to be stepped on."

Savage admitted he hadn't thought of that. Colonel Blount-Buller said it was all barn doors and stolen horses, wasn't it, because no amount of double-knotted shoelaces would undo the harm that had befallen the poor chap. Mrs. Colibri, the older woman who'd been reading Trollope on the sofa while Mr. Rathburn was laboring at the writing desk, asked if the police had been called. No one answered right away, and then Nigel Eglantine said that they hadn't, and that he supposed that would have to be done, wouldn't it?

"Although one hates to bother them," he added, "on a day like this. I suspect they have their hands full, what with better than two feet of snow on the ground." He gestured at the wall of windows. "I couldn't guess what state the roads will be in, and I know there'll be no end of weather-related emergencies. I'm afraid an accidental death will be assigned rather a low priority."

I glanced around. Rufus Quilp, the fat man who'd been reading or dozing the other times I'd seen him, had come in and was not only awake but on his feet. Even as I noted this, he eased his bulk onto a sofa. Off to the side, Lettice Littlefield stood next to her husband, her hand clasped in his. I smiled at her, then curled my lip at him. I don't think either of them noticed.

The colonel was saying something about an unfortunate incident that had happened some years ago in Sarawak. I waited until he slowed down for a semicolon, then said, "Excuse me."

The room went still.

"I'm afraid you ought to call the police right away," I said. "I think they'll want to get here just as soon as they can, no matter how deep the snow is."

"What are you saying, Mr. Rhodenbarr?"

I turned to Molly Cobbett. "When you came in here this morning," I said pleasantly, "just what did you do?"

"I never touched him, sir! I swear to God!"

"I'm sure you didn't," I said. "I believe you said you opened the drapes."

"Sure I did, sir. I'm always to draw them open in the daytime, so as to let the light in."

"And was the room dark before you drew them?"

"It was, sir. Not full dark, as some light came in through the open door, from the other room, like."

"But there were no lights on in this room," I said.

"No, sir."

"No lamps lit."

"No, sir."

"And there was a little light from the open door," I said, "because dawn was breaking. But earlier, when Mr. Rathburn had his tragic accident, it would have been full dark, wouldn't it?"

She looked at me. "I wasn't here, sir."

"Of course you weren't," I agreed. "But if you had been, and it wasn't dawn yet and there were no lamps turned on and the drapes were drawn shut, you'd have found the room dark, don't you suppose?"

Molly stood openmouthed, thinking about it. Nigel Eglantine frowned in thought, looking reluctant to take the thought the next step down the trail. His wife said, "Why yes, of course. It would have been pitch dark in here when Mr. Rathburn fell."

"That might explain his stepping on his shoelace," I said. "He wouldn't have seen it had come untied. But what it doesn't explain is why he'd be up on the steps in the first place. It would have been far too dark in here for him to find the steps, let alone pick out a book to read."

Blount-Buller cleared his throat. "What are you saying, Rhodenbarr?"

"I'm saying it's more complicated than it looks. Jonathan Rathburn would not have had an accident of this sort in a dark room. Either a light was on when he fell or what took place was rather different from your reconstruction of it."

Cissy Eglantine said, "Molly, are you sure you didn't turn off a lamp?"

"I don't remember," the girl wailed. "I don't *think* I did, but—"

"It doesn't seem likely," I said. "The room was dark when she entered it. If there had been a light burning, she'd have noticed it. If she didn't notice it, how would she happen to turn it off?"

"We don't know what step he was standing on," Gordon Wolpert observed. "But suppose he was mounted on one of the top steps. That would be quite a tumble, enough to give him that cut on his head and knock him cold. Might he not have landed with sufficient impact to extinguish a lamp?"

"If he fell on the lamp," I said, "then it would certainly be possible. Or even if he didn't, assuming he landed so hard that a floor lamp was overturned, or a table lamp sent crashing to the floor." Another possibility occurred to me. "Bulbs burn out," I said. "Of their own accord. It's not inconceivable that a bulb was lit when he had his accident and burned out before Molly found him."

"That must be what happened," Nigel Eglantine said.

"In that case," I said, "it's still burned out, because I think we can all agree that Molly hasn't had a chance to replace it yet. Could we try all the lamps and light fixtures?"

"All of them?"

"All of them. A burned-out bulb won't prove the theory, but the lack of one will rule it out."

As indeed it did. Every bulb worked, and once we'd established as much I had them switch the lights off again. We didn't need them; with the whole world outside snow-covered, more than enough light was reflected through the wall of windows.

"Well," I said.

It was a choice moment. They were all looking my way, waiting for me to say something, and the phrase that came unbidden to my lips was *I suppose you're wondering why I summoned you all here.* It's a sentence I've had occasion to utter in the past, and the words have never failed to set my own pulse racing with the thrill of the hunt. But this time they weren't really appropriate. I hadn't summoned anyone, nor had they cause to wonder why they were here.

I was stuck for *le mot juste.* Cissy Eglantine helped me out.

"There must be an explanation," she said.

"I can think of one," I allowed. "Rathburn had a light on when he climbed the library steps and had his accident. He fell like Bishop Berkeley's tree, without making a sound, so no one came running. But sometime afterward someone else passed the room and saw the light on. He or she real--

ized the light shouldn't be on, not in the middle of the night, and came in to turn it out. If it was this lamp, say, or that one, he or she couldn't have missed seeing Rathburn's body, because it would have been right in his or her line of sight. Damn it all, anyway."

"What's the matter, Bern?"

"He or she," I said. "His or her. If nobody objects, I'm just going to use the masculine pronouns from here on." Nobody objected. "Good," I said. "The point is, there are other lamps that could have been lit that a passerby could have turned off without ever coming into line of sight of Jonathan Rathburn's body. He could have walked in, turned off the light, and left the room without the slightest idea there was a corpse on the floor."

A murmur approved this line of thought. Even as it died down, Gordon Wolpert cleared his throat. "I wonder," he said. "Would you turn out a light in the library without taking a look to make sure there was nobody curled up in a chair with a good book? I should think simple manners would demand it."

"Good point," I said.

"And when you looked round, you'd almost certainly see Rathburn."

"If you actually looked," Carolyn said. "But you might just call out. 'I say, anybody here?' And, unless Rathburn managed to say something, you'd figure you had the room all to yourself."

Wolpert thought that made sense, and no one else offered any objection. "Fine," I said. "So there's only one question left to answer. Who turned off the light?"

No answer.

"It would have to have been one of us," I said, "and I

don't think it's the sort of thing we'd be likely to forget having done. Did anybody here come in late last night or early this morning and switch a light out? Any of you?"

They looked at me, they looked at each other, they looked at the floor. Leona Savage whispered discreetly to her daughter, and Millicent piped up to deny that she'd even been to the library at the time in question, let alone turned out any lights. Her father supported her claim, pointing out that the child had never voluntarily turned out a light in her life.

"It seems no one turned off the light," Colonel Blount-Buller said. "So it would appear we're left with two possibilities. Rathburn climbed the stairs in the dark or the light went out of its own accord."

"Neither of which makes any sense," I said. "Here's another—someone did turn off the light, but he can't admit to it because he can't let us know he was anywhere near this room last night. Because he murdered Rathburn, and he turned off the light to delay discovery of the body, never considering how suspicious it would look for Rathburn to be found in a darkened room."

"But that's plainly impossible," Nigel Eglantine said.

"Why?"

"Because it would mean . . ."

"Yes?"

"That someone in this house committed murder," he said.

"I'm afraid so," I said.

"But none of us . . ."

"Not one of us," Cissy Eglantine said stoutly. "If anyone actually did harm poor Mr. Rathburn, there's no way on earth it could have been one of *us*."

"Who else could have done it?" Miss Dinmont wanted to know.

"It must have been someone passing through the neighborhood," Cissy said. "A tramp or vagrant of some sort."

"In this weather?"

Everyone looked at the window. Outside, the snow lay sufficiently deep and crisp and even to gladden the heart of King Wenceslaus, and of almost nobody else.

"He'd want shelter," Cissy said. "He couldn't sleep outside on a night like this. And so he broke in, and—"

"And wanted something to read," Mrs. Colibri suggested.

"And was drawn into this room by the light—"

"Like a moth," Earlene Cobbett said, and then looked quite startled at having spoken the thought aloud, and clapped a freckled hand to her little mouth.

"And found poor Mr. Rathburn," Cissy went on, "who had already died in an accidental fall. And then the tramp, fearing he'd be suspected of involvement in the death, turned off the light and left." She heaved a sigh. "There, Mr. Rhodenbarr! None of us were involved, and it's not a murder after all!"

"Darling," Nigel Eglantine said. "Darling, that was so well said that I only wish it weren't ridiculous."

"Is it ridiculous, Nigel?"

"I'm afraid so, darling."

"Oh. But—"

"There's something else," I said, and stepped closer to the fallen Jonathan Rathburn and pointed down at his eyes, which continued to stare vacantly up at us. I bent down, clucked knowingly, and got to my feet. "If you look closely," I said, "you'll see evidence of pinpoint hemorrhages in both eyes."

No one went over for a closer look. Most of them stared instead at me.

"I don't think he died of loss of blood," I said. "He did bleed quite a bit, and it is possible to bleed to death from a scalp wound, but he didn't lose *that* much blood. And it's possible to strike your head and die of the effects of the blow, but I don't think that's what happened here. The kind of fall that could have caused that much damage would have been a noisy affair, yet nobody here seems to have heard a thing. I don't think Rathburn fell from the library steps. I don't think he mounted them in the first place. I think he was sitting down when his killer struck him."

Greg Savage wanted to know what gave me that idea. I crouched down beside the corpse and pointed to the source of the bleeding, a gash high on the left temple, the area around it showing a lot of discoloration. "If the killer was standing over him," I said, "and if he was right-handed and struck downward, well, that's a logical place for the blow to land."

The colonel wanted to know if a fall couldn't inflict a similar injury. I said I supposed it was possible, but he would have had to bang his head on something—the bottom step, say, or the sharp corner of a table. In that case we ought to see blood on the surface he struck.

"But we don't," I said. "We don't see the proverbial blunt instrument lying about, either, probably because the killer carried it off, but that's very likely what was employed. A bookend, say, or a glass ashtray, or a bronze knickknack like that camel over there. In fact . . ."

The colonel followed me over to the revolving bookcase, and I caught his hand as he was reaching for the camel. "Best not to touch," I said, "although I'll be surprised if it hasn't been wiped clean of prints. There'll probably be microscopic evidence, though. It looks to me as though there's blood on the base of it, but you'd have to run tests to establish that conclusively."

"My God," Cissy Eglantine said. "You can't be saying he was killed with our camel."

"I think he was struck down with it," I said. "But not killed."

"What do you mean?"

"I mean the blow knocked him down," I said, "and drew blood, and may well have rendered him unconscious. It might have eventually proved fatal—it'll take an autopsy to determine that—but it didn't kill Rathburn right away, and the killer didn't want to sit around and wait. He knew better than to strike a second blow and try to pass it off as the result of a fall. So he used something else."

"What?"

I pointed to the couch. "That throw pillow," I said. "No, don't pick it up, but have a look at it. I think the fabric's stained, and my guess is the stain'll turn out to be blood, and the blood'll turn out to be Rathburn's."

Rufus Quilp blinked rapidly. He was sitting on the couch within reach of the pillow in question, and drew away from it now. "I was following you up to that point," he said slowly, his voice thick as if with sleep. I don't think I'd heard him speak before, and had barely seen him awake. "But now you've lost me. Are you suggesting that, having struck the man once with a bronze camel, your killer finished the job by swatting him with a pillow?"

If you'll swallow a camel, I thought, why strain at a pillow? But I couldn't say that, and before I could come up with something else to say, Millicent Savage said, "He didn't hit him with the pillow, silly. He smothered him with it!"

"Millicent," her mother said, "you mustn't interrupt."

"It may have been an interruption," I said, "but she got it right. That would explain the pinpoint hemorrhaging. It's a telltale sign in mercy killings, when a nurse or a relative hurries things along for a terminal patient by holding a pillow over his face."

"If that is blood on the pillow," the colonel said, "it would be damning evidence, eh? Couldn't have got there if Rathburn was alone when he fell." His eyes went to Mrs. Eglantine. "Hate to say it, Cecilia, but it rather knocks your theory of a tramp into a cocked hat."

"I did so want it to be a tramp," Cissy said.

"Because the alternative is insupportable," the colonel said, "but I fear the insupportable in this instance is true. Nigel, there's nothing for it. You'll want to call the police immediately."

Nigel Eglantine drew a breath, swallowed whatever it was he'd been about to say, and left the room. Dakin Littlefield came over for a look at the pillow, the camel, and the fallen Jonathan Rathburn. "I don't get it," he said. "If this killer went to so much trouble to stage an accident, why would he leave a bloodstain on the pillow and blood specks on the camel? He was inches away from a perfect crime and suddenly turned sloppy. It doesn't make sense to me."

"Doesn't it?"

"I just said it didn't," he reminded me. "But I'm sure you've got an explanation."

And I'm sure you've got an alibi was on the tip of my tongue, but I bit it back. "My guess is the accident was staged after the fact," I said. "The assault must have been hasty, even impulsive. Afterward the killer was in a hurry to get back to . . . well, whatever it was he had to get back to. He didn't want to linger there where anyone could walk in and discover him standing over his victim's body. He took a minute to position Rathburn at the foot of the library steps, let him bleed a little into the carpet, then finished him off with the pillow. He gave the camel a quick wipe and put it back on top of the revolving bookstand. He probably didn't see that the pillow was stained. Who knows if there was even a light burning when the murder took place? Rathburn wouldn't have been looking at bookshelves in the dark, but he might have had a quiet talk in a dimly lit room, and how much light do you need to kill a man by?"

"Why not just carry the pillow away?" Littlefield wanted to know. "Why leave it around?"

"Where would he put it? In his luggage? Or on the chair in his room?"

"I don't know, but—"

"It would draw attention anywhere else," I said. "It would be least conspicuous in its usual position, on the couch where he'd found it. Even if he knew there was blood on it, he was better off leaving it there. His hope was that no one would be looking for blood, that the death would get a cursory inspection by the police, that the autopsy would be perfunctory and incomplete, and that Rathburn's death would go into the books as an accident.

"If that happened," I went on, "he was home free. If not, there'd be more of Rathburn's blood to contend with than a stain on the pillow and a drop or two on the camel. A good forensic investigation would turn up blood drops all over the place, probably enough to establish just where Rathburn was sitting when the blow was struck."

Some of the women seemed to draw in their shoulders, as if to avoid contact with all this blood that was allegedly all around them.

"In fact," I said, "we probably ought to leave the room and seal it until the police get here. No one's touching anything, and that's good, but we shouldn't even be here. This is a crime scene."

"Quite right," Colonel Blount-Buller said, "although I don't know that the local police will treat a crime scene quite as Scotland Yard might. But you're correct all the same, sir. Experienced in these matters, are you? Served with the police, I shouldn't wonder."

"Not exactly," I said.

"Not a private detective, I don't suppose?"

I shook my head. "I'm a big reader," I said, "and I read a lot of mysteries. And I watch a lot of TV. You know, locked-room cases? Impossible crimes? English-country-house murders?"

"Poirot and all that," the colonel said.

"That's the idea."

"Never would have guessed it was quite so instructive," he said. "Blood spatters, pinpoint hemorrhages, direction the blow was struck—you certainly seem to know what you're about, Rhodenbarr."

I was preening a little, I have to admit. It's hard to avoid when someone with that kind of accent gives you that kind of compliment. I was busy enjoying the feeling when the good colonel went on to ask me just what it was I did for a living.

"As a matter of fact," I said, "I'm out of work at the moment. My job was eliminated. Corporate downsizing, at least that's what they call it. Getting more work out of fewer people is what it amounts to, and it's a hell of a thing when you're the victim of it."

"Had some of that in the British army," he said, "after we lost India." His face darkened. "Might have put a better face on it if they'd called it downsizing. What did you do for the ungrateful swine before they cut you loose?"

"He's a burglar," Millicent Savage said.

All conversation stopped. I managed a laugh, and what a hollow ring it had in that huge room. "I was joking with the child last night," I said. "I'm afraid she's taken it seriously."

"*You* say it's a joke," said the little horror, "but *I* think it's true. I think you really *are* a burglar, Bernie."

"Millicent," Leona Savage said, "go to your room."

"But Mommy, I—"

"Millicent!"

"It's all right," I said. "I'm sure she didn't mean any harm. At any rate there's no harm done, and—"

I stopped. Nigel Eglantine had come back to the room, a frown darkening his brow.

"I'm sure it's the snow," he said.

We looked at him.

"The phone," he explained. "The line is dead. I'm sure it must be the snow."

THIRTEEN

What we needed to do, Nigel Eglantine insisted, was remain calm. He said this over and over, as if the words were a mantra designed to ward off panic, and with only partial success.

Carolyn rescued him. "Look, Nigel," she said, "there's good news and bad news, right?"

"Good news and bad news? There is?"

"There always is," she assured him. "Suppose you start off by giving us the bad news."

"The bad news," he said.

"Like the phones are out, and whatever else goes with it."

"Ah," he said. "The bad news. Well, the phone service is definitely not on at the moment. I'm sure that's a result of the storm. Bad weather often knocks out our telephones. In the spring and fall the phones are often out after severe electrical storms, and in the winter a bad snowstorm can do it."

"Nothing about *that* in the brochure," Miss Hardesty murmured to Miss Dinmont.

"But the good news," he said, brightening, "is that we're never without phone service for very long. I'd say that we'll have service again within a couple of hours at the most."

"That's good news," Carolyn agreed. "Tell us the rest of the bad news."

"The rest of the bad news?"

"The snow," she prompted.

"Ah, the snow. Well, there's a great deal of it, as you can readily see. Just over two feet of it, according to the newscast, with drifts deep enough to bury an automobile to the roofline. Most of the county roads will be impassable until the plows get through, and that may take quite some time."

"So even if we were to phone the police," the colonel said, "it's doubtful they could get through to us."

"Highly doubtful," Nigel said. "Even if our road were cleared, they couldn't get up our driveway. Nor can anyone else. For the time being, there'll be no deliveries and no guests arriving."

"The last part," Carolyn said, "about no new guests, is more good news than bad, if you ask me. Right now the last thing we need is new people in the house. But the rest is bad news, all right. What's the good news?"

"Even without deliveries," he said, "we've no cause for alarm. The larder's fully stocked with enough food to feed us all royally well into April. That includes an emergency supply of bottled water, which we're unlikely to need because the well is functioning perfectly. And, though it's early in the day to mention it, the Cuttleford cellar is fully stocked. We've enough beer and wine and spirits to carry us well into the next century."

"Well, that's a relief," Carolyn said.

"And actually," he went on, warming to the task,

"there's more good news. It's true we're isolated here, albeit in comfortable isolation, but we won't be confined for long. Orris assures me that as soon as he has the snowblower operating, he'll be able to clear a path to the bridge. Just across the bridge our Jeep is parked, with a stout snowplow attached to it. In a matter of hours, Orris ought to be able to have our driveway cleared all the way to the road."

"Hear, hear!" the colonel said, and there was an ill-coordinated round of applause for Orris, who acknowledged it by dropping his head so that he was staring at his boots, as if to gauge how far above them the snow would reach.

"But before anything else," Cissy Eglantine said, "I think it's ever so important that we all have a proper English breakfast."

"I wonder what this is," Carolyn said. "Maybe it's toad-in-the hole." She looked at her plate, on which reposed a thick slice of toasted white bread. Its center had been re-moved, and an egg cooked in the circular space thus created.

"You sound disappointed," I said.

"Well, it's not bad," she said. "It's a little like Adam and Eve on a raft."

"That's what, two poached eggs on toast?"

"Uh-huh. Except in this case Adam fell off and drowned, and the raft's got a hole in the floorboards. So all that's left is Eve, holding on for dear life." She took a bite. "Not bad, though, I have to admit. Even if it's not what I expected."

"What did you expect?"

"I don't know, Bern. Some exotic form of comfort food, I suppose, if that's not a contradiction in terms. Like this black pudding."

"It's exotic comfort food, eh?"

"Well, kind of." She lifted a forkful to her mouth, chewed thoughtfully. "Very simple," she said, "but very tasty at the same time. And it's black, all right, but it's not like any pudding I ever tasted."

"A far cry from Jell-O," I said.

"They've got funny ideas about pudding, Bern. Look at Yorkshire pudding. I mean, it's good, too, but you wouldn't rush out and squirt Cool Whip on it, would you? Black pudding. What do you suppose they make it out of?"

"Blood."

"Seriously, Bern."

"I'm serious. 'Blood sausage' is another name for it."

"I wish you hadn't told me that, Bern."

"Well, you asked."

"That didn't mean you had to tell me. At least now I know why they call it black pudding. If they called it blood sausage, no one would want any. What about the white pudding, Bern? What do they make that out of, lymph?" She frowned. "Don't answer that. You want more kippers, Bern?"

"I think I've had my limit."

"I guess I should just be grateful," she said, "that they don't use a real toad for toad-in-the-hole. Listen, if they serve us bubble and squeak, do me a favor, okay? If there's something disgusting doing the bubbling and squeaking, keep it to yourself."

"I think it's leftover cabbage and potatoes."

"That would be fine," she said. "Just so it's not recycled reptiles and rodents, Bern? Who do you figure killed Jonathan Rathburn?"

"How should I know?"

She shrugged. "I just thought you might have a hunch. That was pretty cool the way you proved it was murder, and found the two murder weapons and everything. Struck down with a camel, then smothered with a throw pillow. What a way to go, huh?"

"Uh-huh."

"What's the matter, Bern?"

"I was right there," I said.

"So was I, Bern. So was everybody, at one time or another. You want to know something? All the time we were in there standing around Rathburn's body, I couldn't stop glancing up at the top shelf to see if *The Big Sleep* was still there."

"It's still there."

"I know. And I didn't want to stare at it, but I kept looking at it over and over. I don't think anybody noticed. I hope they didn't."

"I think the dead body got most of their attention."

"Yeah, and I wish I knew who killed him." She frowned. "What do you mean, you were right there? You don't mean just now."

"No."

"And you don't mean last night, when we were both there."

"No."

"You mean you were there when he was killed? Bern, you didn't . . . you couldn't have . . ."

"Don't be ridiculous."

"Then what *do* you mean? And why is the book still on the shelf? I thought you were going to get it last night. And how come—"

I filled her in quickly on the events of the previous night.

When I told her about the interlude with Lettice in the East Parlour, her eyes widened and her jaw dropped. "My God," she said. "Imagine doing something like that on your wedding night."

"Lots of women do something like that on their wedding night," I pointed out. "The thing is, most of them do it to their husbands."

"But not Lettice."

"I don't know what she did upstairs with him," I said. "I just know what she did downstairs with me."

"You know," she said, "I was watching her while you were explaining things in the library, and there was something about the way she was looking at you."

"Oh?"

She nodded. "She looked like the cat that swallowed the cream." She frowned. "Make that the cat that ate the canary, okay?"

"Whatever you say."

"Anyway, she looked smug. I guess I know why. You know what, Bern? I think it's something in the air."

"In the air?"

"Last night. Some sex vibe or something. You wouldn't believe the dream I had."

"Oh?"

"Amazingly vivid. I could have sworn—" She broke off in midsentence and motioned to our waitress, who was in fact Molly Cobbett, the downstairs maid who had happened upon Rathburn's corpse and awakened the house with a scream. "Say, Molly," she purred, "do you suppose we could have a little more tea?"

"Why, of course you could, mum."

"I'm Carolyn, Molly. And this is Bernie."

"Very good, mum."

We sat in silence while Molly poured our tea. As soon as she was out of earshot, Carolyn said, "She was in it."

"Who was in what?"

"Molly. In my dream."

"Oh."

"You wouldn't believe how real it was, Bern."

"Yes I would."

"You would? How come? You weren't in the dream, Bernie. It was just Molly and me." She made a face. "That sounds like a song cue, doesn't it? 'My Blue Heaven.' Anyway, it was unbelievably hot. Now I want to blush every time I look at her."

"She's a country girl, Carolyn."

"I know."

"Pretty unsophisticated."

"I realize that," she said. "Her idea of eating out is a burger at the Dairy Queen. I know all that." She pursed her lips. "But in the world of dreams," she said, "the woman is hot hot hot. But I still don't understand what you said before. About being there when it happened."

For a moment I missed the transition, and I thought she meant that I was there when her dream-moment with Molly Cobbett took place. As indeed I was, but that was something she never had to know about.

Then I said, "Oh, when the murder took place. I wasn't, not exactly." And I explained how I'd been about to enter the darkened room when I'd heard two people whispering.

"It must have been Rathburn," she said.

"One of them must have been Rathburn."

"And the other was the man who killed him."

"The man or woman."

"Right, and now we're back to he or she and his or hers. You think a woman could have done it?"

"I think anybody but Millicent Savage could have done it," I said. "It wouldn't take too much strength to hit a person hard enough with a bronze camel to knock him senseless and split his head open. A fatal blow might take more in the way of brute force, although an athletic woman like Miss Hardesty could probably supply as much sheer brute force as most of the men around here. But in this case the blow wasn't fatal, and it may not have been all that hard. So I don't think we can rule out anybody."

"Except Millicent."

"Well, it'd be a reach for a ten-year-old girl."

"And Miss Dinmont."

"What about Miss Dinmont?"

"Well, for openers, she's in a wheelchair." Her eyes widened. "Wait a minute, Bern. You don't think . . ."

"I don't think what?"

"That the wheelchair is a ruse? That she's really physically fit? Is that what you think?"

"Why would I think that?"

"Because you've read Agatha Christie," she said, "and you know that things are seldom what they seem in situations like this one. Bernie, you've got to do something. I hope you realize that."

"I know what I have to do," I said. "I have to get the book, which is going to be a neat trick with the library out of bounds. And I have to get out of here, which is impossible as long as we're snowed in, and probably out of the question until the police send us home. So I can't do either of the things I have to do, not for the time being. In that case, I know what I'm going to do."

"What's that?"

"I'm going to find something to read," I said. "Some book from some room other than the library. God knows there are plenty of rooms, and plenty of books in them, and I ought to be able to find something I feel like reading. I'll take it upstairs and crawl into bed with it, and if it puts me to sleep I won't complain, either."

"Bern, that's not what you have to do."

"I didn't say it was what I *had* to do, I said it was what I was *going* to do, and—"

"There's something else you *have* to do."

"What?"

"You have to solve the murder."

I looked at her. She looked back at me. Conversations, pitched too low to be overheard, continued at the other tables. Outside, you could hear the sound of someone trying to get an engine to turn over. Orris, I thought, having a go at snowblowing.

"That's ridiculous," I said.

"Who else is going to solve it? Nigel Eglantine pours a good drink, but he couldn't solve a jigsaw puzzle. The colonel's used to being in charge, and that's helpful, but he's a straightforward military type. What does he know about the criminal mind?"

"Not much," I said. "On the other hand, what do *I* know about the criminal mind?"

"Well, you've got one, Bern, and you've been using it for years. Come on, who else has a chance of trapping the killer?"

"How about the cops?"

"In the first place," she said, "they're going to be hick cops with a strong family resemblance to Orris. The folks who live around here have been marrying their cousins for centuries. They've been diving into the shallow end of the gene pool, and you can get hurt that way."

"For all you know," I said, "the county sheriff is a retired FBI agent with a law degree and a mind like a steel trap."

"What if he is? And what kind of mind has a steel trap got, anyway? Anyhow, he's not here, and he's not likely to get here for a while, either. Bern, we're snowed in, and that means he's snowed out."

"Hear that?"

"Hear what, Bern?"

I pointed. "The snowblower. He was having trouble getting it started, but it's running now. Pretty soon he'll have a path cleared to the bridge, and then he'll be in the Jeep plowing the driveway clear to the highway. And before you know it this place'll be crawling with cops."

"Retarded cops."

"Well-trained professional law enforcement officers," I said, "led by an L.L.B. from Harvard Law."

"If he's got an L.L.B.," she said, "the chances are he got it from L. L. Bean. But even if he's good, Bern, even if he's another Ray Kirschmann—"

"Bite your tongue," I said.

"—we can't afford to wait for him. Because by the time he gets here it'll be too late."

"Too late for what?"

"Not what. Who."

"Huh?"

"I mean *whom*. Too late for whom."

"What are you talking about, Carolyn?"

She cocked her head. "That doesn't sound right to me, Bern."

"*Whom* doesn't sound right to you? It should, it's the object of the preposition *for*. 'Too late for whom.' Sounds okay to me."

"The engine," she said. "The snowblower. It's making a horrible noise."

It was at that, cranking out an unpleasant metal-on-metal sound, a sort of mechanical death rattle.

"Maybe that's the way they're supposed to sound," I offered.

"Fat chance, Bern."

"How can you be sure? When did you ever hear a snowblower before? Anyway, it stopped. It's quiet now."

"Yeah," she said, and looked around. She might have been sniffing the wind, like a cowboy in a celluloid western. "Too quiet," she said ominously. "It's too quiet, and it's gonna be too late. To late for . . ."

"Whom," I said, feeling like a grammatical owl.

"For the next victim," she said. "Why are you looking at me like that?"

"I don't know," I said. "Maybe it's because I can't believe I really heard you say that. 'For the next victim'? What makes you think there's going to be another victim?"

"There has to be."

"Why?"

"Because there always is."

"There always is?"

"You've read the books, Bern."

"This isn't a book, Carolyn."

"It's not? Well, it might as well be. It's got all the ingredients. It's not Raymond Chandler's mean streets, not by a long shot. It's the kind of setting he despised, where people commit murders with tropical fish."

"How would you kill somebody with guppies?" I wondered.

"Maybe you'd use swordtails," she said, "and run them through. I don't know. All I really know is the killer's already used a camel and a pillow, and you can't make me believe he's going to stop there. He's sure to strike again unless we do something."

"Do what?"

"Catch him," she said. "Unmask him."

"How?"

"Why are you asking me, Bern? You're the expert."

"The hell I am."

"Of course you are. Look at all the times you've solved the mystery and caught the murderer."

"Only because I had to. Every time it happened it was because I fumbled my way into a mess and so I had to fumble my way out of it."

"Well?"

"I didn't fumble my way here," I said. "I came here on vacation."

"And to steal a book, which you haven't stolen yet. And to forget a woman, who's going to be hard to forget the way things are shaping up. Bern, some people would call this fumbling."

"I call it bad luck."

"Call it anything you want. Bern, you know what always happens in the books? The detective hesitates. He's figured things out but he won't tell anybody because he wants to wait until he's absolutely certain. And then, after the killer strikes again, he feels terrible."

"They call that remorse."

"Not the killer, for God's sake. The detective's the one

who feels terrible. 'Soccer blew,' he says. 'It is my fault. If only—' "

"Soccer blew?"

"You know, soccer blew. It's just an expression. Poirot says it all the time."

"Sacre bleu," I said.

"That's what I said, soccer blew. Don't ask me what it's supposed to mean. Bern, all I know is you better do something, or there's gonna be another dead body in the library and you're gonna be saying soccer blew all over the place. Why are you looking at me like that, Bern?"

"You're serious, aren't you?"

"Of course I am."

"You really think there's going to be another murder."

"I'd bet anything there is."

"Unless I do something."

She nodded. "But even if you do," she said, "it's probably too late."

"Too late to keep the killer from striking a second time."

"Right."

"Who's it going to be?"

"The second victim? How can I answer that, Bern? Only one person knows, and . . . God, you don't suspect me, do you?"

"I don't suspect anybody," I said. "I just thought you might have a hunch, that's all."

She leaned forward, lowered her voice another notch. "It'll be somebody who's staying here," she said. "Somebody who was in the library earlier while you were explaining why Rathburn's death had to be murder. Somebody who probably had important information but didn't say anything at the time. Bern, it could be somebody here in this room right now."

Her first three speculations were on the money. But, as it turned out, the second victim wasn't in the Breakfast Room when she spoke those words. He wasn't even in the house.

It was Orris.

FOURTEEN

Thinking back, I saw how close Carolyn had come to being right on all four points. Just moments after she'd said that the next victim might be in the room with us, he made his appearance, walking with cap in hands to the table where Nigel and Cissy Eglantine sat over coffee. He had removed his boots, I saw, and was wearing thick woolen socks. Snow clung to the lower portions of his trouser legs.

After a whispered conference with his employers, young Orris clomped out again. Something—not a premonition, I assure you—urged me to ask Nigel Eglantine if anything was the matter, but I resisted the impulse. It turned out I didn't have to ask, because Nigel came over to our table and made an announcement. There was, he reported, something wrong with the snowblower. Its engine appeared to be damaged. He was going to have a look at it, although he wasn't terribly smart about engines, but even if he proved unable to fix it we were not to worry, because the machine wasn't really essential. Although the snow was deep, with drifts in the yard well over three feet high, Orris was a stout fellow and had insisted he could wade through the snow clear to the bridge and across it. On its other side, of course, was the Jeep, and the Jeep, we could rest assured, was fully reliable.

When he went off to reassure another table, I said to Carolyn, "I bet the truck won't be there, either."

"Did I miss something, Bern? What truck?"

"Oh, it's an ancient joke," I said, and told her about the young Marine making his first parachute jump. He's told how the chute will open automatically, and that there's an emergency ripcord if it doesn't, and that when he lands a truck will pick him up to take him back to camp. So he jumps, and the chute doesn't open, and the ripcord comes off in his hand, and he says to himself, "Hell, I bet the damn truck won't be there, either."

She looked at me. "It's an old joke, huh?"

"The old jokes are the best ones."

"Not necessarily," she said.

This time I didn't hear the scream.

Not the first scream, anyway. I was in a parlor—not the East Parlour, where Lettice and I had misbehaved in front of the stuffed oryx, but in the West Parlour, where I was sitting in a wing chair with my feet up on a needlepoint-covered ottoman, reading *The Portable Dorothy Parker*. The whole idea of a portable Dorothy Parker intrigued me. You could take her along on trips, and every once in a while her head would pop up out of your Gladstone bag and deliver some smartass remark.

I was reading a short story about a woman who was waiting for a telephone to ring, but I wasn't getting very far with it because Miss Dinmont kept interrupting me to ask for help with a crossword puzzle. Did I know a six-letter marsupial, the third letter an *M*? Could I complete the phrase "John Jacob Blank" with a five-letter word ending in *R*?

Why, I've long wondered, would anyone want help on a crossword puzzle? And how does one deal with people who ask for it? If you supply an answer it only encourages them to ask for more, but if you plead ignorance it doesn't seem to discourage them. In fact they seem to ask everything, even the ones where they know the answer themselves, as if determined to plumb the depths of your stupidity.

What might work is to grab the puzzle out of the puzzler's hands, fill in all the squares yourself at breakneck speed (right or wrong, who cares?), and hand it back in triumph. I might have tried it that morning—I was testy enough, even with my stomach full of kippers and porridge and toad-in-the-hole (or wind-in-the-willows, or whatever it was), but I just couldn't be so mean to poor little Miss Dinmont. I was afraid she'd burst into tears. I'd feel terrible, and then Miss Hardesty would come along and beat me to a pulp.

So I was reading, and I'd just been interrupted for perhaps the seventh time, and I'd tried saying, "Hmmm, that's a tricky one, let me think about that one," and there was a scream outside, or at least a great cry.

As I said, I didn't hear it. But Orris was not like Berkeley's tree, and even though I didn't hear him fall, someone else did. Millicent Savage, who was out in front of the house directing her father in the making of a snowman, heard Orris shout. So did her father. "Wait here," Greg Savage told his daughter, and set off toward the source of the cry, walking literally in Orris's footsteps through snow that came up higher than his knees.

Millicent, of course, did not heed her father's command to stay put, but set off in his wake. She found it slow going, however, her precocity being cerebral rather than altitudinal, and before she could reach the bridge, her father had already turned around and was headed back. He scooped her up in his arms and carried her back to Cuttleford House, walking as fast as he could and not bothering to respond to the stream of questions she directed at him.

He reached the door, put her down, threw the door open, and cried out his news to the entire household.

"It's Orris! He's fallen! The bridge is down! He had a long fall and he's not moving! He's just lying there! I think he's dead!"

I heard all that. I heard the scream that followed his announcement, too, but how could I help it? They probably heard it loud and clear in Vermont.

If I'd first seen the bridge in daylight, I don't think I could have crossed it. In the darkness, I'd been able to convince myself that the shallow waters of Cuttlebone Creek were but a few scant yards beneath our feet. In the unlikely event that we fell, at worst we'd get a soaking.

But what I saw, after I'd joined the mad scramble to see what had happened to Orris, was a deep and rocky gorge, its sides near vertical. The suspension bridge dangled like limp spaghetti from its moorings on the far side of the gorge. The connective tissue on our side of the creek had given way before Orris could get himself across. Maybe he cried out the instant of the first snapping of the cable. Maybe he was already falling. He fell clear to the bottom, a drop of at least thirty feet, and when we saw him he lay utterly still on a heap of boulders, his head at an angle that would have been a stretch for Plastic Man.

There was some sentiment for rescuing him. The sides of the gorge were too steep for a safe descent in good weather, and out of the question now, with snow covering everything and making it impossible to see where you could or could not get a decent foothold. According to Nigel, if you followed the creek a mile or so downstream, you'd reach a spot where the stream could be easily crossed, and from that point you could wade upstream until you reached Orris. Of course it would take a long time to walk a mile cross-country through two feet of snow, and it would take at least as long to return along a frozen creek bed, not to mention the risk of putting a foot wrong and spraining an ankle or breaking a leg.

"Leave him," Dakin Littlefield counseled.

"But he'll die!" one of the women wailed. (I believe it was Earlene Cobbett. Her cousin Molly had had a busy night, starring in Carolyn's dream and then screaming when she discovered Jonathan Rathburn's body. Now it was the heavily freckled Earlene's turn, and she'd let out a scream of her own at Greg Savage's report of Orris's fall; a propensity for full-throated shrieking seemed to run in the Cobbett family.)

"Not likely," Littlefield said.

"I don't see how you can say that," Mrs. Colibri said. "It seems to me that people die of exposure all the time. And they die of shock, too, when they suffer severe trauma and don't receive medical attention."

"Happens all the time," Littlefield agreed. "But only to people who are alive to begin with."

"What do you mean?"

"I mean he's already as dead as a doornail," Littlefield said, his words as cruel as the mouth they came out of.

"He had a long drop and a hard landing. He probably dashed out what brains he had on that rock, and if that didn't kill him the broken neck did. See how he's lying?"

"It's an awkward lie," Colonel Blount-Buller allowed.

"It's not a hard position to get into," Littlefield said, "as long as you're a chicken and somebody's already wrung your neck for you. Face it, the man's toast. His future is all in the past. Anybody else goes after him, he's odds-on to take the same kind of spill this guy took and wind up in the same kind of shape. We already have two men dead, which is on the high side for a quiet weekend in the country. Somebody else wants to round out the hat trick, be my guest, but I think you're out of your mind."

"But what are we to do?" Nigel Eglantine asked. "We can't just leave him there, can we?"

"Why not? He's not going anywhere."

Somebody said something about predatory scavengers, and a few heads looked heavenward, as if to spot a vulture circling patiently overhead. There was nothing up there but the sky.

"He's reasonably safe in this weather," Dakin Littlefield said. "And the longer he lies there the safer he gets, because once he freezes solid he can quit worrying that something's going to start gnawing on him. Not that he's doing any worrying of his own as it is."

A sob, wrenching enough to melt a heart of stone, tore from the throat of Earlene Cobbett.

It had no discernible effect on Lettice's new husband. "Say a couple of us managed to get to him," he went on mercilessly, "which'd be a neat trick, and say we got the body up, which'd be a neater one. Then what?" He didn't wait for an answer. "We'd just have to leave him outside," he said. "On the back porch, stacked like cordwood and with a rug tossed over him. We may be a few days waiting for the rest of the world to reach us, and he'll keep a lot better outside in the cold than inside where it's warm." His nose wrinkled at the notion. "Where would we put him, anyway? The library's already out of bounds because there's a dead body in it. If that genius over there"—a wave in my direction—"hadn't managed to sell everybody on the idea that Rathburn was murdered, we could have moved him outside before he started to get ripe."

"I say," the colonel reminded him. "There are ladies present, Littlefield."

"Did I curse without knowing it, Colonel? When did 'ripe' get to be a swear word?"

Blount-Buller cleared his throat. "All a bit indelicate, wouldn't you say?"

The debate went on, but I'd lost interest in it. I didn't much want to walk over to the gully's rim, but I forced myself, and had a look at the rope cables that had given way, sending poor Orris to his death.

I remembered the words of the clown who'd driven us from the station at Pattaskinnick. Good strong rope, he'd called it, and then he'd gone on to describe how rain could soak into the rope, and how it would swell when it froze, severing fibers, and go on thawing and freezing until it had sustained enough invisible damage that it would, as he'd put it, snap like a twig.

I looked closely at the good strong rope and saw where it had snapped like a twig. And then I turned my head quickly, to make sure nobody was standing too close to me. I was, after all, right at the edge of the gorge, and a quick shove would send me plummeting to a fate worse than Orris's.

And someone might be inclined to supply that little push.

No one was standing dangerously near me, but I drew back from the brink all the same. Greg Savage was saying something, but I wasn't paying attention to the words, just waiting for a pause. When one came along I grabbed my chance.

"The body has to stay where it is," I said. "That's the way the police will want it."

Someone wanted to know what the police had to do with it. "You don't need the police when someone dies accidentally," I was told. "Not when it's an obvious accident, not out here in the country. All you need is for a doctor to sign a death certificate."

I hadn't known that, and still wasn't sure it was true. But it didn't matter.

"It wasn't an accident," I said. "There were two ropes securing the bridge on this side of the creek, one on the left and one on the right. These were stout ropes, fully half an inch thick. There's no reason why they would have snapped."

"They weren't steel cables," Miss Hardesty said. "Rope is rope. It's strong, but it doesn't last forever."

I started to say something, but there was a gasp from Lettice. "My God," she said, and clutched her husband's arm. "We were the last people on that bridge!"

"We were the last to cross it," he corrected her. "The guy down there was the last person on it."

"Dakin, we could have been killed!"

"We could have been struck by lightning," he said, "or swept away in a flash flood. But we weren't. And we weren't on the bridge when the ropes broke, either, which was lucky for us and not too lucky for that poor slob who was."

Calling Orris a slob, while perhaps unimpeachable on

grounds of fact, seemed to me a clear case of speaking ill of the dead. But I let it go, figuring the lousy maid service the Littlefields could now expect to receive from the scowling Earlene Cobbett was answer enough.

"One rope might break," I said. "But not two, not both at once."

"I wonder," the colonel said. "If one rope was frayed or weakened by the elements, wouldn't its fellow be similarly stressed?"

"To a degree," I admitted. "But not to the point where they'd both go at the same instant."

"I see your point, Rhodenbarr. But say one rope gives way. Wouldn't that place additional stress on the other? And wouldn't *that* be enough to finish off an already weakened rope?"

"There'd be a delay," I said. "One rope would give way, and there'd be a few seconds while the fibers parted on the other one. Probably enough time for anyone on the bridge to get the hell off it."

"Perhaps," he said, "if he had his wits about him. Orris was by no means an imbecile, but none would call him quick-witted. He was unquestionably slow."

"And he crossed the bridge every day," Nigel Eglantine put in. "He wouldn't have been thinking about it while he crossed it, as those of us who are nervous on bridges might. His mind would have been occupied with thoughts of what he was going to do next—starting up the Jeep, plowing the drive."

"There you are," the colonel said. "He'd scarcely have noticed when the first rope failed. He'd have registered the sound, and by the time he'd identified it, well . . ."

"Bob's your uncle," Carolyn said.

"I beg your pardon?"

"Just an expression," I said. "It seems to me it would take a lot longer than that for the second rope to give way, but it's not a hypothesis we can test, so let's let it go."

"Then there's no reason to assume it was anything other than an accident," Dakin Littlefield said.

"But there is," I said.

"Oh?"

"The rope ends," I said. "The fibers don't look frayed to me. I'd say somebody cut them most of the way through. When Orris walked onto the bridge, it was literally hanging by a thread. Well, two threads, one on each side. And they did give way at once, and before he'd taken more than a step or two."

Someone asked how I knew that.

"Look at the bridge," I said, and pointed across the gorge, where the thing hung down from its two remaining ropes. "It was covered with snow," I said, "like everything else in the county, and most of the snow's spilled into the gorge now. But you can see footprints at one end, where Orris's weight compacted the snow underfoot. He only got a chance to make two footprints."

This brought fresh sobs from Earlene Cobbett, whose freckled face was now awash with tears.

"I'm not a forensics expert," I said, with just the faintest sense of *déjà vu*. "The police will have someone who can examine those rope ends and determine for certain whether or not they were cut. But it certainly looks to me as though they were, and that just strengthens the argument for leaving Orris's body where it is. I suppose someone could go down there to inspect him, just to make sure that he's dead, but I don't really think there's much question of that, not with his head at that angle."

"I say," the colonel said. "Whole thing's a bit rum, eh?

Someone right here at Cuttleford House set a trap for this man and murdered him."

"Not exactly," I said.

"Not exactly? But you just said—"

"Let's get back to the house," I said, "before we freeze to death, or somebody puts a foot wrong and winds up in the ditch with Orris. And then I'll explain."

FIFTEEN

"Someone set a trap," I said. "That much is true. The ropes supporting the bridge were cut through to the point where the slightest stress would finish them. But it wasn't a trap for Orris."

We were back inside Cuttleford House, the whole lot of us crowded into the bar and spilling over into the room adjoining it. Nigel Eglantine was pouring drinks and the Cobbett cousins were handing round trays of them, offering us a choice of malt whisky or what we were assured was a fine nutty brown sherry. It wasn't even noon yet, but nobody was saying no to a drink, and most of us were going straight for the hard stuff.

Rufus Quilp was among us, I was pleased to note, and so was Miss Dinmont, her wheelchair now once again in the capable hands of Miss Hardesty. They had been the only members of the party who had not rushed out to the fallen bridge, and I had not been surprised at their absence. Neither Miss Dinmont's wheelchair nor Mr. Quilp's great bulk could have had easy passage through the deep snow. All the same, I was happy to see them again, comforted by the knowledge that neither of them had seized the moment to kill the other, nor had some third party knocked off both of them.

"What do we know about the sabotage of the bridge?" I went on. "First, let's set a time. We know the bridge was intact when the Littlefields arrived last night. That was around ten or ten-thirty. The snow continued to fall after their arrival, because by this morning their footprints were completely covered." I paused significantly. "And so were the footprints of the person who sabotaged the bridge. Orris walked through two feet of virgin snow to get to that bridge. Whoever sabotaged it must have done so not long after the Littlefields crossed it."

"I told you," Lettice said, gripping her husband's arm. "We could have been killed."

"If you'd arrived later," I said, "or if the killer had gone to the bridge sooner, you might have been on it when the ropes broke. But you weren't his target, and I don't think Orris was, either. Not specifically."

Someone wanted to know what I meant.

"He couldn't be sure who he'd get. Maybe someone else would arrive from outside. Maybe someone other than Orris would be the first to leave. The more I think about it, the more I'm inclined to believe that the damage he did to the bridge wasn't designed to kill anybody."

"Then what was the point of it?"

"To prevent anyone from crossing the bridge. To keep us all here, and keep the rest of the world on the other side of Cuttlebone Creek."

The colonel was nodding in understanding. "A bridge too far," he said thoughtfully. "He sabotaged the bridge—when would you say, Rhodenbarr? Before or after he struck down Rathburn?"

"I don't know."

"Hard to say until we know who he is and why he did it, eh? But if he just wanted the bridge out, why stop at cutting the ropes halfway through? Why not make a good job of it and drop the bridge into the gorge in one shot?"

"He may have been concerned about how much noise it might make when it fell," I said. "And worried that someone within earshot might catch him in the act. From what I saw of the rope ends, he didn't leave a great deal uncut. He may have expected the bridge to fall by itself in a couple of hours, from the weight of the snow that was continuing to fall. If that had happened, Orris would still be with us."

That last observation tore at the heart of Earlene Cobbett. The poor thing cried out and clutched her hand to her bosom, a task to which one hand was barely equal. The other hand, though, held a tray containing two glasses of sherry, and it wasn't equal to the task, either; the tray tilted, the glasses tipped, and the sherry wound up spilling onto Gordon Wolpert.

"A little while ago," I said, "Orris fired up the snowblower. It didn't start right away, but once he got it running he managed to clear a path ten or twelve feet long. I heard him trying to get it started, though I didn't pay much attention. I heard it a lot more clearly when it cut out."

"It made an awful sound," Miss Dinmont recalled. "As though everything inside was being ground up."

I turned to ask Nigel if that had ever happened before. He said it seemed to him that the snowblower, while occasionally difficult to start in cold weather (and of no use whatsoever in warm weather), had in all other respects performed perfectly the entire winter.

"Here's what I think," I said. "My guess is it was deliberately sabotaged. I don't know if anyone else noticed, but when we all rushed out of the house there was a faint smell in the air."

"Gasoline," Millicent Savage said. "From when Orris was running the snowblower."

"I noticed it while we were working on the snowman," her father confirmed. "What about it?"

"There was more to the smell than gasoline."

He thought about it. "You're right," he said. "There was another element to the odor, but I can't tell you what it was." And his nose wrinkled, as if to pursue the scent through the corridors of memory. "Millicent," he asked his daughter, "what was the smell like?"

"When I had the toy stove," she said. "With the light bulb for heat? And you could bake your own cookies?"

"Not very good cookies," he remembered.

"Not like Mummy's," she said, winning a smile from Leona. "But they weren't as bad as when I tried to make candy. *That's* what it smelled like."

"Made a mess, too," Greg Savage said. "Jesus!" He looked at me. "Burnt sugar," he said.

"That's what I smelled," I said.

"Sugar in the gas tank?"

I nodded.

"An old standby," Colonel Blount-Buller said. "Readily available to any local wog bent on mischief or any malcontent in the ranks. Engine starts up, runs for a bit, then ruins itself entirely. If it's been sugared, Eglantine, you'll never get that snowblower working again, not without replacing the engine."

Nigel just stared. Cissy, who had just come back with a cloth to sponge off Gordon Wolpert, wanted to know why anyone would want to ruin their snowblower. "It does make a racket," she said, "but it's ever so useful when it snows."

"Someone wanted to prevent Orris from clearing the path to the bridge," I said. "Perhaps they thought that would keep us from setting foot on the bridge, or at least delay our doing so until the bridge had fallen of its own weight."

"But why?"

"To keep us here," I said.

"And why keep us here?" It was Dakin Littlefield, holding out his glass to be refilled. "I suppose we can take it for granted that the person who sugared the snowblower and cut the ropes on the bridge was the same nut who killed the poor sap in the library."

Heads nodded in assent.

"What's the stiff's name, Rathburn? He kills Rathburn, he bundles up warm, he goes out and saws the ropes halfway through and sugars the gas tank. Then he slips back inside and goes to bed. Why, for Christ's sake?"

"Maybe he did what he did to the bridge and the snowblower before he killed Mr. Rathburn," Carolyn suggested.

"That seems even wackier," Littlefield said, "but even if he did, same question: Why? I know, I know, to keep us here, but *why* keep us here? Unless he didn't come back to the house but got the hell out, and the business with the snowblower and the bridge was to keep us from following him."

"The bridge supports were cut through on this side," the colonel reminded him. "He'd have been burning his bridge before he crossed it, so to speak."

"Then I don't get it. I don't know anything about Rathburn, so I won't even try to guess why somebody would want to kill him. But I suppose there's always a reason. Once Rathburn's dead, though, wouldn't the killer just want to get away from here and back to his life as quickly as possible? Instead he's stuck here with the rest of us. Or did I miss something?"

"No," I said. "Whoever he is, he's still here."

"Well, where's the sense in that? By keeping us stuck here, he keeps himself stuck here, too. Why?"

"Maybe he wanted to keep the police away," Leona Savage said.

"The police," Nigel said. "I ought to call them."

"But the phone—"

"They may have restored service by now," he said, and went off to find out.

While he was gone, we batted around theories and arguments. Keeping the police away didn't make sense, someone said, because they'd still get here before anybody here could get away. So what was gained? I let them talk it through, sustaining myself with small sips of malt whisky. It wasn't Glen Drumnadrochit, but it wasn't bad.

I didn't want to take too much of it, though. Even if Nigel got through to them, it would be a while before the police could reach us. A plow would have to precede them down the long driveway from the road to the bridge, and then they'd pretty much have to throw up a new bridge. The distance wasn't that great, so maybe they could heave a rope across the gap. Once we'd secured it, they could make their way hand-over-hand.

Of course they'd have to be young cops, in good condition, and either brave or stupid enough to try it. I thought of the cops I knew back in New York and tried to picture any of them dangling above a rock-strewn gorge. I had gotten so far as to put Ray Kirschmann in that unlikely picture, and the resulting image had me working hard to keep from giggling. It wouldn't have been terribly appropriate, not with Rathburn and Orris dead and the rest of us marooned here, but it was hard to keep a straight face.

I had help when Nigel came back. His own expression was not merely grave but troubled.

"Still no phone service," he said.

"You were gone a long time," Gordon Wolpert said

"Yes."

"Longer than you might think it would take to lift a telephone receiver and listen for a dial tone. Of course it would be natural to jiggle the receiver and poke the disconnect button a couple of times, but even so it seems to me you were gone quite a while."

"Quite a while," Nigel agreed.

"I realize there's no television here," Greg Savage said, "but someone must have a radio. Maybe one of the local stations will have something to say about when telephone service is likely to be restored."

"The cook has a radio," Cissy Eglantine said. "But it only gets one station, and it doesn't come in very clearly. We mostly play tapes on it."

"Still, if you could bring in that station—"

"There won't be anything about the resumption of phone service," I said. "Or if there is it won't apply to us."

"Why do you say that, Rhodenbarr?"

I glanced over at Nigel. "Better tell them," I said.

"I don't know what made me check," he said. " 'You're being silly,' I told myself, but I couldn't dismiss the thought, so I pulled on my boots and put a jacket on and went outside. That's what took me so long. It was slow going, you see, because it's all the way round the back of the house, and you've already seen how deep the snow is."

Rufus Quilp wanted to know what it was that was all the way in back of the house.

"That's where the telephone lines come in," I guessed.

"Quite right," Nigel said. He sighed heavily and his shoulders sagged. "Someone's gone and cut them," he said.

SIXTEEN

There were no screams or gasps in response to Nigel's revelation. The general reaction was not so much one of panic and alarm as it was a sinking feeling, a bottomless dread. A couple of the guests voiced the thought that they just did not understand what was happening to us or why, but that sounded like denial to me. We all knew what was going on.

Carolyn spelled it out. "It's all straight out of Agatha Christie, sort of a combination of *The Mousetrap* and *And Then There Were None*. We're isolated, all of us. We can't get out of here and nobody can turn up to rescue us. And it's that way because that's how the killer wants it."

"He couldn't have arranged the snow," Gordon Wolpert pointed out.

"No," she said, "but he could have picked a weekend when a heavy snowfall was forecast. Or maybe he decided to take advantage of the snow once it fell. Outside of the snow, it was all his doing. He clubbed Rathburn and smothered him, he cut the phone wires, he fixed the snowblower so it would be ruined and the bridge so it would fall if anybody set foot on it. It's pretty obvious why he wants us stranded here. He's not through."

There was a sort of general intake of breath at this announcement. I don't think it was a new thought for most of the people there, but no one had put words to the tune until now.

Colonel Blount-Buller looked at the drink in his hand as if wondering what it was, then set it aside and cleared his throat. "There will be more killings," he said. "That's what you're getting at, isn't it, Mrs. Rhodenbarr?"

"Well, why else would he seal us off like this?"

"You're assuming he's still here, and he wasn't merely seeking to discourage pursuit."

"Pursuit?" She spread her hands. "What pursuit? Who's gonna pursue him? If this guy wants to get away from here, that's fine with me. I'll pay for his cab."

The colonel nodded slowly. "And there's really no way he could have left, is there? The snow and all, and the bridge. He's elected to remain at Cuttleford House."

"I don't see where else he could have gone to," Carolyn said, and drew a breath. "Matter of fact, he's probably right here in this room."

It was comfortable enough in the house, even without central heating, and there was a fire in the bar's fireplace that had that room warm as toast. But right about then you got a sense of what absolute zero must be like, with the cessation of all molecular activity, because that's the kind of silence that greeted Carolyn's observation.

Nigel Eglantine broke it. "I say," he said. "That's a bit rich, isn't it? 'In this room.' Why, there's no one in this room but . . ."

"But us chickens," someone said softly.

"But ourselves," Nigel managed. "There's only guests and . . . and staff . . ."

"A tramp," Cissy Eglantine said. "Are we all that certain it might not be a tramp?"

"I'm afraid not," the colonel said.

"Oh, I do so wish it could be a tramp," she said. "It would be so much nicer for everyone."

"It's not a tramp," her husband said heavily.

"But you said it couldn't possibly be one of us, Nigel, and—"

"It can't be," he said, "but it must be. That's what's so awful. This is such a blessed spot, Cuttleford House, a haven from the cares of the world, and only truly nice people are drawn here. And nice people do not murder." He set his jaw. "Or sugar snowblower engines, or sabotage suspension bridges, or cut telephone wires. Yet all these actions have been performed, haven't they? Apparently by one of us."

"That's so dreadful, Nigel."

"It is," he agreed. "It's quite insupportable, and that's why it would be wonderful to blame it on a tramp, or the Bosnian Serbs, or the IRA."

"I never thought of them. . . ."

"Well, you needn't think of them now, dear. I'm afraid Mrs. Rhodenbarr is correct. The killer is one of us."

There was another silence, until Carolyn said, "Oh, the hell with it. It's Ms. Kaiser."

"But that's remarkable," Leona Savage said. "You mean you actually know who the murderer is? But which one of us is Ms. Kaiser?"

"*I'm* Ms. Kaiser," Carolyn said.

"You mean . . ."

"No, for God's sake! I wasn't saying Ms. Kaiser was the murderer."

"But you distinctly said, 'It's Ms. Kaiser.' I'm positive that's what you said."

"Oh, Mummy," Millicent said, exasperated. "Carolyn said 'It's Ms. Kaiser' because she's sick and tired of being called Mrs. Rhodenbarr. She's not married to Bernie."

"Well, I know that," Leona said. "Neither of them wears a ring. I was being polite, in view of the fact that they're here together and sharing a room."

"I wouldn't ordinarily mind what anybody called me," Carolyn said, "but we're all getting more involved than I thought we'd be, since one of us seems to be busy trying to kill the rest of us."

"Quite right," the colonel said. "When it's 'Nice day today' and 'Please pass the salt,' one doesn't much care what one's called. But it's a different matter when we're thrown together to fight for our lives."

Dakin Littlefield suggested that was a rather dramatic way of putting it. "If there's a killer among us," he said, "and that's a pretty big *if*, all we have to do is wait him out. Yes, the phone lines are down and the bridge is out, but sooner or later someone's going to fail to reach us and inform the authorities, and the next thing you know there'll be a helicopter full of state troopers landing on the front lawn. How long can that take, a day or two? Three days at the most?"

No one had any idea.

"Say three days," Littlefield went on. "I understand there's plenty of food and water, and the bar's not about to run out of Scotch. We came here to get away from it all and I'd have to say we've succeeded beyond our wildest dreams."

"But what do we do now?"

"Whatever we please," he said. "Play Scrabble, read a good book, sit by the fire." He glanced at his bride, and I suppose he had the right to look at her that way, running his eyes insolently over her body. After all, he was married to her and they were on their honeymoon. All the same, I can't say I liked it. "I'm sure we can all find something to keep us amused," he said, and his tone made it clear what form of amusement he was thinking of for himself.

"That's great," Carolyn said. "The two of you can run off and make a Dakin-and-Lettice sandwich. Meanwhile the killer sees who he can knock off next."

That brought everybody up short. Miss Hardesty wondered how long we could expect the killing to go on. Miss Dinmont admitted she was frightened, and asked if anyone could furnish her with a pistol for her own protection, as she could neither fight off nor flee from an attacker. Mr. Quilp, who had appeared to have dozed off, straightened up in his seat and demanded to know what we were to do.

Someone suggested that we had to defend ourselves. That got the colonel's attention. "Have to do more than that," he said. "Best defense is a good offense, wot? Can't just wait for the cavalry to arrive. Have to meet them halfway, don't wo? Find the damned murderer ourselves."

"How?"

"Smoke him out," he said. "Trap him, chase him into a corner, harry him until he drops. Attack him on the right, attack him on the left, attack him in the center. Cut off his escape route, sever his supply lines. Then crush him."

It was quite a performance. You could almost hear a tinny little orchestra in the background, belting out the theme from *The Bridge on the River Kwai*. In the respectful silence that followed I said, "I think we have to mount both a defense and an offense. The first thing we have to do is make sure that no more killings take place. While we're seeing to that, we can also put our heads together and pool our information. It's possible that we already know enough about one another to be able to determine the killer's identity."

"Good thinking," the colonel said. "Daresay you've put on a uniform yourself, eh, Rhodenbarr?"

That made me stop and think. I knew what he meant, and the answer was no, I'd never been in the military. But had I ever worn a uniform? I went to prison once, I blush to admit, and they did dress us all alike, and not very stylishly, either. But would you call those prison grays a uniform?

Then I remembered my Boy Scout uniform.

"It's been a few years," I said.

"There's a way of thinking that once learned is never forgotten, Rhodenbarr. Defense and offense, that's the ticket. You have a plan in mind? An approach?"

"In a manner of speaking."

"Good man. Let's hear it."

"First of all," I said, "we have to make sure there are no more murders, and we'll do that by sticking together."

"You mean like this, Bern? All of us hanging out together in one room?"

"Not exactly," I said. "That won't always be convenient. But what each of us can do is make sure we're never completely alone. If I always have somebody with me, then the killer can't cut me out of the herd and do away with me."

"Suppose the person you pick for company turns out to be the killer?"

It was Gordon Wolpert who offered this objection, and it was a good one. Others elaborated on the theme. If one of us was the killer, and if everybody was paired off with another person, that meant somebody would be buddied up with the killer.

"No problem," Dakin Littlefield drawled. "Everybody pick a buddy and stick with that person. Then, next time somebody turns up dead, we'll know it's the person's buddy who did all the killing."

"That's appalling," Mrs. Colibri said. "But it's not a great deal more appalling than the notion of being tethered night and day to another person. It's all well and good for those of you who are married"—she glanced significantly at me and Carolyn—"or intimately allied, if unmarried. But what about those of us who are here alone?"

Someone said something about Greta Garbo.

"I don't mean that I want to be alone," Mrs. Colibri said icily. "But I'd as soon not share my bed with anyone, thank you very much, and I'm afraid I'm old-fashioned enough to prefer privacy in the bath. Add in the virtual certainty that one of us would be paired with the murderer, and you begin to see the dimensions of the problem."

"Threesomes," I said.

"I beg your pardon!"

"Not at night," I said hastily. "During waking hours. If we divide into groups of three, that means two people will be buddied up with the murderer."

"Safety in numbers," the colonel murmured.

"Just that," I said. "If A and B are buddies, and A's the killer, he can wait for a quiet moment and knock off B. But if C's part of the party, then he can't."

"What about bedtime?" Miss Hardesty wondered.

"That's more complicated," I admitted. "Millicent, I'm afraid you're going to have to go back to sleeping in your parents' room. Sleeping arrangements for the rest of us will need a little more thought. I think, though, that Mrs. Colibri's concerns about bathroom privacy are satisfied by this approach."

"If I don't want one person in the bath with me," Mrs. Colibri said, "what on earth makes you think I'd be happier with two?"

"Because they'd be waiting outside," I said, "keeping an eye on the door, and on each other. I'm sure there will be lots of details that need work, but I'm equally certain we can work them all out. We're well motivated, and that's a help."

"That's good sense," the colonel said. "Carry on, Rhodenbarr."

"Well," I said, and put my glass down, wanting a clear head. "I guess the first thing to do is make sure we're all here. I can't think of anyone who's missing, but I don't have a list of all of us." I patted my pockets. "Or anything to make a list with, either."

"One moment," Nigel said. He ducked out of the room and came back minutes later with a clipboard holding a yellow legal pad. The top sheet was blank, but a skilled investigator could have rubbed the side of a pencil point very gently over its surface to raise an impression of what had been written on the sheet above. Why anyone would want to do so, however, was quite beyond me.

"Thanks," I said, and clicked the cap of my ballpoint pen a couple of times, and tested it with a quick squiggle in the margin. "This will do perfectly. But I should have stopped you." He looked at me. "You went off by yourself," I explained. "And that's something none of us ought to do. Until we've got ourselves organized, can we agree that no one will leave the immediate area without a companion?"

"Two companions," Lettice said. "Threesomes, remember?"

Threesomes indeed. Somehow the word had a special flavor coming from Mrs. Littlefield's lips, and it threw me offstride for a moment. "Two companions," I agreed. "Although one companion might be enough on a brief errand of the sort Nigel just ran. Just so no one goes off on his own." Or her own? Or their own? The hell with it.

"Now," I said, clicking my pen again. "Let's start with the staff. Nigel Eglantine. Cissy Eglantine. Present and accounted for." I wrote down both their names.

"And the two serving wenches," Dakin Littlefield said.

"The upstairs maid," I corrected, "Earlene Cobbett, and the downstairs maid, Molly Cobbett. Both here, I see."

"Yes, sir."

"Good," I said, and jotted down their names. "And Orris, of course, who is accounted for but not present. How do you spell his name?"

Cissy Eglantine spelled it. "Like the root," she said.

"And his last name?"

"Cobbett," Cissy said, and Earlene Cobbett let out a desperate sob. She seemed utterly undone by Orris's death, and I'd wondered what they'd been to each other. The news that they shared a surname failed to clear up the nature of their relationship. Were they brother and sister? Husband and wife? All of the above?

My confusion must have shown, for Nigel Eglantine moved to clear it up. "There are a lot of Cobbetts in the region," he said. "Molly and Earlene are cousins, and they're both Cobbetts. And Orris was a cousin of both of them. Have I got that right, Molly?"

"Orris was cousin to Earlene, sir," she said. "And cousin and uncle both to me, cousin on my father's side and uncle on my mother's."

"My God," Dakin Littlefield said. "They must all have webbed feet."

"Or royal blood," Nigel said. "The Cobbetts show about the same degree of inbreeding as the crowned heads of Europe."

Orris, I'd written down, and now I wrote *Cobbett* after it. I looked at the name for a moment and then put a checkmark alongside it. I didn't much like the way that looked, but decided that crossing it out would be even worse.

"Is that all?" I asked Nigel. "I know there are sometimes people behind the scenes whom one never sees, but who keep things running smoothly. Is there anyone else on staff I've left out?"

"I'm afraid that's the lot," he said. "We all work hard, you see, and put in long hours, so it doesn't require very many of us."

"Of course there's Cook," Cissy put in.

"Oh, yes," Nigel said. "Quite right. Mustn't forget Cook."

I scanned the room. She'd been among us earlier, a comfortingly stout woman of a certain age who'd taken a glass of sherry and refilled it twice that I'd noticed.

"I don't see her," I said.

"I expect she's gone to the kitchen."

"But everyone's supposed to stay right here."

"I expect she slipped out before we decided that," Nigel

said, "or else she didn't consider that rule as applying to herself."

"Cooks are a law unto themselves," the colonel agreed.

"She'd be preparing lunch now," Cissy said. "I know it must seem as though we just got up from breakfast, but it's been longer than that, actually, and she has lunch to prepare. I'd hate to call her away from the kitchen."

Miss Dinmont wanted to know if she was alone in the kitchen. Because, she pointed out, we'd just agreed that no one was to be alone.

"It's a bit different for Cook," Nigel said. "She doesn't much care for company in the kitchen."

"And I'm sure she'll be safe in there," Cissy said. "Since we're all out here, aren't we?"

That brought another brief silence, reminding us that the "we" in that sentence presumably included the murderer. You'd think we'd have gotten used to the idea, but it kept taking us by surprise and bringing us up short.

"I'll just put her on the list then," I said. "I don't believe I caught her name."

Nigel and Cissy exchanged glances. "We just call her 'Cook,' " Cissy said.

"She must have a name."

"Of course," she said, "but I can't think what it is. Molly? Earlene?"

"Just 'Cook,' mum."

" 'Cook' is all, mum."

"She has a name," Nigel said. "I could look it up, but . . ."

"Not now," I said, and wrote *Cook* on my list, then looked up. "I don't suppose her name would be Cobbett," I said. "Or would it?"

Nigel shook his head, and Molly assured me that Cook was no Cobbett, nor any kind of kin to Cobbetts.

"Just a wild guess," I said. "And that's all for the owners and staff of Cuttleford House? Now for the guests."

Bernard Rhodenbarr.
Carolyn Kaiser.
Gregory Savage.
Leona Savage.
Millicent Savage.
Anne Hardesty.
Gloria Dinmont.

"I wonder," Miss Dinmont said. "I don't suppose I should say this, but . . ." She paused significantly and looked around. When no one urged her to go ahead and say it, she shot a peeved glance at her companion.

"Perhaps you should," Miss Hardesty said obligingly.

"Well, I was just wondering. Of course the cook will be quite safe in the kitchen, if all the rest of us are out here, the murderer included. But what if the murderer is not included?"

"How could that be?" Colonel Blount-Buller demanded. "If we're here, and if the killer is one of us—"

"Unless it's the cook," Miss Dinmont said, and lowered her eyes. "I'm sure I'm just a foolish woman."

Dakin Littlefield rolled his eyes at that, while Leona Savage closed hers. The colonel said he somehow doubted that Cook was the sort to club and smother a man, then dash about cutting phone lines and bridge supports and destroying snowblowers.

"Of course she'd have no trouble getting sugar," Greg Savage said. "There must be an abundant supply in the larder. She could have helped herself to a cup of it, and a funnel to channel it into the snowblower's gas tank."

"Anyone who walked into the kitchen could get all the sugar he wanted," Nigel said, "and there are sugar bowls on all the tables in the breakfast and dining rooms as well. As for a funnel, well, how hard is it to pour sugar into a gas tank?" No one admitted to personal knowledge of the degree of difficulty of such an act. "In any event," he said, "I'm sure she wouldn't do any such thing."

"How can you say that?" Miss Dinmont wondered. "You don't even know her name."

"And do you really want to check her off the list of possible murderers?" Gordon Wolpert asked. "Because if we start eliminating people like a trial lawyer issuing peremptory challenges, we'll very quickly eliminate everyone. What you're saying, Eglantine, is that the cook's not the sort to commit murder. Well, neither is anyone else in this house, I'm sure. We're all decent, upstanding people. That's quite obvious. And I'm afraid it's every bit as obvious that one of us decent, upstanding people has so far been responsible for two deaths. So I'm going to suggest that no one be eliminated from our working list of persons under suspicion except for cause. There'll be no peremptory challenges."

This soaked in, and we all looked at each other again. It seemed to me that I was being eyed with suspicion by some of our party, even as I was eyeing them with suspicion in turn.

"Let's move on," I suggested, and brandished my pen and clipboard.

Gordon Wolpert.
Bettina Colibri.

Dakin Littlefield.
Lettice Littlefield.
Col. Edward Blount-Buller.

"I was just thinking," the colonel put in, "about the cook and her absence. It seemed at first a dangerous violation of a safety procedure almost as soon as we'd initiated it, but in fact it's really entirely safe."

"How's that?" Wolpert asked him.

The colonel cleared his throat. "If the cook is entirely innocent of the crimes which have taken place here, as seems likely, then the killer is one of us. And in that case the cook is in no peril in the kitchen, because all of us are here."

"Didn't I say that?" Cissy wondered aloud.

"But," he went on, "if by some chance the cook *is* the murderer, then we're all quite safe. Because we're here and she's elsewhere."

"In the kitchen," Mrs. Colibri said.

"Quite so."

"Preparing our lunch."

The room went very still. Miss Gloria Dinmont broke the silence. "She could poison us all," she said softly. "We'd drop like flies, never knowing what hit us."

"Or writhe in agony," her companion chimed in, "knowing we'd been poisoned, but unable to get hold of the antidote."

"A tasteless and odorless poison," Miss Dinmont said.

"A poison that leaves no trace," said Miss Hardesty.

"Oh, come on," Carolyn said. "What difference does it makes if the poison leaves a trace or not? If we're all discovered lying dead all over the house, what do you figure the cops are going to think? That somebody said something so shocking we all popped off with heart attacks?"

"Besides," young Millicent said, "I don't think there's any such thing as a poison that doesn't leave a trace."

"It seems to me most toxic substances leave some sort of evidence that would show up in an autopsy," I said, "but you generally have to look for it."

"How do you know that, Bern?"

I knew it from *Quincy* reruns on Nick at Nite, but I didn't want to say that. "We're out in the country," I said, "and a rural cop who walked in on a roomful of dead people with no marks on them would probably write it off as carbon monoxide poisoning from a defective furnace."

"But there's no central heating."

"That might not occur to him. Still, we've got what, fifteen or sixteen people in the room? Safety in numbers."

"What do you mean, Bern?"

"I mean that many people dying all at once under mysterious circumstances would trigger a full-scale investigation. The state troopers would run it, and there'd be a complete toxicological workup. If we'd been poisoned it would show up."

"Well, that's a load off my mind," Dakin Littlefield said. "I can't tell you how relieved I am to hear that."

"All I'm trying to say—"

But he didn't want to hear it. "For God's sake," he said, "if the cook was bent on lacing our porridge with rat poison she wouldn't start off by killing people with a camel and a pillow and a cup of sugar. If Gloria over there in the wheelchair is seriously worried about poison, I'll volunteer to eat her lunch for her. Assuming we ever got lunch."

"Ha!" Rufus Quilp thrust his head forward, his little eyes beady and bright. "Lunch," he said. "Breakfast was ages ago and no one's serving us lunch. What about that, Eglantine?"

"I'm sure lunch won't be long now," Nigel said.

"If we're not going to get it right away," Quilp said, "I don't see why we can't at least have our elevensies."

"Elevensies?"

"Normally served at eleven," Quilp said dryly, "as you might guess from the name. Too late for that now, of course, so you could call it something else, or call it nothing at all, just so one has the opportunity to eat it. A cup of coffee, say, and a scone or some crumpets. Anything that will do to tide one over between breakfast and lunch."

"Nigel," Cissy said, "perhaps someone could fetch Mr. Quilp a cup of coffee."

"And a scone," Quilp said.

"And a scone."

"Or perhaps a croissant," the fat man suggested, "if there are any left, and perhaps with some of those gingered rhubarb preserves."

"Yes, those are lovely, aren't they? I'm sure we've some left, Mr. Quilp. Nigel, why don't I just fetch something for Mr. Quilp?"

"Not by yourself," her husband said.

"Oh. But if I simply went to the kitchen . . . oh, but . . ." She frowned, troubled. "Oh," she said.

"I don't want to cause a fuss," Rufus Quilp said. "And if lunch should turn out to be imminent, well, I wouldn't want to spoil my appetite."

"Fat chance," Carolyn muttered.

"But if lunch is destined to be rather a distant affair," he went on, "then I do think I could do with a bit of tiding over. There's my blood sugar to be considered, don't you see."

I found myself considering Mr. Quilp's blood sugar, and wondered idly if it could render a snowblower *hors de com-*

bat. While I pondered the point, the colonel took command, dispatching a patrol on a reconnaissance mission. Cissy Eglantine, flanked by the Cobbett cousins, were to go to the kitchen and inquire of the cook just how long it would be until lunch. If our estimated waiting time was thirty minutes or less, they would return empty-handed; if longer, they'd bring back something designed to tide us over.

They were no sooner out of the room than Raffles turned up, threading his way through the room, getting petted and cooed at and fussed over as he went, and rubbing up against the odd ankle along the way. "Oh, it's Raffles," Lettice said, reaching to scratch him behind the ear. Her husband asked her how she happened to know the cat's name, and she said she must have heard someone call him that.

When, he wondered. Last night or this morning, she said, and why did he want to know? Because this was the first he'd seen of the cat, he replied, and he wondered when she'd had time to see it, and make its acquaintance.

"Why, Dakin," she said, arching her eyebrows. "Don't tell me you're jealous of him. He's a pussycat!"

"How do you know it's a male?"

"Because he miaows in bass," she said. "Darling, how do I know? I suppose whoever called him by name also referred to him with a male pronoun."

"And he's the resident cat here, is he? What happened to his tail?"

"He's a Manx," Millicent Savage said helpfully. "And he doesn't live here. He came here with Carolyn and Bernie."

"Well, I don't suppose he's the killer," Littlefield said. "He might have clubbed the poor jerk in the library and clawed the bridge supports, but I can't imagine him doing a number on the snowblower."

"He's been declawed," Millicent said.

"I give up," Littlefield said. "He's innocent." He started to say something else but stopped, probably for the same reason that everyone else in the room had stopped talking. Cissy Eglantine, back from the kitchen, stood framed in the doorway. The Cobbett cousins stood just to the rear of her, as if they were trying to shrink into her shadow.

She looked across the room at her husband. For a moment she didn't say anything, and then she said, "Nigel, I spoke with Cook."

"And what did she say, dear?"

"I'm afraid she didn't say anything."

"It's hard to get much out of her, I'll grant you that. Did you ask her directly when lunch will be ready?"

"No."

"You didn't? Whyever not?"

"I couldn't," she said, and her lip trembled. "Nigel, mind you, I'm not absolutely certain, but—"

"But what?"

"Oh, Nigel," she said, and sighed. "Nigel, I believe she's dead."

SEVENTEEN

"She was a good cook," Cissy Eglantine said.

There's a short story of Saki's that begins like that. *She was a good cook, as cooks go, and as cooks go, she went.* The stout woman who presided over the Cuttleford kitchen had indeed been a good cook, even an excellent cook, and she, like her fictional counterpart, had gone. She had taken her leave of this world, although she had done so without leaving the kitchen.

She was as Cissy and the Cobbett girls had found her, seated in the oversize oak armchair to the left of the old six-burner gas stove. A low flame kept a cauldron of thick soup simmering on a back burner. In the large old-fashioned sink, water dripped from a leaking faucet onto a coffee mug, a couple of spoons, and a shish kebab skewer. A radio, its volume turned way down, brought in a mixture of country music and static.

"That's where she always sits," Cissy said, "and that's *how* she always sits. I thought she'd just nodded off, you know, with the cookbook open on her lap. But then she didn't answer when I spoke to her, and I made myself touch her, you see, and, and give her a little shake, and—"

"Steady, Cecilia."

"I'm actually quite all right, Nigel." Her eyes sought mine. "Is she dead, Mr. Rhodenbarr? I don't suppose she could be sleeping soundly, could she?"

Her hands, large for a woman, reposed in her lap, the fingers of one still curled around the handle of a wooden cooking spoon. I pressed my fingertips to the back of her hand, her upper arm, her broad forehead.

"I'm afraid she's dead," I said.

But she was a good deal subtler about it than either of her two predecessors in death had been. One look at either of them and you knew what you were dealing with. Cook, on the other hand, looked as though she might be sleeping, and her body temperature, while discernibly lower than the traditional 98.6°, had not yet dropped down to the level of luncheon meat. I supposed she'd get there soon enough, even in a warm kitchen, but she had a ways to go yet.

"How did she—"

"I don't know," I said. "I don't see any signs of violence. She wasn't shot or stabbed or dropped from a height." I raised an eyelid and stared. I didn't see any sign of pinpoint hemorrhage, or anything else but a rather glassy eyeball. I closed the lid and straightened up.

Everyone was talking at once, filling the air with questions and suggestions. We'd all rushed there in a body at Cissy's announcement, although I couldn't swear that no one had slipped off along the way.

"Maybe it was natural causes," I heard someone say.

"Around here," someone else countered, "murder is a natural cause."

"Shock. Don't people die of shock?"

"If they're struck by lightning. Or touch an electrical wire."

"I mean the kind of shock that gives you a heart attack. She might have had a weak heart, and I don't suppose she was on a low-fat diet. The shock of the two deaths earlier—"

"Cook didn't even say anything," Cissy remembered, "or look much disturbed. After the first death she made breakfast, and after the second she came in here and started lunch."

"And a good lunch, too, from the smell of it." Rufus Quilp had pushed his way through to the stove, and was lifting pot lids and sniffing. "Lamb stew," he announced. "Seasoned with rosemary and thyme, and can that be fresh dill? Wherever would she get fresh dill?"

"Not this time of year," someone said.

"And here's a lovely pot of rice," he said, "all nice and fluffy, and there's a big wooden bowl of salad on the counter, just waiting to be tossed." He replaced the lid on the stew pot. "I think we should eat," he said. "I think we'll all be much better able to cope once we've eaten."

There was a general murmur of assent, which died down when Carolyn stuck her face up next to the cook's, then stepped back shaking her head. "Didn't work," she said. "I was trying to smell her breath, but she's not breathing."

"Why would you want to smell her breath?"

"I thought there might be the odor of bitter almonds, Bern."

"If she'd ingested cyanide," I said. "But doesn't she look awfully peaceful for a victim of cyanide poisoning?"

"I don't know, Bern. Does it make you writhe in agony? If she was poisoned, it must have been with something nonviolent."

Leona Savage remarked on the irony of it. Minutes ago we'd discussed the possibility of our being poisoned by the cook, and now it looked as though the cook herself might have been poisoned.

"And she's holding a spoon," her husband observed. "A cooking spoon. I think I see what happened." He gestured, miming the action. "She was at the stove, stirring the stew. She took a taste of it. When the poison hit her—"

"The poison?"

"In the stew. At first maybe all she thought was it needed more salt, but then it hit her and her legs got weak and she had to sit down."

"Is that what happens when you take poison? Your legs get weak?"

"It must depend on the poison," he said. "At any rate, she didn't feel too hot and she sat down. Evidently it was a gentle poison, and it just made her nod off and then killed her in her sleep."

"Cook didn't like people in her kitchen," Molly Cobbett said. "If anybody tried to put anything in her stewpot, Cook would pitch a fit."

Nigel confirmed this. "If you wanted to get taken to task, all you had to do was lift the lid of one of her pots. I can't think she'd have stood still for it if someone salted her stew for her."

"She wouldn't have known," I said. "Because she wouldn't have been here when it happened."

"But she was always in the kitchen."

"She was in the bar with the rest of us a little while ago,

remember? She slipped off to the kitchen while we were arguing about one thing or another. Did anyone notice when she left?" No one had. "Well, she was in the back, she could have slipped out unobtrusively enough."

"And someone slipped off after her? And poisoned her, and then slipped back again?"

I shook my head. "It would have happened earlier," I said. "She didn't toss this stew together in a few minutes. She must have started preparing it while we were eating our breakfast. It's been cooking all morning. When Orris had his accident and Earlene screamed almost loud enough to wake him, Cook would have left the kitchen to find out what was the matter."

"She was outside," the colonel recalled. "I remember noticing her when we were weighing the merits of attempting to retrieve poor Orris's body."

I thought that would bring a fresh sob from Earlene, but perhaps she'd begun to get over her loss. "And after that," I said, "she wound up in the bar. So she was out of the kitchen for a while, and in her absence someone could have gone in and put anything at all into that pot of stew."

Carolyn said, "Like what, Bern? Mrs. Murphy's overalls?" Everyone stared at her and she said, "Like the song, 'Who threw the overalls in Mrs. Murphy's chowder?' Oh, come on. I can't be the only person who remembers that one."

"Sure you can," I said. "And as far as what the killer put in the stew, I couldn't begin to guess. I don't know much about poisons."

"Mushrooms," Miss Dinmont said. "Are there mushrooms in the stew?"

"I would certainly hope so," Rufus Quilp said. "Who in

his right mind would make a lamb stew without mushrooms?"

"Poisonous mushrooms," Miss Dinmont cried. "Deadly nightshade!"

"That's not a mushroom," Gordon Wolpert said.

"It's not?"

"No. But there are a lot of poisonous mushrooms, or toadstools, or whatever you want to call them. The amanitas are particularly deadly. One's called the death angel —that may be what you were thinking of. But you couldn't go out and gather mushrooms in this weather. It's not the season for them, and even if it were you'd never find them under the snow."

"If deadly nightshade isn't a mushroom," said Miss Dinmont, "then what in heaven's name is it?"

"A vine," Wolpert told her. "A close relative of the tomato and the potato. Not to mention the eggplant."

"Why not mention the eggplant?"

"There's tomato in here," Rufus Quilp announced. "And potato, of course. And mushrooms and barley." If there was an airborne poison as well, I figured his days were numbered, the way he was inhaling. "I don't believe there's any eggplant. It's not usual in lamb stew, though it wouldn't matter if there were some. I'm sure there's nothing in here to be concerned about. Why would anyone poison a splendid pot of lamb stew?"

"Why would anyone kill the cook?" Carolyn asked him in return. "Or wreck the bridge and the snowblower? Or kill Mr. Rathburn?"

"I'm sure I have no idea, young lady. What I do have is a gnawing in my belly, and what I intend to have is a bowl of this stew."

"But if it's poisoned . . ."

"If it's perfectly wholesome," he said, "then we ought to be eating it. If it's toxic we ought to keep it at arm's length. But how are we to tell which it is?" No one had the answer, so he supplied it himself. "What's required is a food taster. One man has a bowl of stew. If he lives, everyone may freely join in the feast. If he dies, well, at least the others are spared." He squared his shoulders. "I shall be that man," he said.

"But Mr. Quilp—"

"Please," he said. "I insist."

"But if you should die . . ."

"Then I suppose you'll leave me lying where I fall, as seems to be the custom of the house. If you actually go so far as to put me in the ground, an appropriate phrase for the tombstone might be 'He ate that others might live.' Hand me down one of those bowls, will you? And the ladle, if you don't mind."

In the dining room, Quilp took a seat at a table set for two. He tucked in his napkin and lifted a fork. " 'It is a far, far better thing that I do,' " he said, " 'than I have ever done,' and I fear that's all I remember of that passage. I'd say grace, but if the stew turns out to be laced with arsenic, that might be a thumb in the eye for the Man Upstairs. So without further ado . . ."

He speared a morsel with his fork, put it in his mouth, chewed thoughtfully. He took another bite, smacked his lips.

"There," he said with satisfaction. "As you can see—"

He broke off the sentence and a look of alarm spread on his florid face. The hand not clutching his fork moved to the middle of his chest, just over his heart. His lower lip trembled and he slumped in his chair.

Why hadn't I stopped him? How could I let the man kill

himself like this? Oh, in a sense he'd been doing so for years, digging his grave with his knife and fork, but . . .

"Ha!" He straightened up in his seat, gave a little yelp of laughter, and looked positively delighted by the expressions on our faces. "Oh my," he said. "Oh my, oh my. Terrible of me, I know, but I couldn't resist. You will forgive me my little joke, won't you?" He plunged the fork into the bowl of stew. "It's wonderfully flavorful, I assure you," he said, "and it couldn't possibly harm anyone. May I urge you all to fill bowls for yourselves and join me?"

"We can't be sure it's safe," Miss Hardesty said. "There are slow-acting poisons, aren't there?"

"If Cook was poisoned," said Quilp, "the poison seems to have worked at the speed of light. But I'm sure you're right. The stew contains a slow-acting poison, and I'm doomed. In fifty years' time I'll be stone dead." He rolled his eyes. "With that timetable, young Millicent might want to hold off. The rest of you can afford to take your chances."

Mrs. Colibri said she thought she'd wait, not fifty years but, oh, fifteen minutes or so, just to be on the safe side. Several others murmured their agreement. Quilp told us to suit ourselves, but by then he'd very likely have had a second helping, and perhaps even a third. "And if Molly or Earlene could bring me a plate of that salad," he said, "and some of the seven-grain bread, I think there must be some left. And some butter, of course. And beer, I think, would provide a better accompaniment than wine. Is there some of that nice brown ale, Nigel?"

EIGHTEEN

"Jonathan Rathburn," Nigel Eglantine said, and put the tips of his long fingers together. "I'm afraid I don't know much about him at all. He rang up early in the week to ask if he could come up for a short stay. You both arrived yesterday, didn't you? Mr. Rathburn preceded you by a day. It was Wednesday when he turned up, early in the afternoon."

"How did he get here?"

"I don't know that he said. If he drove, his car would be parked on the other side of the bridge. But we can't get there to look for it, and we wouldn't know it if we saw it, would we?"

"We wouldn't even see it," I said, "under all that snow."

It was snowing again, though not as heavily as before. Carolyn and I were in the Great Library, along with Nigel and Colonel Blount-Buller. That room was pretty much as we'd left it, down to the copy of *The Big Sleep* still perched on the topmost shelf. There was, however, one significant change. Jonathan Rathburn was no longer crumpled at the foot of the library steps. The steps remained, and his blood still discolored the carpet, but Rathburn was gone.

He hadn't risen from the dead, nor had he been mysteriously spirited away. The decision to move the body had been a collective one, taken up with not much argument in the aftermath of a satisfying if initially unnerving lunch of lamb stew and salad and seven-grain bread, all washed down with Newcastle brown ale or California zinfandel or Deer Park spring water, as one preferred. Someone, I'm not sure who, made the point that we now had two rooms off-limits and out of bounds because there were bodies in them. While it was no more than a nuisance to be unable to go into the library, we would be hard pressed to make do without the kitchen.

Furthermore, it was noted, our initial decision to give up the library to the late Mr. Rathburn had been founded on the belief that the police would be appearing shortly. With the phone disabled and the bridge down, and with more snow falling, there was no way to guess when the police would actually show up. In the meantime, neither corpse was improving with age.

"Rathburn's gone off," the colonel reported, "and the cook can't be far behind. It's unfortunate about young Orris, but there's no denying he's a good deal more conveniently placed than the other two."

Now, halfway through the afternoon, Rathburn and Cook were conveniently situated as well—outside, though not at the bottom of the gully. They reposed side by side in lawn chairs immediately to the rear of Cuttleford House, each covered with a bedsheet which was being covered in its turn by a fresh fall of snow.

We'd taken crime-scene photographs before we moved the bodies, making use of a Polaroid camera the Savages had brought. Greg had snapped half a dozen shots of each of them from a variety of angles. He had more film in his room, he assured us, but thought he ought to save some. For the next victim, I suppose.

Someone proposed outlining the bodies before moving them, either with chalk or strips of tape, but both were in short supply. Nor could anyone quite say what point there was in outlining the corpses. We'd all seen them do it on TV and figured you were supposed to.

Once the library was clear, we opened a window to air it out, then assembled there and divided into groups of three. It was the colonel's suggestion that he make up a trio with Carolyn and me, and that the three of us initiate an investigation, interviewing each of the others in turn and holding our interviews in the library, at the very scene of the first murder. "I do have a lifetime of military experience," he said, "and sat on my share of courts-martial over the years. And Rhodenbarr here has had investigative experience."

What sort, someone wondered. Millicent, bless her heart, piped up again that I was a burglar. "Maybe the police investigated him," she said. "And he assisted them in their inquiries."

"Cut the crap," Carolyn told her. "If you want to know what Bernie is, he's what you could call an amateur sleuth. With a house like this, I'm surprised you haven't got an amateur sleuth on staff year round." Someone wanted to know just what an amateur sleuth was, and what they did. "Sometimes they're busybodies," Carolyn explained. "But other times they're ordinary people like Bernie, just minding their own business, and getting mixed up in murder investigations through no fault of their own. That's what keeps happening to Bernie. He can't go away for a quiet weekend in the country without stumbling over dead bodies."

"And then he solves the crime?"

"I've had some good luck in the past," I admitted.

"Is it a hobby?" someone wanted to know. I felt like saying that staying out of jail was a hobby, and solving other people's crimes had occasionally served as a means toward that end. But I just lowered my head and tried to look modest.

And now our investigation was underway. We'd begun with Nigel, and had learned that he didn't know much about Rathburn, except that Nigel had thought he'd said over the phone that he was calling from New York, but that he'd written "Boston, Mass." in the guest register. "Of course he could have called from New York even if he lived in Boston," Nigel added.

"Or he could have lied over the phone," Carolyn said, "and remembered it wrong when it was time to sign in. For all we know he's from Ames, Iowa."

"I don't think we've ever had a guest from Iowa," Nigel said. "That's not the same as Omaha, is it?"

The colonel asked him where he'd been at the time of the first murder, and Nigel said he didn't know when the murder took place, but he rather thought he must have been asleep at the time. "In our own private quarters," he said, "which isn't one of the named rooms, I'm afraid. Cissy and I have a suite on the other side of the kitchen."

"On the ground floor?"

"Yes."

"And do you know when you retired for the night?"

He frowned. "It's difficult to be precise," he said. "Last

night you'll recall we had a sort of informal trial of the Glen Drumnadrochit." I said I remembered it well. "I remember *it* well enough," he said, "but I find that when I drink a good deal over a period of several hours, the tail end of the evening tends to be the slightest bit difficult to recall. The details blur, as it were."

"No need to apologize," the colonel said. "It could happen to a bishop."

"It seems to me I had a walk round the downstairs," Nigel said, "to see the house was settled in for the night. Cissy was already in bed when I returned to our room, and I joined her and, well, I must have dropped off right away. Next thing I knew it was morning."

He'd been awake and dressed when Molly Cobbett discovered the body, he said, but hadn't yet left the bedroom quarters. "We've our own en-suite bathroom," he explained. "I say, I hope you won't need to mention that to the others? All of the guests have to share, and they might resent it."

"It's your house, Nigel," the colonel said. "You're in it twelve months a year. I don't imagine anyone would begrudge you a bog of your own. Was Cissy there when you awoke?"

"She woke up before me. But she was in our quarters, yes."

"And neither of you left your quarters during the night?" I asked.

"Well, we wouldn't have had occasion to, would we? Having the bath en suite and all."

Cissy was next. She'd had hardly any contact with Rathburn beyond taking the imprint of his credit card when he checked in. She was quick to assure us, though, that he had seemed like a very nice man. All of the guests were nice people, she added, which was what made things so impossibly difficult.

"I know you're all quite certain it couldn't be a tramp," she said wistfully, "and I do understand, believe me. But it would be ever so much nicer if it were. You can see that, can't you?"

We agreed that we could.

"Because all of us here at Cuttleford House, guests and staff alike, are unassailably *nice*, don't you see? And this is just not the sort of thing nice people do."

I thought about this, while Carolyn and the colonel asked various logistical questions in an attempt to determine who was where when various acts occurred. I found myself contemplating various murderers over the years, trying to determine if any of them had been what you could legitimately call "nice." Murder itself was not nice, not by any stretch of the imagination, but it seemed to me that it was occasionally committed by nice people, or at least by people who appeared unequivocally nice on the surface.

Such was the case in my own experience, and such was most definitely the case in what I'd read, especially when English country houses came into the picture. A good part of the appeal of books set in English country houses, it seemed to me, lay in the fact that one wasn't forced to read about the sort of person with whom one wouldn't care to associate in real life. All of the characters were just as nice as you could hope, and yet you always seemed to wind up with dead bodies all over the place.

"Mrs. Eglantine," I said. "Or should I call you Cecilia?"

"Or Cissy," she said. "Everyone calls me that."

"Cissy," I said, "I'm sure you're an observant woman.

You'd have to be, running an establishment like Cuttleford House."

"One has to keep one's eyes open," she agreed.

"So I'm sure you've noticed some unusual behavior."

"Unusual behavior?"

"Perhaps some of the guests are not quite what they seem."

"Not quite . . ."

"Or a little more than appears on the surface."

"I'm not sure I understand," she said.

"Some of the others have noticed things," I said. "Inconsistencies, odd behavior."

"They have?"

"And reported them to us."

"Oh, dear," she said, frowning. "But you've only just spoken with Nigel, haven't you?"

"There were some other informal discussions earlier. With some of the others."

"I see."

"And I can't violate a confidence, but—"

"No, of course not."

"But if everyone adds a little piece to the puzzle, soon the whole picture may emerge."

"Yes, I see what you mean," she said. "And there is something."

"I thought there might be."

"Except It's really nothing, you see."

"Well, of course it would seem like nothing."

"It would?"

"It always does."

"Ah," she said. "I see. It always seems like nothing."

"Always."

"Well," she said, "it was a look."

"A look?"

"A glance, really. One person glanced at another."

"And who did the glancing?"

"Mr. Rathburn. Poor Mr. Rathburn."

"And he glanced at—"

"Mrs. Savage."

"Leona Savage."

"Yes. Millicent's mother."

"And Greg's wife," I said. "And Mr. Rathburn glanced at her?"

"He did."

The colonel cleared his throat. "Men do glance at women," he said, "although with every passing year I find it a little more difficult to remember why. But they do, and Mrs. Savage is an attractive young woman, and Mr. Rathburn is a vigorous young man. Or was, that is to say. So if Mr. Rathburn glanced at Mrs. Savage the way a man glances at a woman—"

"I'm sure that's all it was," Cissy Eglantine said.

"No," Carolyn said, "you're not. Are you?"

Cissy sighed, set her shoulders. "No," she admitted. "I'm not. It wasn't that sort of glance at all."

"It couldn't have been, or you wouldn't have mentioned it. What sort of glance was it?"

"It was just a glance," Cissy said, "and perfectly innocent, I'm certain, but the thought that came to me—"

"Yes?"

"—was that they knew each other, and that they weren't keen that anyone else should know this. But I'm sure there was nothing to it. I'm sure there was just something about her that reminded him of someone he'd known years ago, but only from a certain angle. And then when she turned her head the resemblance was gone. That happens all the time, doesn't it? You think you recognize someone, but once you take a second glance you realize there's really no resemblance at all."

"That fellow Wolpert," Rufus Quilp said. "He talks like a lawyer. You may have noticed."

"Everyone talks like a lawyer," Carolyn said. "I think Court TV's what did it, that and the OJ trial."

"Perhaps that's all it is," Quilp said with a sigh, settling his clasped hands upon his ample stomach. "He can't actually be an attorney, can he? Because they're all terribly busy, and Wolpert has the time to come here for a lengthy holiday."

"He was talking about extending his stay," I remembered.

"We're all extending our stay now, aren't we? Like it or not. No TV to be watched, either, *Court* or otherwise, so perhaps our Mr. Wolpert will lose his lawyerly aspect. If that's where he got it." He sniffed. "He certainly doesn't dress like a lawyer. No Brooks Brothers suits in his closet. Tweed jackets with elbow patches, that's more his line. Knows a lot about poisons, did you notice?"

"About mushrooms, anyway."

"About everything. Could be a professor. Dresses like a professor, wouldn't you say? Ought to be fiddling about with a pipe, forever taking it apart and cleaning it. Fit the image to a T."

"You don't like him," Carolyn said.

"Don't dislike him, either," Quilp said. "No need to feel one way or the other about him, actually. Wouldn't have said boo about him, but you did ask about little suspicions and observations." He leaned forward. "I'll tell you what it is. I've watched him eat."

"You have?"

"I have. He picks at his food. I never trust a man who picks at his food."

"Miss Dinmont can walk," Millicent Savage reported.

"I think she said as much," I said. "She was telling me that she has a first-floor room because of the wheelchair. She can manage stairs if she absolutely has to, but then somebody has to carry the wheelchair upstairs. If she can get up a flight of stairs, I suppose she can walk."

"She was dancing," the child said.

"Dancing?"

"In her room. She was all by herself, too, in her room with the door locked and the curtain drawn."

"If the door was locked and the curtain drawn," said the colonel, "then how could you possibly have seen her?"

"Maybe I was wrong and the door was open," Millicent suggested.

"And maybe it wasn't," Carolyn said. "Maybe you looked through the keyhole."

Millicent giggled. "Maybe I did."

"I say," the colonel said. "That's no way to behave, young lady."

"I know," she said. "But I'm only ten years old. It would be a lot worse if a grown-up did it. And I never would have done it except for the music."

"The music?"

"That she was dancing to. It was all dreamy and gooey and romantic, and I heard it coming through the door, and that's what made me look."

"I don't believe you," Carolyn said. "I bet you look in keyholes all the time."

"Not all the time." The imp giggled. "You'd be surprised what you can see that way."

"And what did you see this time?"

"Miss Dinmont dancing, and she was very graceful, too. She had her arms held out as if she was dancing with a partner, but she was all by herself. Unless she was dancing with a ghost. But I'm sure she wasn't."

I'd have let that pass, but Carolyn thought to ask her what made her so certain.

"Because it wouldn't have been decent."

"To dance with a ghost?"

"Not like that."

"Not like what?"

"Naked," Millicent said. "Miss Dinmont didn't have any clothes on."

Rufus Quilp was apt to drop off to sleep at any moment. It might be Pickwickian syndrome and it might be apnea. And it might be feigned—sometimes he appeared to be sleeping, but something he said later would indicate that he'd overheard what was being said during his little nap.

Miss Hardesty had been seen in urgent conversation with the cook. Greg Savage, who mentioned seeing the two of them, had assumed the conversation had something to do with Miss Dinmont's dietary requirements, which one somehow knew would be complicated. Now, though, it seemed to him that Miss Hardesty had appeared a bit agitated, and the cook faintly disgruntled.

Jonathan Rathburn, whom I had observed writing at the desk in the library, had been spotted doing the same thing in other parts of the house as well. There was some disagreement as to what he'd been writing. I'd sort of assumed he'd been writing letters, as that's one of the things people are forever doing in English country houses, but someone reported him as having written on a pad, and another thought he had been making entries in a diary. Neither letters nor a diary had been found on his body, or elsewhere in the library, which might mean that the murderer had carried them off, or that he hadn't had them with him when he was murdered.

No one admitted to having met Rathburn prior to his arrival at Cuttleford House. Hardly anyone could recall exchanging a word with him. Several people described him as preoccupied, and Leona Savage, who'd also seen him scribbling away, had thought he might be a writer. "Struggling to make headway on a book or story," she said. "He had that air about him, as if he'd come to the country to free himself creatively."

"And she never laid eyes on him before," the colonel said after she'd left the room, "and yet Cissy Eglantine saw Rathburn give her a significant glance."

"Cissy could be mistaken," Carolyn said, "or Rathburn could have recognized Leona even if Leona didn't recognize him. Or he could have thought he knew her even if he didn't."

"Or she could be lying," I said.

"Or she could be lying. Anybody could be lying about anything, couldn't they? You know those party games where one person's the murderer, and when you interrogate all the players, everybody except the murderer has to tell the truth? Well, that's what this is like, except it isn't." The colonel looked puzzled, and I suppose I did, too. "Because any of them could be lying and it wouldn't prove anything," she explained. "Not necessarily. Suppose Jonathan and Leona had a brief fling twenty years ago when they were both counselors at Camp Yahrzeit. That would be reason enough for him to give her a significant glance, and it might also be reason enough for her to insist she'd never met him before, no matter who killed him."

We tossed that back and forth, and wound up agreeing with her. Anybody could lie, not just the murderer. It didn't seem fair, but that's the way it was.

It left me wondering at the point of our efforts. I'd deliberately turned things around during our session with Cissy, switching from a clinical look at alibis and schedules to a more gossipy, anecdotal approach. After she'd left the room I had explained why.

"You described me as an amateur sleuth," I told Carolyn, "and that's what all three of us are, amateurs. We all have a little experience that might prove useful, but we're not cops. A professional approach won't work for us. But an amateur approach, where people wind up telling us the kind of observations and inferences they wouldn't dream of sharing with a policeman, well, that might be fruitful."

And I suppose it had been, in a way. We'd since learned from Quilp that Gordon Wolpert was a picky eater and not to be trusted, and in due course we learned from Wolpert that Earlene Cobbett, the freckled chambermaid so distraught over Orris's fatal fall, had been noisily ill several mornings in succession. "Now that doesn't mean the girl is in the family way," he said, "or that Orris put her there, and even if she is and he did, that doesn't begin to implicate either of them or anyone else in the events you're attempting to investigate." But we'd said we wanted to know what he had observed, and he'd heard her retching three mornings in a row, so he was reporting it.

But what good did it do us to know it? What profit was

there in having learned that Miss Dinmont danced in the nude, or that Millicent Savage peeped at keyholes? What difference did it make if Miss Hardesty had had words with the cook, or that Dakin Littlefield had been spotted casting speculative glances at Molly Cobbett?

It was Mrs. Colibri who'd reported Littlefield's evident interest in the downstairs maid. Lettice in turn had Molly sized up as a saucy tart ready to throw herself at anything in pants. (The most interesting thing about her observation was Carolyn's reaction to it; she looked down at herself to make sure she wasn't wearing a skirt.) "My own husband hasn't noticed the little tramp," Lettice added, "but we're on our honeymoon, and that makes a difference. I'm sure the rest of the men have noticed, and I wouldn't be surprised if some of them have given her a tumble."

If Dakin had entertained thoughts of luring the downstairs maid upstairs, he was keeping them to himself. According to him, he hadn't paid a great deal of attention to the staff, or to the other guests either. Nor was he much interested in our inquiry, or in staying any longer than he had to at Cuttleford House.

"In the morning," he said, "we're out of here." He tossed his head, a gesture that someone must have told him showed off his wavy hair. "I understand if you walk downstream a ways there's a place where you can get across the creek without breaking your neck in the process. Then it's just a matter of finding your way out to the main road. It's too late to try it now, but as soon as the sun's up that's what Lettice and I are going to do."

"But there's been murder done," the colonel told him. "I thought it was agreed that we would all remain here until the police arrive."

"Maybe that's what you thought," Dakin said, "but so what? I didn't agree to anything, and the rest of you haven't got any authority over me. Once we get out of here we'll call the cops and they'll be out here like a shot, and isn't that what you people want?"

"Yes, but—"

"I don't know why the hell I ever came here in the first place," he went on. "It was Lettice's idea, and don't ask me where she got it from. This place is supposed to be so exclusive and special, and all I see is a run-down pile of bricks run by a dizzy dame with a drunk for a husband. Every place you go nowadays you got satellite TV with fifty or a hundred channels, and this dump can't even put together an old black-and-white portable set with a rabbit-ear antenna. Who in his right mind would come to a place like this?"

"Mrs. Eglantine is perfectly stable," the colonel said, "and Nigel is hardly an alcoholic simply because he's developed a palate for malt whisky. And there are special pleasures to be found in the absence of television. As for what sort of person would willingly come here, I may say that I myself am pleased to spend six months a year here."

"I rest my case," Dakin said. "This investigation of yours is a lot of crap, and so's the idea of everybody tripling up in kinky little trios. I'm with my wife, and the two of us'll be sticking together, and everybody else can just stay the hell away from us. And in the morning we're gone, and I'll tell you, I'll be glad to get out of this nuthouse."

I could see his point.

"It's hopeless," I announced. "I've got a notebook full of scribbles, and I'm no closer to naming the murderer than I was when we started. When the police crack this case, they'll do it by breaking down alibis and asking hard questions and analyzing physical evidence. We can't do any of that. We've got no authority, and when people tell us things anyway we don't know what to make of it. All we can hope to do is keep everyone else alive until the cops get here, and I don't know when that will be, and neither does anybody else. Jesus, is it snowing again?"

"I think it's just blowing around," Carolyn said.

"Well, I don't. I think it's fresh snow, and I think it's falling, and maybe it'll go on like that all night. I don't know what to do."

"Keep a stiff upper lip," Blount-Buller advised.

"I'll certainly try," I said, "but . . ."

There was a knock on the door. I went over and opened it, and Raffles came in. He usually scratches, and he's not very good at that, and I was trying to figure out how he'd managed to knock when I realized that Molly Cobbett was standing there, waiting to be acknowledged before she said anything.

"Yes, Molly," I said.

"Begging your pardon, sir," she said, "and yours, ma'am, and yours as well, sir—"

"What is it, Molly?"

"It's dinner, sir. Not wanting to disturb you, but it's served, and they're all in the dining room. Except for those as are in the bar, having a drink before dinner."

"A drink before dinner," I said.

"Yes, sir. It sharpens the appetite, Mr. Eglantine says."

"Well, then," I said. "We'd all better have one, don't you think? Everybody knows you can't trust a picky eater."

NINETEEN

Dinner, it turned out, was the joint effort of Cissy Eglantine and the Cobbett cousins. There'd been some leftover ham in the refrigerator, and they'd combined it with mashed potatoes and boiled cabbage and diced carrots and bacon drippings in what Cissy called an old English recipe. It was evidently something of a staple in the Cobbett clan. "You takes what you has got left," Earlene explained, "and you cooks it all together like. If your people be really hungry, they will eat it."

It was actually rather tasty, once you sat down and tucked in, but it offered little in the way of eye appeal. A quaint name would have helped—dog's breakfast, say, or Taffy-in the-woodpile. As it was, guests would slip into the dining room, then reconsider and visit the bar first. Once in the bar, one tended to linger, counting on malt whisky to heighten the appetite for the evening meal.

Eventually, though, everyone got to table, and the main course turned out better than it looked or sounded. There wasn't much of a market for second helpings, aside from

Rufus Quilp, who'd probably have asked for seconds on death angel mushrooms. For everybody else, one portion was plenty. I kept an occasional eye on Gordon Wolpert, but as far as I could see he wasn't any more picky an eater on this occasion than the rest of us.

There was good bread on the table, and some sort of custard for dessert. The coffee was weak.

We were in the library with fresh mugs of coffee when the colonel found us and announced he was going to make it an early night. "I shall return to Trevelyan," he said, "and slip into a simpler world."

I asked which door he'd be using to enter that world, Trevelyan's one-volume *History of England* or the more specialized *England Under the Stuarts*.

"Neither, I'm afraid. I'm reading his three-volume history of England under Queen Anne. Halfway through the middle volume."

"*Ramillies and the Union with Scotland*," I said.

He looked startled. "Quite," he said. "However do you happen to know that?"

"Just a lucky guess."

"Hardly that. I gather you're a student of English history."

"Some college courses," I said. "Years ago. And I never actually read the three volumes on Anne's reign. I just remember the titles."

"*Marlborough and Prince Eugene*," he said. "*The War of the Spanish Succession. The Battle of Blenheim.*"

"A famous victory," I said, echoing the Robert Southey poem.

"Famous once. Forgotten nowadays, I shouldn't wonder. I don't know what young people remember these days.

Shouldn't think they recall anything much earlier than the day before yesterday. It's stirring stuff, Trevelyan's history. You should read it sometime."

"One of these days."

"Well," he said, setting his shoulders. "You'll forgive me for breaking ranks, won't you? I know we're supposed to hold in squads of three, but I'm sure I'll be all right in my quarters, and just as confident you two can see to each other's safety. So, if you've no objection . . ."

I could hardly object. They'd all agreed readily enough to hang out in trios earlier, but that had gone by the boards as the day wore on, and by the time dinner was over it had ceased even to be honored in the breach. I'd overheard Millicent Savage whining about having to stay in Lucinda's Room with her parents instead of being all by herself in Uncle Roger's Room. So far Greg and Leona seemed to be holding out, but I had a feeling the child would have her own way in the end.

"Nobody's taking it seriously," I told Carolyn. "I don't get it. There are three people dead and an unknown killer in our midst, and they'd rather grumble about dinner than make sure they're still alive for breakfast. What's wrong with these people?"

She thought about it. "I think they're just good at adjusting," she said.

"At adjusting?"

"I think so, Bern. They were all really spooked earlier, when we found the cook cooling off in the kitchen. There were bodies all over the place and nobody had a clue who was gonna be next."

"There still are," I said, "and they still don't, but all of a sudden nobody gives a damn."

"Right. They've adjusted. Rathburn and the cook are

outside where nobody has to look at them, and Orris is way down at the bottom of the gully. You know what they say, Bern. Out of sight, out of mind."

"The bodies are out of sight," I said, "and the rest of us are out of our minds."

"People adjust," she said. "Take you and me. Last night the coffee was strong and full-bodied, and we enjoyed it. Tonight it's weak, and we're still enjoying it."

"We didn't adjust to it."

"We most certainly did."

"We put Scotch in it, Carolyn."

"That's how we adjusted," she said, "and I'd have to say we made a good adjustment, Bern. It tastes a lot better this way. Somehow you don't notice that it's weak. You know, that might be a good way to stretch coffee, as a sort of economy move. Use less coffee and add whisky to taste."

"For economy," I said.

"Well, if there was a major coffee shortage, say, or if we went to war with Brazil."

"Why would we do that?"

"Why does anybody do anything?" She frowned. "Where was I?"

"You were drinking fortified coffee."

"Fortified," she said. "That's a good word for it. I suppose it's a crime against nature to put single-malt whisky in coffee, but that coffee was a crime against nature to begin with and I figure they cancel each other out. At least we didn't use the Drumnadrochit."

"God forbid."

"I hope we get out of this place soon, Bern, but not before I get one more crack at the Drumnadrochit. Anyway, the answer to 'Where was I?' is I was talking about people adjusting."

"To murder."

"Uh-huh. They're not really concerned anymore, Bern, not the way they were. Some of them are taking the tack that there weren't any murders in the first place."

"Then where did all those bodies come from?"

"Jonathan Rathburn fell off the ladder, Orris fell off the bridge, and the cook—"

"Fell into a deep and dreamless sleep," I said, "and lo, she doth be sleeping still. That's ridiculous, for God's sake."

"I know."

"The cook could conceivably have had a stroke or a heart attack," I said, "although it strikes me as unlikely. But Orris and Rathburn were murdered, pure and simple. And if their deaths were accidental, how do you explain the sugar in the snowblower's gas tank and the severed phone wires? Acts of God?"

"They say He works in mysterious ways. I heard someone say that phone wires get disconnected all the time in bad weather. And somebody else was saying that the snowblower probably had a perfectly ordinary mechanical breakdown, and that nobody really smelled burnt sugar after all."

"That's ridiculous."

"I know, Bern."

"I ought to siphon a cup of gasoline from the snowblower's gas tank," I said, "and make them all taste it."

"We may want it tomorrow," she said, "for dessert, if there's no more custard. Look, not everybody thinks the deaths were accidental. The rest of them think the cycle's complete."

"The cycle?"

"Three deaths, Bern. Deaths are supposed to come in

threes, remember? Now that the cook's dead, everybody can relax."

"That doesn't make any sense."

"I know. But what's the difference, Bern? It's not as though we're going to solve the puzzle. You said so yourself, that all the bits and pieces we picked up interrogating people this afternoon wouldn't do us any good at all."

"I didn't say they wouldn't do any good. I just said we weren't getting anywhere."

"Close enough. So we'll hang out here, and the colonel can read English history. Hey, you never went to college. How come you knew all that about Queen Anne?"

"I don't know anything about Queen Anne," I said. "I had a set of the books in the store. I was beginning to think I ought to have a look inside the covers, and then somebody came along and bought them."

"Hey, it happens. She was gay, you know."

"Queen Anne?"

"Uh-huh. Had a thing with Sarah Churchill, whose husband was the Duke of Marlborough that the colonel was just talking about. Why are you looking at me like that, Bern? It's herstory."

"Herstory?"

"History for girls. Anyway, you can read about Queen Anne, or about just about anything else, with all these books staring us in the face. And we can drink fortified coffee, and sooner or later the police will turn up and rescue us. And then they can do all those sophisticated tests, DNA and blood spatters and autopsies, and they can run background checks on all the guests, and—"

"And Bob's your uncle," I suggested.

"Well, something like that." She sighed. "You know

something, Bern? I never thought I'd sit around wishing the police would turn up, but that's exactly what I'm doing. Because right this minute I'd actually be happy to see that door burst open and Ray Kirschmann come lumbering through it. I . . ."

"What's the matter, Carolyn?"

"Huh?"

"You broke off what you were saying and started staring at something."

"The door," she said.

"What about it?"

"I was sure it was gonna fly open," she said, "and I was sure he was gonna be there."

"Who, Ray?"

She nodded. "Dumb idea, Bern. He doesn't even know we're here, does he?"

"I can't see how he would even know we left town."

"Still, it shows you the state I'm in. You know what it all means, Bernie?"

"No."

"It means the day of the amateur sleuth is over. If ever a case looked made to order for amateur sleuthing, this would have to be it. A snowbound English country house with corpses piling up faster than the snow? And here we are, throwing up our hands."

"I'm glad that's all we're throwing up," I said. "When I got my first look at dinner tonight my heart sank. Does that dish have a name, do you figure? Something like Cobbett surprise?"

"Oh, that reminds me," she said, getting to her feet. "I promised I'd help."

"Help what?"

"In the kitchen."

"That's not what," I said. "It's where."

"I said I'd help with the cleanup."

"You?"

"Why not?"

"Well, for one thing," I said, "it's not your job. For another, you happen to hate helping in the kitchen."

"It's an emergency," she said. "They're short-handed, what with the cook being dead and all."

"And all," I said.

"So I thought I'd help."

I noticed the way she was avoiding my eye, and light dawned. I asked who she'd be helping.

"Whoever's in there," she said. "Look, I'll just—"

"Molly Cobbett," I said.

"She's probably in there, yeah. So?"

"And her cousin Earlene?"

"She's probably got other jobs to do."

"So Molly's alone in the kitchen."

"She probably is," she said, "and now that you mention it, that's probably not safe. So that's all the more reason for me to go keep her company."

"Maybe I should come too," I said.

"No need, Bern."

"Two's dangerous, remember? Suppose Molly turns out to be the killer?"

"Very funny."

"Or suppose you turn out to be the killer."

"Even funnier, Bern."

"I just don't want to see you make the wrong move," I said. "I know you dreamed about her, but—"

"It was some dream, Bern. You have no idea."

Oh, no? "She's a country girl," I went on, "from a sheltered background, and she probably doesn't know the first thing about lesbians."

"You didn't see the way she was looking at me."

"Well, you're exotic," I said. "Hip and urban and—"

"And gay," she said. "And she's a Cobbett, which means there's probably not a whole lot she hasn't done. The only thing that makes me exotic is that I'm not a blood relative. Listen, I'm not looking to put the moves on her. I just want to go keep her company in the kitchen."

I couldn't think of anyone else I wanted to keep company with, in the kitchen or elsewhere. The only object of my affections in the neighborhood was Lettice Littlefield, and I wasn't too sure how affectionately I felt toward her just now. Anyway, they were on their honeymoon and there was a killer on the premises, so her sneering husband was likely to be keeping her on a short leash.

What I really wanted to do was escape, and there's one tried-and-true way to manage that feat without actually going anywhere. I remembered Emily Dickinson's words on the subject: *There is no frigate like a book.* "Frigate," I said, more or less, and went into the library.

I looked up at Raymond Chandler, looked over at the library steps, looked at the camel and the throw pillow. I wondered if a person could actually sit down and work out a murder scheme involving a camel and a pillow. It had to have been improvised, I decided, or else the whole thing had an impossibly Monty Python tone to it.

It was a pity, I thought, that I hadn't heard any of the conversation that had been murmured in this very room while I lurked in the doorway. One of the participants had almost certainly been Jonathan Rathburn, the other the person who cameled and pillowed him to death. Had I crept in a little way I might have found out what they were going on about, and might have learned the identity of the other party. Conversely, if I'd just blundered in noisily, switching on lights and begging pardon for the intrusion, I might have prevented a murder. And, if that first killing hadn't taken place, perhaps the others would have been nipped in the bud as well.

I could have saved them all, I thought. If only I'd been a little more furtive, or a little more oafish. Either extreme might well have done the trick. It was this middle-of-the-road crap that caused all the trouble.

Well, as Emily D. would say, frigate. High time I sailed away from all this. I went over to the shelves and started looking at the books.

I stayed there in the library, reading, then went upstairs to Aunt Augusta's Room and ran into Millicent Savage in the hallway. She'd won, she told me triumphantly. She was going to be allowed to remain in Uncle Roger's Room. I told her I thought she should stay with her parents.

"Why?" she demanded. "So you can burglarize Uncle Roger?"

"What's he got to steal besides a pipe and slippers?"

"And the pipe's smelly," she said, getting into the spirit of things. "And the slippers have holes in them."

"Poor old Uncle Roger."

"No, it's Poor Miss McTavish! *Gross* old Uncle Roger."

"I still think you should stay in your parents' room," I said.

"Why?"

"I just think it would be a good idea."

She looked at me. "You think there's going to be another murder," she said, "but you won't come right out and say so because you don't want me to be scared. But if I'm not scared, I'll want to go on staying in my own room."

"It's a poser," I agreed.

"I think you're right," she said. "I think there's going to be another killing. But I won't be the victim."

"How can you be sure?"

"Because I'm just a little kid," she said. "Nobody's going to bother killing me. You're the one who should be scared."

"Me?"

She nodded solemnly. "Somebody's going to be murdered tonight," she said, "and it might be you."

An hour or so later I was in yet another sitting room. This one boasted no antelopes on the wall, just a couple of edged weapons. One of them had a wave-shaped blade about eight inches long, and I took it down from the wall to admire it. I couldn't swear to it, but what it looked like to me was a Malayan kris, a frequent denizen of the very same crossword puzzles that welcomed the oryx and the zebu. I ran my thumb across the blade, decided it was sharp enough for headhunting, and hung it back on the wall.

I'd stopped at the bar first, where I'd poured myself a drink and made the appropriate notation in the book. I was making the drink last, just wetting my lips every few pages while I worked my way through *Scoop*, Evelyn Waugh's wonderful novel of journalists in Africa. There's a passage fairly early on in which a dour newspaperman reminisces about once having made and launched a dugout canoe, whereupon the thing sank like a stone. I was a little vague on the details, but I remembered that I'd laughed for ten minutes the first time I read the book. I didn't know when I'd be likely to hit it, and I was a little worried that it wouldn't be as funny this time, and that I'd wind up wondering why I'd ever thought it was funny in the first place.

Better to be anxious about that than to worry about being bridged and mushroomed and cameled and pillowed to death. While I couldn't be sure how my favorite passage would hold up, so far the book was an excellent choice. There were, to be sure, hundreds if not thousands of books on the shelves that I hadn't read, but this was a night to be reading something I could count on. I wanted to escape, but on familiar paths.

I'd passed Raffles earlier in the upstairs hall, and you'd have thought I'd done something to offend him; he paid me no attention at all, and he'd have sailed on by with his tail held high if he'd had one. He turned up again after I'd been reading for half an hour, having undergone a personality transplant in the interim. He came over, rubbed against my ankle, draped himself over my feet, and purred with such energy that I felt the vibrations clear to my knees.

He was still in place, still revving his motor, when I heard footsteps and looked up at Carolyn. "You know," I said, "I've got a good book to read and good whisky to drink and a comfortable chair to sit in. I've got a cat who has the decency to act as though he loves me, even though we know how unlikely that is. It's not a bad life. I hope I don't get killed."

She stared. "Why even say something like that?"

I told her what Millicent had said.

"Oh, come on," she said. "She's just a creepy little kid,

Bern. It's not like she's holding down the first chair at the Psychic Friends Network."

"I know that," I said, "but it's spooky all the same. It gives me a funny feeling."

"Don't *say* that, Bern."

"Why not?"

"It sounds ominous, that's all. And I'm feeling pretty spooked to begin with. I went upstairs just now and the door to our room was locked."

"Well, sure," I said. "That's because neither of us was in it."

"I know."

"You've got a key, right? We've each got one. You didn't lose yours, did you?"

"Of course not. But I was scared to use it."

"Why?"

"I was afraid of what might be inside."

"Like a dead body?"

"Or a live one, waiting to kill me. I don't *know* what I was afraid of, Bern. I knocked, hoping nobody would open the door, and nobody did, and I came downstairs to look for you."

"And here I am," I said. "Let's go upstairs. Maybe tomorrow'll be better."

"That's what people are always saying," she said, "and it never is. But this time it almost has to be. Maybe the cops'll come and we can all go home. Except I love it here, or at least I did until everybody started getting killed."

"Wait a minute, Bern."

We were skirting the library on our way to the stairs when she tugged at my sleeve. I waited, and she darted inside. She came out with a facial expression I recognized from Japanese films—the samurai, moments before committing hara-kiri.

"Bern," she said through clenched teeth, "go in there!"

"Why? I've already got a book."

"Just do it. And look at the shelf."

"What shelf?"

"*The* shelf."

I went and looked, knowing what I'd see. The shelf held no surprises. And it didn't hold *The Big Sleep*, either. Just a space where the book had been until someone snatched it away.

TWENTY

"I'm not surprised," I said. "I don't really want to talk about it, to tell you the truth, but I can't say I'm surprised."

"I don't suppose it's really very important, Bern. With people getting killed left and right, a rare book doesn't seem all that significant. But the idea that it could just disappear like that . . ."

"You're right," I said. "It's not important."

We were in our bedroom, and I didn't want to talk about *The Big Sleep*, so I asked about Molly Cobbett. Carolyn's expression turned wistful.

"She's sweet," she said, "and she's full of stories about this part of the country, and about the Cobbetts clear back to Revolutionary War days. But I guess she's more innocent than I thought, Bern."

"You mean she's only been sleeping with boy cousins?"

"That's about it. Remember how I told you she was looking at me before? Well, I'm beginning to get the sense that she just stares that way at everybody. It's what passes for manners in Cobbett country."

"So I guess you won't be sneaking off in the middle of the night to pay a visit to the servants' quarters."

"Only in my dreams," she said, and grinned. "And if tonight's dream is half as good as last night's, I won't have anything to complain about."

Getting ready for bed wasn't all that much of a problem. Occasionally on a late night one of us stays over at the other's apartment, and the business of changing to sleepwear isn't all that awkward, even in close quarters. It was being in the same bed together that was strange, and stranger still for my recollection of her dream of the night before.

I sat up and read, willing Evelyn Waugh to take my mind off pretty much everything it was on, and Carolyn sat beside me reading a book of her own, and I wondered who'd be first to switch off the bedside lamp. And then, of course, there was the sound of scratching at the door.

"Raffles," she said.

"I'm afraid you're right."

"You want to let him in?"

"If we let him in," I said, "we'll just have to let him out."

"Can't we just leave the door open? That's what we did last night."

"Sure," I said. "In a house where three people have been murdered so far."

"You think a locked door could keep a murderer away?"

"I'd prefer a clove of garlic on a string," I said, "but I don't want to go all the way down to the kitchen at this hour. I don't know if a locked door would keep anybody out who was really determined to get in, but an open door's an invitation. 'Here I am, murder me.' "

"Leave it locked, Bern. Maybe he'll go away."

Fat chance. The scratching was repeated half a dozen times in the next few minutes, and at that point I gave up and let him in. And left the door ajar.

He came in, made his rounds, nibbled some dried food, invited strokes and behind-the-ear scratches, and took his leave. I watched him go and stared for a long moment at the open door.

Then I went back to my book.

"Bern? When I was in the kitchen with Molly? I thought I might learn something that would help us figure out who the killer is. But I didn't get anywhere."

I closed the book.

"I'm completely lost," she said. "Stumped. And I guess you're the same way, huh?"

"Not exactly," I said.

"What do you mean? Don't tell me you know who did it."

"Well," I admitted, "I sort of have an idea."

"Well, for crying out loud, let's hear it!"

I shook my head. "Not now," I said.

"What do you mean, not now?"

"It's just a hunch," I said, "and I could be completely wrong. And I haven't worked it all out in my mind yet."

"So what? Bern, there's nobody in the room but you and me. Nobody's gonna sue you for slander."

"I know."

"So?"

I considered, then shook my head. "It wouldn't be right."

"Bern!" She grabbed my arm. "Don't you see what you're doing? You're refusing to act."

"I am?"

"I've read hundreds of books," she said, "where the detective does just what you're doing. And he says the same kind of harebrained thing you just said, about how it's too early to tell what he knows. And the next thing you know there's another corpse on the floor, and he's saying something like 'Dash it all, it's all my fault. I waited too long.' And that's what you're doing, Bern. You're waiting too long."

"But it's just a hunch," I said, "and I'm probably wrong, and the puzzle's still got too many pieces missing."

"That's what they all say."

"And it's the middle of the night."

"That's not what they all say. But what difference does it make?"

"Even if I'm right," I said, "I can't run out now and do anything about it. So what's the point in talking about it?"

"For one thing, it'll keep me from going crazy."

"Maybe, but it would have been better if I hadn't said anything in the first place."

She shook her head. "You've got to tell me, Bernie. Suppose that creepy little kid is right and you get killed tonight. If you don't tell anybody, your secret will die with you." She held up her index finger, pointing at nothing in particular. "That's another thing you read about all the time," she said. "Somebody has it all worked out and won't tell anybody, and then he's the next victim."

"I don't want to be the next victim," I said.

"Don't even say it, Bern."

"You're the one who said it. You really think I'm in danger?"

"You might be. Anybody might be."

"And you really think I'll be safer if I tell you?"

"All I know," she said, "is I'll never be able to sleep unless you do."

She was sleeping.

I'd been the first to turn out my bedside lamp, but I never even came close to dozing off. I lay there in the dark, listening to the creaking and groaning of the old house. I wasn't any drowsier when Carolyn put her book aside and switched off her lamp, and I was still wide awake when her breathing slowed and deepened.

I was at least lost in thought, if not yet actually sleepy, when she stirred beside me and rolled over onto her side. Her arm reached out and draped itself over me, and she drew close, ready to start playing softball on the Field of Dreams.

Gently, gingerly, I disentangled myself and got quietly out of bed. Carolyn's arm, deprived of a body to clutch, pawed at the air. I took the pillow I'd been using and slipped it into the circle of her embrace. She held off for a moment, as if weighing the pillow's merits as a Molly Cobbett surrogate, then decided in its favor.

I dressed in the darkness, quickly and silently. The door, I noted, was still ajar, and the game was afoot.

I let myself out.

TWENTY-ONE

It was around seven in the morning when Carolyn Kaiser awakened. Her eyes barely open, she put on a robe and walked down the hall to the bathroom. It was on her return to the bedroom that she noticed that the bed was empty.

"Hey, Bern," she said. "Where'd you go?"

She glanced at the wooden chair where her friend had hung the clothes he'd been wearing the night before. It was empty. She got dressed herself and went out into the hallway again, where she saw Bettina Colibri a few doors down fitting a key into a lock.

"Have you seen Bernie?" she demanded.

"Bernie? Your uh friend?"

"Yeah, my uh friend. Bernie Rhodenbarr. Have you seen him?"

"I haven't seen anybody," the woman said. "I'm just on my way down to breakfast now. If there's actually going to *be* breakfast, in the absence of the cook."

"I don't care about breakfast," Carolyn said. "I'm just worried about Bernie."

"Why, for heaven's sake?"

"Why? Because he's my best friend in the world, that's why."

"And friendship is a wonderful thing," Mrs. Colibri said, "but what possible cause have you to worry? If he's not in your room he's very likely gone downstairs himself."

"I hope you're right."

She hurried downstairs, and her state of mind was evident, because everyone she met asked her if something was the matter. "I'm trying to find Bernie," she told them all. "I don't know where he is and I'm worried."

Downstairs, she made her way from room to room. Bernie Rhodenbarr was nowhere to be found. She checked the Breakfast Room, the Morning Room, the Great Library, the various parlors. She inquired of everyone she encountered.

No one mentioned having seen Bernie Rhodenbarr, not since the previous evening. No one had any idea where he might be.

"Maybe he got the hell out," Dakin Littlefield suggested. "Which is what my wife and I are planning to do as soon as our breakfast has had time to settle. That's what I told him I was planning yesterday, and maybe it gave him an idea."

"He wouldn't do that," Carolyn insisted. "And he certainly wouldn't leave without saying anything to me."

"Well, you know him better than I do," Littlefield said, with the sort of smirk on his face that suggested she didn't really know Rhodenbarr well at all.

A more systematic search of the downstairs, with others lending a hand, was no more successful. Colonel Blount-Buller was clearly troubled by Rhodenbarr's disappearance, although his temperament was such that he showed far less agitation than Carolyn Kaiser. "You're quite right," he told her. "Rhodenbarr's a level-headed chap. It's not like him to disappear this way, without a word to anyone."

"I'm afraid," Carolyn said.

"In the ordinary course of things," Blount-Buller said, "there'd be no reason to suspect foul play. But in the present circumstances, with three suspicious deaths already—"

"Oh, no," she cried. "Not Bernie!"

"He's so alive," Lettice Littlefield said. "I can't imagine him being—"

"Don't say it," Carolyn begged her.

Lettice left her sentence unfinished. Millicent Savage, wearing bib overalls and rabbit slippers, finished the sentence for her. "Dead," she said.

Everyone looked at her.

"I told him he might be the next to die," the child said, her lower lip trembling. "I don't know why I said it. It just came into my mind and I said it without thinking about it. And now it's come true!"

It hadn't necessarily come true, people rushed to tell her, and even if it had it wasn't her fault. Millicent looked unconvinced.

There was more than a little confusion in the ranks. Nigel Eglantine snatched up the telephone and poked at its buttons, as if in the hope that the severed wires had somehow knitted themselves back together during the night. Carolyn somehow got hold of the colonel and asked him if he could do something, and he took command, silencing the throng with an elaborate clearing of his throat, then summarizing the situation for them.

There were, he told them, insofar as Bernie Rhodenbarr was concerned, two possibilities. One, Rhodenbarr had quit the premises and gone home, without a word to his faithful companion or anyone else. Two, Rhodenbarr was somewhere in the house or on the grounds, but was deaf to the present hue and cry because he was in a deep sleep, or drugged and/or tied up, or . . .

"Or dead," said Millicent Savage.

The thing to do, the colonel said, was muster everyone into a great body and give the house a systematic room-by-room search. Cissy Eglantine produced a master key which afforded entry to each of the second-floor bedrooms, including Young George's Room, earlier occupied by the late Jonathan Rathburn.

"This was the son of a bitch who started the whole thing," Dakin Littlefield remarked from the doorway to Young George's Room. His wife, Lettice, objected that Rathburn was a victim, that he had been killed. "Serves him right," Littlefield told her. "Look what he started. Look at the mess he created."

But there was no mess within Rathburn's room. It was neat as a pin, unlike more than a few of the bedrooms, whose occupants apologized for their untidy state. "You'll pardon the disorder," Rufus Quilp said dryly, "but I wasn't expecting guests." And Lettice Littlefield, on opening the door to their bridal chamber, rushed to the window and threw it open, as if the room was in urgent need of airing out before anyone could set foot in it. "What's that smell?" Millicent Savage wanted to know, while her father winced, her mother told her to be quiet, and Lettice herself managed an uncharacteristic blush. Her husband, Carolyn noticed, preened a little, looking pleased with himself.

The search moved to the servants' quarters and storage areas on the top floor, then back to the ground floor, with its maze of public rooms, its kitchen and pantry, and the guest bedroom shared by the Misses Dinmont and Hardesty, as well as the Eglantines' private suite. The whole mass of guests and staff trooped through room after room, like Japanese tourists at the White House, determined to see everything.

They didn't find Rhodenbarr. Not a trace of him, living or dead.

"He's not in the house," the colonel told them. "It would seem that he's cut out on his own, though how or why escapes me."

"Maybe he went to get help," Carolyn suggested. "But all by himself? In the middle of the night? Without a word to anybody?"

"It's hard to credit," Blount-Buller agreed. "But we've searched everywhere, and if he's not here he must be elsewhere. Point of elementary logic, wot?"

"Unless . . ."

Everyone looked at Carolyn.

"Unless something's happened to him," she managed, "and he's with . . ."

"With?"

"With the others," she said.

"The others," several people repeated, puzzled, and then Miss Dinmont, who'd missed the action on the upper two floors but had wheeled herself gamely from room to room on the ground floor, said, "Oh, of course. The other victims."

"Actually," Greg Savage said, "I thought of that."

"You did?" his wife said, surprised.

"It seemed like something a compulsive killer might do, keep all his victims together. So I looked out the back door, where we moved the bodies, and they're right where we left them."

"Untouched," someone said.

"Far as I can see. The lawn chairs we used, each with a body on it and a bedsheet tossed over it. Actually I couldn't swear about the bodies, or even about the bedsheets, on account of the snow, but that's how we left them yesterday and that's what it looks like today. Three lawn chairs out there in the snow."

"Three," someone said.

"Right. Three bodies, three lawn chairs."

"There should only be two bodies," Mrs. Colibri said.

Savage rolled his eyes. "One—Jonathan Rathburn. Two—Orris Cobbett. Three—the cook, and I *still* don't know her name, but she makes three, and—"

"Orris fell off the bridge," someone said.

"And we left him where he fell," someone else said.

Earlene Cobbett let out a reflexive yelp at this last announcement, but no one paid much attention. "My God," Greg Savage said. "I figured three deaths, three bodies. But if Orris is still at the bottom of the gully, that means—"

And they rushed off to see just what it did mean.

Three lawn chairs, three bodies wrapped in sheets and covered with snow. They gathered around, no one quite daring to be the first to yank a sheet off a chair and display its contents. "Oh, somebody do something!" Carolyn cried, and the colonel cleared his throat and grabbed a sheet and gave a yank, sending powdery snow flying and displaying the frozen corpse of Jonathan Rathburn.

The second bedsheet went the way of the first, revealing the late cook.

"I can't stand it," Carolyn groaned, and the colonel tore away the third sheet, and somebody let out a scream, but it wasn't Carolyn. Her worse fears went unrealized.

Because, while there was indeed a fresh corpse in the third chair, it wasn't her uh friend Bernie Rhodenbarr.

It was Gordon Wolpert.

Rhodenbarr did it.

That was the clear consensus. Bernie Rhodenbarr, evidently some sort of crazed mass murderer, had claimed his fourth victim. While pretending to spearhead the investigation, he'd bided his time before adding one more to his chain of murders.

"But that's impossible," Carolyn said. "You people don't know him. He's a good, decent human being."

"He proved that Mr. Rathburn had been murdered," Cissy Eglantine remembered, "when we all thought it was an accident. Why would he do that?"

"To draw suspicion away from himself," her husband suggested.

"But there was no suspicion, Nigel," she said. "Not until he told us it was murder. You don't suppose . . ."

"No," he said firmly. "No, darling. It was not a tramp all along."

"Rhodenbarr did indeed identify Rathburn as a murder victim," the colonel said, picking up the ball. "And he went so far as to spearhead the investigation, if our amateur efforts were worthy of the label. The bloody cheek of the man!"

More than a few eyes turned toward Wolpert, their owners having taken the colonel literally. But there was no blood to be seen upon the dead man's cheek. There were ligature marks on his throat, however, and it appeared that he had been strangled.

"And now he's gone," Rufus Quilp said. "Vanished, into thin air."

"Why?" Carolyn demanded.

"Why?"

"Yeah, why? If he's this diabolical killer who's knocking people off and pretending to investigate all at the same time, why would he cut out and run? Did anybody see him kill Wolpert?" No one had. "So none of us would have had any reason to suspect him. So why wouldn't he stick around and keep on playing the game?"

Someone asked her what she was getting at.

"The truth," she said. "Bernie's here somewhere. He's got to be. He wouldn't kill anybody. And he wouldn't have left, not without me."

"If he's still here," Dakin Littlefield said, "maybe you'd like to point him out to us."

"I thought that was him on the third lawn chair," she said, "and so did everyone else. We were all surprised when it turned out to be Mr. Wolpert."

"I was surprised," Millicent piped up. "But I didn't think it would be Bernie. I thought it would be Orris."

Everyone looked at her. "Orris is dead," her father said patiently.

"I know that."

"He's at the bottom of the gully," her mother put in. "Did you think somebody would go to the trouble to move him?"

"I thought he walked," Millicent said. "You know how people sometimes walk in their sleep? Well, maybe sometimes they walk in their death the same way. It happens a lot in the movies."

"You're not supposed to watch those pictures," Greg said, but Carolyn was wide-eyed, gesturing wildly with her hands.

"Sleepwalking," she said. "That's it! Bernie must have walked in his sleep."

"And while he was sleepwalking," Rufus Quilp murmured, "he went in for a bit of sleep-strangling."

"He must have thought he was going to get help," Carolyn went on, "and he must have forgotten the bridge was out, and—this way, everybody! Hurry!"

And off she went, and off they went after her.

"Look!"

But they were already looking—at a crumpled form down at the bottom of the gully. It lay a few yards distant from another crumpled form, the snow-covered remains of Orris Cobbett. The new crumpled form had a light dusting of snow on it, but not enough to obscure it completely. You could see the pants, the jacket, the shoes.

"That's his jacket," Carolyn cried. "That's his pants. Those are his shoes. Ohmigod, it's him!"

There was a certain amount of discussion as to what ought to be done next. Someone suggested that Rhodenbarr might still be alive. While the same fall had broken Orris's neck, the gully's latest victim might have landed differently, merely breaking a dozen bones and knocking himself senseless. But would he have died of exposure since then? Or might he be still alive, and might quick action prevent his dying of exposure?

"Before you rescue him," Earlene Cobbett said doggedly, "you has got to rescue Orris. Orris fell in first."

"But Orris is dead," someone pointed out.

"Don't matter," Earlene said. "Fair is fair."

"Wait a minute," Carolyn said, pointing. "What's that?"

"What's what?"

"It looks like something poking out of his jacket. You see it? Sort of angling back?"

"Probably a stick," someone said. "Probably a branch dislodged by his fall, so that it tumbled after him and landed on top of him."

"It doesn't look like a stick to me," Carolyn said.

"It doesn't," the colonel agreed, and produced a small pair of field glasses from his jacket pocket. He peered through them, working the knob to adjust the focus. "I say," he said.

"What is it?"

"Nigel," he said, "have a look, why don't you?" And he passed the binoculars to Eglantine.

"I say," Nigel Eglantine said.

"Quite."

"Isn't that—"

"I believe it is, yes."

"Bone handle fitted on a steel tang and wrapped with copper wire, it looks like to me."

"It does, yes."

"Tapering hilt with a slight flare."

"A slight flare, yes."

"And the blade. You can only see two inches of it, but wouldn't you say it's . . ."

His hand scalloped the air.

"Wavy," the colonel said. "Quite."

"I say," Nigel said.

"But you don't," Carolyn cried. "Or if you do say, I can't figure out what you're saying. What's that sticking out of Bernie?"

"It would appear to be a kris," Nigel Eglantine said.

"A crease? You mean it's a shadow where his jacket's creased? It looks like more than that to me."

"K-R-I-S," the colonel said. "It's a dagger, traditional weapon in the Malay States. Saw my share of them in my time, in Sarawak and Penang and other Eastern hellholes. Catch a bleeder skulking around with one of those, you knew he was up to no good."

"I never knew what it was," Nigel put in, "until the colonel identified it for me. It came with the house, you see, like almost all of the decorations, and was hanging on the wall when we bought the place. I'm quite certain it's our kris, though I couldn't swear to it, not from this distance in this light. But it does look as though someone's gone and thrust it into Mr. Rhodenbarr."

The reaction was what you might expect—except, curiously enough, for Ms. Carolyn Kaiser. You might have missed it unless you were watching carefully, but for a moment her expression was one of genuine relief.

TWENTY-TWO

At least that's how I figure it went.

Oh, come on now. You didn't actually think that was *me*, did you? Down at the bottom of the gully? Don't tell me you figured I'd developed a late enthusiasm for body piercing, and the Malayan kris was my idea of a fashion statement.

No, of course not. The crumpled form a few yards from Orris Cobbett's wasn't me. It was a dummy—no cracks, please—a quickly wrought creation consisting of some of my clothing stuffed with the pillows from Jonathan Rathburn's room. I'd fetched the kris from the wall on which I'd noticed it earlier, and it was not without a pang of regret that I stabbed my inoffensive parka in the back. I'd found a spool of fishing line in one of the cupboards, and I'd attached an end of it to the faux Rhodenbarr and lowered it —him?—to the bottom of the gully.

Then I cut the line and tossed the end I was holding into the abyss, figuring nobody would be able to see it. I certainly couldn't, but then I could barely see the dummy, either; it was full dark when I performed these maneuvers, and the little pencil-beam flashlight that goes wherever I go is for peering into drawers and safes in dark apartments, not for gazing into near-bottomless ravines. Its narrow little beam had pretty much petered out by the time it got all the way down there.

I had a reason for all of this.

A good reason, too. It stemmed from more than an urge to be present, à la Tom Sawyer, at my own funeral, or to assert, à la Mark Twain, that reports of my death were greatly exaggerated.

If I was dead, I could move around a little.

Officially dead, that is. Generally Regarded as Dead, say. If everyone took it for granted that I was sprawled lifeless in a frozen creek bed at the bottom of a ravine, I could have the run of the place without people wondering where I was and what I was up to.

Because the immobility was driving me nuts.

At a glance, it might seem odd that I was feeling cramped at Cuttleford House. I'm a New Yorker, and it's not as though I have the space requirements of a rancher in Montana. I live in a small one-bedroom apartment and spend my days in a cluttered bookstore, and I get from one place to the other in a subway car, generally packed shoulder to shoulder among my fellow citizens.

At Cuttleford House, on the other hand, there were more rooms than anyone knew what to do with, and acres of grounds, and plenty of country all around. All of this capaciousness was occupied by a scattering of guests and a small staff, and this human aggregate was itself shrinking on a daily basis. So why was I feeling claustrophobic?

Well, see, in New York the people you see all over the place are strangers. They don't know you and you don't know them, and thus even when you're crammed sardine-style into the rush-hour IRT, you're essentially alone. Anonymous, really. The next thing to invisible.

So I was used to zipping around the city, dashing to and fro, slipping in and out of offices and residences, not always with the tenant's knowledge or permission. That was how I operated. It was the way I earned my living, and it had served me well on the handful of occasions when I'd found myself up to my ears in a homicide investigation.

Carolyn had called me an amateur sleuth, and if I'm any kind of a sleuth at all I'm certainly an amateur. I'm a pro in two other areas, burglary and bookselling, and I know the difference between amateurs and professionals, and when it comes to sleuthery I'm not about to hang out a shingle. I know what detectives do—I ought to, I've read enough books about them. They knock on doors and ask impertinent questions and check alibis and gather evidence and do all sorts of things I'd be no good at.

I don't do that. I sort of slip around and sneak around and stir things up, and sometimes things work out.

But at Cuttleford House everybody was right there. There was never a question of rounding up the usual suspects, because they never strayed very far. They couldn't. The bridge was out and the phone lines were down and the whole place was piled deep with snow.

So what had I done? Well, I'd tried approaching the situation like a real detective, interrogating everybody one at a time, and that hadn't been a great success. Even so, by the end of the day I had a couple of ideas buzzing in my brain. I even had a strong hunch as to the identity of the killer, but it seemed impossible. I needed more information than I had, and I couldn't get it because there were all these people all over the place, watching my every move even as I was watching theirs. (And who could blame them? For all they knew, I was the murderer and they were next on my list.)

And so I worked out a different approach. While the rest of the household slept, I'd skulk around with my flashlight, like Diogenes looking for a dishonest man. While I was at it, I'd take a shot at faking my own death, leaving an apparent corpse in a spot inaccessible enough to discourage close investigation. That would give me a chance to continue skulking in the daytime.

I explained what I had in mind to Carolyn before we turned out our respective bedside lamps. At first she thought I was going to lie down at the bottom of the gully and play dead, and she was concerned that I might catch a bad cold and wind up with pneumonia.

"I might even freeze to death," I told her.

"Then don't do it," she said. "Why take the chance, Bern? It's not worth it."

The news that it wouldn't actually be me down there reassured her, and when I'd run through it a couple of times she said she had it down pat. "The tricky part," I said, "is getting somebody to think of looking in the gully."

"Why don't I just say, 'Hey, guys, maybe he fell in the gully'?"

"That would work," I allowed, "but it would be better if someone else thought of it."

"So they don't think it's a setup."

"Right."

"I'll work on it," she said. "And you'll be out of the way somewhere while we're all running around searching the house?"

"Snug," I said, "as a bug in a rug."

"But that's hours from now. What'll you be doing between now and then?"

"Setting the stage," I said. "Going places. Doing things."

"Going where? Doing what?"

"Here and there," I said. "This and that."

"And you're not gonna tell me who the killer is."

"Not until I know for sure."

She yawned. "I'd argue the point," she said, "if I weren't so tired. Aren't you tired, Bern?"

"Exhausted."

"Can I ask a dumb question? How are you gonna stay up all night sneaking around in the dark? You'll be dead on your feet tomorrow."

"Never mind tomorrow," I said. "I'll be dead on my feet tonight."

"So why not forget it, Bern? Get a good night's sleep. Sleep late, in fact, and take a nap tomorrow during the day, and if the police don't turn up by then you can stay up tomorrow night."

"You're tempting me."

"So? Do what I always do when I'm tempted."

"Surrender to it?"

"Hey," she said. "Works for me, Bern."

I said I'd let my body decide. I read for a few minutes and turned off the light, and there was a moment when I almost drifted off, but it passed and I knew it wasn't going to happen. But I waited until Carolyn was sleeping, snug in the arms of Morpheus or Molly Cobbett, before I got out of bed.

And then I got dressed in the darkness and let myself out of the room. But I already told you about that, didn't I?

I had things to do and I got busy doing them. My first stop was Young George's Room, way down at the other end of the long hallway. I didn't have to worry that someone would catch sight of me, because I wasn't doing anything all that suspicious. I could always say I was looking for an unoccupied bathroom, or stretching my legs, but I didn't encounter anyone so it didn't matter.

The only thing that would have been hard to explain was picking the lock and letting myself into Rathburn's room, and to minimize the chance of discovery I spent as little time at the task as possible. Earlier I'd tried my own key in the lock for starters, and I wouldn't have been much surprised if it had worked. Those old skeleton keys are often virtually interchangeable, especially when the locks are old and well used.

The key didn't work, but my picks did, and in not much more time than it would take to turn a key. I darted inside, closed and locked the door, and stopped myself even as I was fumbling for the light switch. No need to let light leak out into the hallway from underneath the door. The average person would never notice, but there was a murderer in our midst. He was the one person likely to notice, and the one whose attention I most particularly wanted to escape.

I stayed put for about an hour and a half, going through the effects of the late Jonathan Rathburn and searching for something in writing that he might have left behind. I found enough to keep me interested until I figured the household had had a chance to settle in for the night. Then I raided the closet for clothes and took the pillow from the bed and let myself out of there.

I was downstairs and headed out the door when I remembered the kris. I remembered what room it was in but wasn't sure how to get there, and I was tempted to settle for some other imperial artifact—an assegai spear, say, or a horn from the oryx. But I found the kris in due course. Next I rifled a pantry, looking for some kind of twine or cord, and couldn't come up with anything better than a ball of cotton thread. It didn't seem very strong to me. Then I came across the fishing line, and took them both.

The line was what I used for actually lowering the dummy, but the thread came in handy for stitching the thing together. I used the pillow and some of Rathburn's clothes for stuffing, and I tied a pair of his shoes to the pants cuffs by their laces, and tied the cuffs of the jacket sleeves tight around a pair of my own gloves. (If he'd had any gloves, I couldn't find them.) I couldn't get the head so it looked right—it was just a ball of clothes tied in shape with string—and up close it was about as deceptive as a scarecrow, which, come to think of it, it rather resembled.

I reminded myself that no one was going to get a close look at it, but all the same I retied it. I wrapped a dark shirt around the top portion, so that it looked like a cap of dark hair over the white undershirt that was supposed to look like a face. Lowering the sucker turned out to be one of those things that are easier said than done, and it wasn't made any easier by the fact that (a) I was lying on my belly with my arms out over the edge and the flashlight in my mouth and (b) I was still petrified of falling. I had to lower it slowly, too, because I knew how amateurishly I had constructed it. If it landed with any impact I was sure it would come apart, and while that may also happen with real people dropped from a great height, I somehow didn't think the results would be convincing in the present instance.

So I lowered the dummy slowly and gently, resisting the impulse to jiggle the line and adjust its position once it had come to rest. I gave the end of the fishing line a toss, transferred the little flashlight from my mouth to my hand, and looked at what I'd done.

Was it deceptive?

Hard to say. It didn't fool me, but then how could it? I knew better. It could pass for a bundle of rags, certainly, but so could the mortal remains of poor Orris. Could it pass for a body?

Not if some passing animal pawed at it, like a mad laundress bent on separating whites and colors.

Not if anyone took a really close look.

On the other hand, what would happen if my little subterfuge was spotted? The logical assumption, it seemed to me, would be that I had done the faking. And why would I have done such a thing? Because I was a murderer, obviously, and because I had hotfooted it, and wanted to delay pursuit.

In which case they'd assume I was off the premises, which, for my purposes, was the next best thing to being dead.

No time to brood about it, though. No time to worry and wonder. I had things to do.

I got busy doing them.

I'd been on the verge of sleep earlier, lying next to Carolyn in Aunt Augusta's Room, but once I was up and dressed I'd caught a second wind, and it carried me a long ways. I was still going strong when the eastern sky began to show the first signs that eternal night had not yet descended upon the planet. There would indeed be a dawn, and it looked as though I'd be around to see it.

I was perhaps fifty yards from the front door of Cuttleford House when I noticed that faint glow in the east. You might think it would have heartened me, but all it really did was make me aware of the lateness of the hour, which in turn served to remind me that I'd been awake for almost twenty-four hours, that I was cold and wet and exhausted, and that if I didn't get into a warm bed soon I might very well drop in my tracks.

I walked the rest of the way along the path to the front door, past the sugar-sabotaged snowblower, past the little red wagons. I used my picks on the lock and tickled it open, but the door wouldn't budge. A close look showed why. Someone had slid the heavy bolt across.

It was hard to imagine why. There we were, out in the middle of nowhere, cut off utterly from the rest of the world and snowbound in the bargain. Cissy Eglantine's fixation on the proverbial passing tramp notwithstanding, I had a hunch the nearest indigent wayfarer was hustling passersby in Boston Common, trying to raise busfare to Miami. So why bolt the door?

Habit, I guessed. It had been bolted until I let myself out earlier, and evidently someone had passed it during the night, noticed the unbolted state in which I'd left it, and shot the bolt home. Had I world enough and time I could have dealt with it, but it was simpler by far to walk around the house and find an unbolted door.

There was always the kitchen door, which may or may

not have been bolted, but I didn't get to find out. Before I reached it, in fact just after I'd passed the three lawn chairs with their grisly burden, I came to the door of a glassed-in back porch, the sort of room where people go to take the sun without having to endure fresh air. The door was all small panes of glass, and there's not much point fastening elaborate hardware on a door like that, as anyone who wants to get in can just break one of the panes and reach in. So the lock was about what you'd expect. A clever woman could have opened it with a bobby pin. I used my picks. There was a latch as well, one of those hook-and-eye arrangements. All you have to do to defeat them is slip a wallet-size plastic calendar between the door and the frame and give a flick upward, lifting the hook from the eye, and that is precisely what I did.

I locked up after myself, slipping the hook back into the eye, and inclined my head respectfully when I caught sight of the three lawn chairs, each bearing a late member of our little company. Then, without further ado, I quit the little sunroom and began working my way through the maze of rooms.

The house was not entirely silent. There was the odd creaking noise to be heard, and the occasional footfall. With that many people under one roof, it was unlikely that there was ever a moment when not a creature was stirring. If that created the possibility that I might run into somebody on my way back to Mr. Rathburn's room, it also meant I could put a foot wrong and step on a creaking board myself without raising suspicion. It didn't matter greatly if people heard me moving about, just so nobody had a clear view of me.

So I kept to the shadows and scouted out each room before I entered it. The staircase and the upstairs hallway were dangerous areas, open and exposed, and I intended to spend no more time traversing them than I absolutely had to.

I was two-thirds of the way up the stairs when it hit me. Three lawn chairs?

I kept going.

I'd left Rathburn's door unlocked in the interest of saving time going and coming, and for a change no one had happened along to alter the status quo. I let myself in, closed the door, and concentrated on picking the lock shut, which is essentially the same process as unlocking it, though understandably less exciting. It gave me something to think about, which kept me from having to consider the implications of the third lawn chair. But it didn't take very long, and it took no time at all to work the little sliding bolt, and there I was, tucked safely away in Rathburn's room, with plenty of time to wonder what that third lawn chair was doing there and just whose mortal remains might be weighing it down.

How, I wondered, could I have failed to notice the three chairs? Well, I told myself, I'd had a long day and a busy night, and it was fair to say I was exhausted. Nor was it entirely accurate to say I'd failed to notice the chairs. Obviously I'd noticed them, or I wouldn't be agonizing over them now. What I'd done was fail to register the fact that there was one more corpse-laden chair than there ought to have been.

What did it mean?

Maybe it didn't mean anything at all. Maybe there'd always been three chairs there, two of them pressed into service to hold the bodies of Rathburn and the cook, and one holding something completely uninteresting. Lawn and garden supplies, say. Perhaps all three chairs had been so encumbered originally. Then the clutter on two of the chairs had been transferred to the third, and the bodies shifted, and all three draped with sheets.

Possible, I decided, but not probable. It was far more likely that the third chair, like its fellows, had a corpse on it.

But whose?

The answer would have to wait. For all I knew it could be just about anybody. The only person I could rule out with any real certainty was Bernie Rhodenbarr. Last I saw of him, poor devil, he was at the bottom of the gully.

What I needed was an hour of sleep.

Well, no. What I *needed* was more like eight hours, but that was out of the question. Failing that, an hour or so would give me a chance of functioning with some semblance of efficiency. It wouldn't set me up so that I'd be operating at the top of my game, but that was all right. After all, I wasn't planning to drive or operate machinery. I just wanted to solve a few murders and go home.

Rathburn's effects didn't seem to include a travel alarm clock, and Cuttleford House wasn't the sort of establishment where you could ring the desk and leave a wake-up call. I thought maybe I could just lie down with my eyes closed and rest rather than sleep, but I saw right away that wasn't going to work.

So I just gave up and let go. I'm usually a fairly light sleeper, and I figured I'd wake up when Carolyn raised the alarm. If not, well, I'd hear them banging on the door. The bolt would keep them on the outside, and they wouldn't figure it was bolted, they'd figure their key wasn't working, and when that happened . . .

I don't know what I thought would happen after that. Because by the time I'd got that far in my thoughts I was asleep.

I slept for an hour and a half, and nothing in particular woke me. There were sounds to be heard—people walking around, stairs creaking, old plumbing making the sounds old plumbing makes—but none of them sufficiently intrusive to wake a person up. But they say everybody has a personal inner alarm clock, and evidently mine was working.

I listened at the door, fairly certain Carolyn had not yet gone into her act. I couldn't detect anything out of the ordinary, so I drew back the bolt and started to ease the door open a crack, but of course I couldn't. I'd picked it shut. Now I could pick it open again, only to pick it shut once more in a minute or two, and for what? So that I could watch Rufus Quilp waddle across the floor to the bathroom? It hardly seemed worth it.

I grabbed a chair and sat on it. A pair of walkie-talkies, I thought, would have simplified operations considerably. I could get Carolyn out of bed and into action. The sooner she got moving, the sooner I'd be able to move. I could get to work. I could get to business. I could go to the bathroom.

Ah, yes. There's that bit of business Ben Franklin stole from George Herbert: "For want of a nail a shoe was lost, for want of a shoe a horse was lost, for want of a horse a rider was lost." I don't know how many riders—and battles, and wars—have actually been lost for a nail, but I've sometimes wondered how often the course of history has been changed in one direction or another because somebody had to pee. I don't know if its results are quite as dire as losing a nail out of a horseshoe, but I have a feeling it comes up more often.

It would have been nice if Cuttleford House's commitment to quaintness included a chamber pot beneath the bed, but if such a thing had ever existed, some prior occupant of Young George's Room had taken it home for use as a soup tureen.

Of course, I thought, if Carolyn would quit dreaming about unavailable chambermaids and raise the alarm for her absent best friend, the problem would soon be resolved. Once everyone gathered together, all I had to do was wait until the group had removed to the ground floor. Then I could have my pick of bathrooms, but until then it wasn't safe to set foot in the hallway.

And how long, really, could a person be expected to wait?

I don't want to dwell on this subject, it's not a fit one for polite discourse, but neither do I want to leave you wondering.

So how will it be if I simply state that there was a time when I opened the window and held out a shoe which had once belonged to Jonathan Rathburn, and for which he could be presumed to have no further use. I turned the shoe upside down, and then I brought it back in again, and closed the window.

So much for that. Now all I had to do was wait for Carolyn to wake up, and hope she hadn't forgotten what she was supposed to do. We're none of us at our best first thing in the morning, and Carolyn had had the odd wee dram of malt the night before. I could picture her wondering where I'd disappeared to and dismissing the question with a shrug as she tucked into a hearty breakfast of fly-in-the-oatmeal or some such traditional British treat.

"And wherever is your uh husband, Mrs. Rhodenbarr?"

"You mean Bernie? Gee, I dunno. . . . Omigod, we've got to find him! He's disappeared!"

She'd get it right, I assured myself. And until she did, all I could do was wait.

No problem. I had something to read.

No problem at all, as it turned out. Carolyn did wake up, and did remember her lines, and did succeed in communicating her feigned panic to the rest of the household. My door (or Rathburn's, if you prefer, or Young George's) was unbolted but still locked when they got to it, and the lock yielded readily enough to the master key.

"No one here," Nigel Eglantine announced, and the horde gathered itself and prepared to head elsewhere. I distinguished various voices in the throng—Carolyn sounding on the brink of panic, Leona Savage murmuring reassurance—and then Dakin Littlefield's voice rang out like a cracked bell.

"Not so fast," he said. "Nobody checked the closet."

"Why bother?" Carolyn said quickly. "He's not here. What would he be doing in the closet?"

"Dropping down to room temperature," Littlefield said. "If he's dead somebody must have stowed him somewhere, and the closet's as good a place as any. If it was worth looking in this room, it's worth looking in the closet."

"Let me," Carolyn said. "Bernie? Bernie, are you in there?"

"If he's dead," Littlefield told her, "you'll be a long time waiting for an answer. Open the door, why don't you?"

"It's stuck. This is ridiculous, he's not in here, and we're wasting time when we could be—"

"Stuck?" Littlefield did a lot with the one syllable, making it clear somehow that an inability to open the closet door indicated not only physical but mental and moral weakness. "Let's just see how stuck it is," he said, and flung the thing open.

TWENTY-THREE

There was a sound that may have been Carolyn catching her breath, then a snort of disappointment from Littlefield. "Zilch," he announced. "Just poor Rathburn's clothes. He bought cheap crap, didn't he?" He sniffed. "Smells a little funky in here, like somebody took a leak in one of his shoes. Probably that damned cat."

"Raffles is toilet trained," Carolyn said.

"Good for him. Anyway, it'd smell a lot worse if there was a body turning sour in here. We're wasting time."

And off they went. The last person out closed the door, remarkably enough, and nobody bothered to lock it, which would save me a minute or two, and spare that much wear on my burglar's tools.

I waited another minute, just to make sure nobody came back for a last look, and crawled out from under the bed.

See, you had nothing to worry about. You were not fooled. You already knew they were still looking for me when they spotted the dummy at the bottom of the ravine.

So your heart didn't threaten to seize when Littlefield opened the closet.

Carolyn's did. She was sure I was in Rathburn's room, because I'd said that was where I'd probably be. They might very well pass up searching the room altogether, I'd told her, but if they looked they wouldn't find me, because I'd be tucked away somewhere, probably in the closet.

I don't know what made me dive under the bed instead. Maybe I was reluctant to share close quarters with Rathburn's shoes. More likely I remembered all the closets I'd stowed away in over the years and figured I'd be pushing my luck to try that old trick yet again. I'd been under Rathburn's bed earlier, looking for the chamber pot that wasn't there, so I knew I'd fit, albeit snugly. So that's where I was, and a good thing, too.

If I'd thought of it, I'd have left the closet door wide open. They wouldn't have had to cross the threshold to see that the room was empty, and after a glance or two they'd have been on their way. But I'd left the door closed—Rathburn's shoes may have had something to do with it—and that was enough to catch Littlefield's interest. Carolyn was certain I was in the closet, and thus tried to keep the door closed. For my part, I wished they would open the damn thing and be done with it, before someone else got the bright idea to look under the bed.

Later, when they uncovered the corpses on the three lawn chairs, Carolyn didn't have to work at it to look frightened. Because if I wasn't in Rathburn's closet she didn't know where I was, so it was entirely possible that was me on one of those lawn chairs.

Once they were done checking the bedrooms and had begun the process of searching for me on the ground floor, it was my turn to return the favor and give their rooms a toss. I'd gone door-to-door in much the same fashion many years ago, when a fellow named Louis Lewis sold me a passkey that would open every room in the old Taft Hotel. I'd considered spacing my visits over a week or two, hitting a half-dozen rooms each time, but this was a while ago, and the fires of youth burned in my blood. I was impatient. I wanted instant gratification, and I didn't want to wait for it, either.

So I booked a room at the Taft under a name selected for the occasion and let a bellhop bring my two large suitcases to my room. I checked in at three in the afternoon and checked out at seven the following morning, and by the time I left I'd been in more rooms than the Gideon Bible. The Taft was a huge hotel, and there was no way to hit every room, but I did my best. I'd go up to a door, knock gently, wait a moment, knock again, and then let myself in. It doesn't take long to search a hotel room—the occupants haven't been there long enough to build up an accumulation of clutter—so it's just a matter of checking the drawers and closet, going through the luggage, and dipping into the pockets of clothes in the closet.

More often than not there was nothing to take. But here and there I found jewelry, some of it worth lifting, and here and there I found cash. During the early-evening hours most of the rooms I hit were empty, but as the night wore on guests came back to the hotel and turned in for the night. Some growled at my knock, or came to the door; a simple apology sent them back to bed. Others didn't hear me knocking, nor did they hear me open their doors and pad softly around their carpeted floors. My visits were briefer when the occupants were in, but they were also more profitable, because if they were home so were their purses and wallets. I didn't have to look hard to find them, either.

Then back to my room to stow my prizes. Then off, pass-key in hand, eager as a kid on Christmas morning, wondering what the next pretty package would hold.

Ah, youth! When I left the next morning I'd jettisoned the phone books that had given my suitcases a feeling of respectable substance, and I'd filled both bags with well-gotten gains. I don't know how I wound up after I'd tallied the cash and fenced the rest of the swag, and I'm sure it didn't add up to what I'd expect to net nowadays from a single halfway decent stamp or coin collection, but it was a decent night's work all the same. And I felt like a hero, a veritable superman of burglars. I'd pulled not one job but dozens of jobs, one right after the other.

Of course, it's not all that tricky when you've got a key.

I didn't have a key this time, and it would have speeded things up, no question about it. No matter how quick you are with your picks and probes, a key makes it quicker. Still, a couple of guests had leveled the playing fields for me a bit by neglecting to lock their doors. I was grateful, if a touch bemused. It's nice, I suppose, to go about assuming one's fellow guests are as honest as oneself, but doesn't the illusion get harder to maintain when people are getting bumped off left and right? I suppose a properly brought up murderer will still draw the line at entering another person's private quarters, but even so . . .

I went about my work. I had to remind myself not to steal—old habits die hard—but the situation was urgent enough to keep me pretty well focused on the business at hand. I made sure I stayed a floor away from the rest of them, and I ducked out of sight when I heard someone on the stairs. When they were all on the ground floor I had a quick look at the servants' quarters up above. A little later, when I looked out the window and saw them heading down the path toward the fallen bridge, I seized the moment and made a foray into a couple of rooms on the ground floor.

I came out of the Eglantine apartment knowing I wasn't going to have much more time. It was cold out, and they'd been in too much of a hurry to bundle up, so they'd want to get back inside the house as soon as possible. I was counting on it, as a matter of fact; the more uncomfortable they were out there, the less time they'd waste on a good look at the late Bernard Grimes Rhodenbarr.

But I wanted a look at those lawn chairs.

The voices had been too muffled earlier for me to tell what had excited them, though I suspected it might be the lawn chairs out behind the house. Was there a fresh corpse on one of those chairs? And, if so, whose was it?

I found my way to the sunroom. Through its windows I saw the three chairs, and I could tell I wasn't the only one who'd noticed. The snow was tamped down all around them, and the snow-covered sheets that shrouded them had been removed.

But, alas, they'd been replaced. They weren't covered with snow now, but they still hid the chairs' contents from view.

Three bodies. I could tell that much, given a good look in decent light. But who was the latest victim?

All I had to do was go out and have a look. But I could already hear them on their way back to the house, all talking at once, their voices a discordant blur. By the time I got out the door and ran over to the chairs and had a look—

No time.

I raced for the stairs.

Back in Young George's Room, which I found myself regarding less and less as Jonathan Rathburn's and more and more as my own, I sat on the edge of the bed and tried to figure out what to do next. I had a pad of paper in front of me and I had drawn a rough diagram, with a lot of circles and X's and arrows. It was supposed to represent how the sequence of killings had taken place, and a look at my handiwork suggested that the killer must have been a geometry teacher. No one else could have made sense of it.

When I wasn't looking at the diagram or off into space, I was checking my watch. Sooner or later I was going to have to leave my comfy little hiding place and show my face in the world, or at least in the more populated regions of Cuttleford House. I'd bought some time by faking my own death, and I'd spent some of it to good effect in my room-by-room tour of the place. Now I had all the data I was likely to get, and I had things figured out.

Well, almost figured out.

Sort of.

And now it seemed to me that timing was critical. I didn't want to make my move too early, nor did I want to leave it too late. After breakfast, say, but before they'd all scattered to different parts of the house. And certainly before anyone could take it into his head to leave.

Tricky.

So I kept glancing at my watch, and an ineffectual gesture it was, since I couldn't have told you what time I was waiting for it to be. And then, just sitting there like that, it became evident to me that I wasn't going to be able to allow myself the relative luxury of waiting until it was time to leave.

I needed to go to the bathroom.

Well, it happens, for God's sake. It never happens in Agatha Christie's books, and I can't recall it ever posing a problem for an earthy guy like Philip Marlowe, either, but that's not a whole lot of consolation when the necessity arises.

It had arisen before, you're probably thinking, and I dealt with it, if not elegantly, at least effectively. Couldn't I just do again as I did before? And, preferably, without talking about it?

Believe me, I'd just as soon not talk about it. And, not to put too fine a point on it, let me just state that the function I needed to perform was different in kind from the previous instance, and that the shoe-and-window number simply would not do at all.

I've thought about this since, and it seems to me that one's behavior in such a situation varies with the direness of one's circumstances. If I'd been hiding from the Nazis in war-torn Belgium, say, I'd have fouled my nest and learned to live with it. But I just wasn't that desperate. I didn't know who might be lurking in the hallway outside my door, but I could be fairly sure it wasn't the Gestapo.

I eased the door open a crack and took a look-see. I couldn't spot anybody, and the only sounds of human activity I could make out were a floor away. I opened the door a little farther and scanned the long hall. I caught a trace of movement out of the corner of my eye, and that might have inspired more in the way of reconnaissance at a less urgent moment, but I couldn't wait. I rushed down the hall to the bathroom, darted inside, and, well, let's for God's sake draw the curtain on the next several moments, shall we?

Thanks. I feel better already.

———

I'd closed the bedroom door when I left it, but of course I hadn't wasted time locking it, so I didn't have to waste time unlocking it on my return. I slipped inside, heaved a great sigh, and slid the bolt across. Then I sat down once again on the edge of the bed and tried to remember what I'd been thinking about before Nature had called.

Timing, that was part of it. And some of the details about the string of murders. A thought came along and I frowned at it, trying to pin it down and think it through. I was getting somewhere in the old ratiocination process, it seemed to me, and then Raffles brushed against my ankle and began purring, and my train of thought was shunted off on a sidetrack.

I patted my lap, a clear invitation for him to spring up, but he didn't seem to notice. His purring picked up in volume, and he was really busy rubbing his head against my ankles, which meant either that he was damned glad to see me or that his ear itched and this was the best way he could think of to scratch it.

Of course, I thought, the two possibilities were not mutually exclusive. He could have an itching ear *and* still entertain a feeling of abiding affection for the chap who kept him in Meow Mix. For my part, I was pleased to discover that I was glad to see him. So I reached down and scooped him up and plopped him down on my lap, where he continued to purr up a storm.

"Good old Raffles," I said aloud, and gave him a scratch behind the ear. "Didn't see much of you last night. How'd you get through the hours?"

He didn't answer, but then he never does. But I went on looking at him and petting him, and another far more unsettling question came to me.

How the hell did he get in the room?

He would have had to come in while I was in the john down the hall. Because he certainly hadn't been in the room before then, and here he was, big as life.

But how did he do it?

Simple—he followed me home. He was in the hallway when I finished up in the bathroom. I hadn't noticed him because I wasn't looking at the floor when I scanned the area, being on the lookout for a taller specimen.

Could he have done that? Scooted in right behind me without my noticing?

No, I decided. I would have noticed.

He couldn't have managed it when I first eased the door open a crack, either, or when I let myself out. And then I'd closed the door.

Could I have unwittingly left it slightly ajar? If so, he could have come on in. But it had definitely been closed when I came back. He wouldn't have closed it, let alone slammed it with enough force to make it click shut.

Why was I making so much of this? The steps were clear. A—I leave the room, thinking I've closed the door but failing to engage the latch. B—Raffles, finding the door ajar, enters. C—An air current closes the door again, and makes a better job of it than I had done. D—I return, find the door closed, which is how I incorrectly believe I've left it. E—I enter, close the door, fasten the bolt, and am subsequently bewildered to find myself with a cat on my lap.

I decided it was possible. Not too probable, however. Then I remembered the old dictum about ruling out everything that was strictly impossible. If you did that, whatever possibility remained, however improbable, had to be the truth.

Had I ruled out every other possibility?

A chill came over me, along with an awareness of a possibility I had not ruled out, because I hadn't thought of it. I took a deep breath and let it out, and I sent my eyes on as much of a tour of the room as they could manage without moving my head. And then I said, in what was supposed to be a forceful but low-pitched voice, "Now would be a good time to come out of the closet."

There was no response, not even from Raffles.

"I mean it," I said, wondering if I did. "You can come out of the closet now."

"No I can't," came the reply, in a small high-pitched voice. "I'm under the bed."

And then she giggled, the imp. I stood up. Raffles sprang forward involuntarily when my lap disappeared, landing predictably enough on all four feet and giving me a look. And, even as I had done a while earlier, out from under the bed crawled the improbable person of Millicent Savage.

TWENTY-FOUR

"You're not a ghost," she said. "At least I don't think you are. Are you?"

I considered the question. "No," I said. "I'm not."

"Would you tell me if you were?"

"That's hard to say," I admitted. "Who knows what a ghost would do?"

"Not me," she said. "I don't even know if I believe in them. And when I saw you in the hallway I didn't think you were a ghost."

"How come?"

"I didn't think you were dead. In fact I thought you were right here, in Young George's Room. You know what my father calls it? 'Boy George's Room,' "

"He's probably not the only one. How come you didn't think I was dead?"

"Because I saw you under the bed."

"You did?"

She nodded. "When Mr. Littlefield wanted to open the closet door, and Carolyn didn't want him to. At least I thought I saw you under the bed. I saw *something* under the bed, but I couldn't be sure what it was unless I got down on all fours and checked, and I couldn't do that because my father was holding my hand."

"Good for him," I said.

"Then Mr. Littlefield opened the door," she went on, "and there was nobody there. And I almost said something."

"I'm glad you didn't."

" 'Look under the bed,' I almost said. But I didn't want to help Mr. Littlefield. I don't like him."

"Neither do I."

"And besides," she said, "how could I be sure it was you?"

"It could have been anybody."

"I wasn't even sure it was a person."

"That's a point. It could have been a monster."

She rolled her eyes.

"Well, maybe a troll," I said.

"They live under bridges," she said. "*Not* under beds."

"I stand corrected."

"When there was an extra body on one of the chairs behind the house," she said, "I thought it was you, and I was positive I made a mistake thinking I saw you under the bed. But then it wasn't you, it was someone you killed, and . . ."

"I didn't kill anybody."

"Are you sure?"

"Positive."

"Because everybody thinks . . ."

"I know what everybody thinks. I didn't kill anybody."

"Not ever? Not in your whole life?"

"Well," I said, "I'm still young."

She giggled. "I believe you," she said, "because you say funny things. I don't think a murderer would say funny things, do you?"

"No," I said, "and neither would a ghost."

She thought that over, shrugged. "Anyway," she said, "it turned out you were dead after all. Somebody stabbed you and threw your body off the cliff. I wasn't supposed to look, but I did."

"And?"

"And what?"

"Well? Did it look convincing?"

"I didn't get a very good look," she said. "I guess it looked like a body, and somebody recognized the clothes. But you know what I kept thinking about?"

"What?"

"The crease."

"The crease? Oh—" I drew a wavy line in the air. "The kris."

"That's what I said."

"I know. What about it?"

"If *I* stabbed somebody," she said, "I don't think I would drag him all the way to the edge of the cliff and push him over. And if he was already standing at the edge I wouldn't stab him first, I'd just push him in. And if I did stab him for some reason, and then I wanted to throw him in to make it look like he fell, I'd remove the kris and hang it up on the wall again."

"I guess the kris was overkill."

"I just kept thinking about it," Millicent said, "and I started thinking maybe that was you under the bed after all. And then I thought maybe it was a *ghost* under the bed.

Do you ever have times when the more you think about something, the more confusing it gets?"

"Boy, do I ever."

"After everybody came back to the house, I waited until nobody was paying attention. And I came upstairs and I put my ear to the door of this room and listened real hard."

"What did you hear?"

"Nothing."

"Oh."

"I was too scared to open the door. So I went down the hall to my room and sat in the doorway and watched. I can be very patient."

"An uncommon trait in one so young."

"Well, I can. And I was watching when you stuck your head out, and I quick drew back so you wouldn't see me. But I saw you hurry down the hall to the bathroom."

"And not a moment too soon," I recalled.

"I was pretty sure it was you and not a ghost. You know why?"

"Why?"

"Ghosts don't have to go to the bathroom."

"Sure they do."

"They do not."

"They most certainly do. Haven't you ever gotten a package in the mail? And when you opened it up, did it have some packing material to keep it from getting broken?"

"So?"

"Little white stuff the size of your thumb," I said. "You probably were told it was Styrofoam."

"It *is* Styrofoam."

"Nope."

"Then what is it?"

"Ghost turds."

I thought that would get a laugh, but all she did was roll her eyes. *"Anyway,"* she said heavily, "Raffles came along while you were in the bathroom, and I figured he would know."

"If I was a ghost or not."

"Right. So I grabbed him and brought him with me and came in here. At first we were both under the bed, but when you opened the door he trotted out to see what was going on. Can I ask a question?"

"I don't see how I could stop you."

"Why are you pretending to be dead?"

"Because I'm going to trap the killer."

"Do you know who it is?"

"I think so, yes."

"Tell me!"

I shook my head. "Not now," I said. "But there's something you've got to tell me."

"What? I don't know anything."

"You know who the latest victim is."

"It's you," she said, "or at least it's supposed to be. Down at the bottom of the gully."

"That's just smoke and mirrors," I said.

"Smoke and mirrors?"

"Well, clothes and pillows. It wasn't really me down there, Millicent, and it wasn't anybody else, either."

"I know."

"But there was a real Latest Victim," I said. "On one of those lawn chairs out behind the house. There was Jonathan Rathburn and there was the cook, and there was a third victim on a third chair."

"So?"

"So tell me who it was."

Light dawned. "You don't know," she said. "Everybody thinks you know because everybody thinks you killed him, or at least they did until it turned out that you were dead, too. But you didn't kill him, even if you don't happen to be dead yourself, and . . ."

"Right."

"So you don't know."

"But I will," I said, "as soon as you tell me."

She looked at me.

"What's the matter?"

"I know who got killed," she said, giving it a sort of singsong cadence, "and you don't. And *you* know who the killer is, and *I* don't."

"Time to strike a deal, huh?"

She nodded solemnly.

"Okay," I said. "You tell me who was on the chair, and I'll tell you who put him there."

" 'Him'?"

"You mean it was a woman?"

"Maybe," she said. "Maybe it was a woman and maybe it was a man. That's for me to know."

"And for me to find out," I finished, "and the way I'll find out is by you telling me."

"And then you'll tell me who did it."

"Right."

"Okay," she said.

"It's a deal?"

She nodded. "It's a deal."

"So?"

"So what?"

"So tell me."

She frowned. "I think you should go first."

"Why? Don't you trust me?"

She didn't say anything, which was answer enough. I could have gone first, but if she didn't trust me, why should I trust her? I dug out my wallet, looked for scraps of paper, and wound up drawing out a pair of dollar bills. I gave one of them to Millicent.

"In the space alongside Washington's portrait," I said. "Just print the victim's name there, and I'll do the same with the killer's name."

"I think it's against the law to write on money."

"If they arrest you for it," I said, "tell them it was my idea. No cheating, now. No writing 'Mickey Mouse' to fake me out. Okay?"

"I wouldn't do that."

"Sure you would," I said, "and so would I, but not today. Deal?" She nodded, and I printed the name of my favorite suspect, shielding the action from view with my left hand. When I finished I folded the bill, folded it again, and held it out to the child. With my other hand I took hold of the bill she was offering, similarly folded. Our eyes locked, and she counted to three, and at once we completed the exchange.

I unfolded the bill, looked at what she'd written. I looked at Millicent, and found her looking back at me.

"You're sure of this?"

She nodded, her eyes enormous. "I thought it was going to be you," she said, "but it was him instead."

"Gordon Wolpert. With the tweed jackets and the elbow patches and . . ."

"That's him."

"And he was dead." I frowned. "Do you suppose it was accidental? Maybe he was overcome with remorse and he pulled up a chair to sit next to the two people he'd killed, and before he knew it he'd fallen asleep and frozen to death."

She gave me a look. "Anyway," she said, "there were marks on his neck. They said he'd been strangled."

"Strangled.

"Did anybody look at his eyes? I wonder if he had pinpoint hemorrhages. But maybe you only get those if somebody smothers you. Wait a minute. Strangled? Maybe he hanged himself. Maybe he was overcome with remorse"—I seemed attached to the phrase—"and he hanged himself from a beam or something, and—"

"And what?"

"And cut himself down and went outside and sat on a lawn chair with a blanket over him. Never mind. Gordon Wolpert, for God's sake. You're sure it was him? Of course you're sure."

"And you're sure he was the killer?"

"Well, no," I said. "I was a few minutes ago. Now I'm not sure of anything."

I got to my feet, crossed to the chest of drawers, and picked up a book I'd been reading earlier, holding it as though absorbing its essence might somehow empower me. Gordon Wolpert, who I'd somehow managed to convince myself was a multiple murderer, had in turn managed to persuade someone else to murder him.

I opened a drawer, put the book inside. I opened the closet door, got a whiff of Rathburn's shoes, and closed it again.

"It's time," I said.

"Time for what, Bernie?"

"Time for action. You know what Chandler said, don't you? When things start to slow down, bring in a couple of guys with guns in their hands."

"Have you got a gun?"

"No," I said, "and I'm only one man, but it's high time I found a couple of mean streets to walk down. I want you to go downstairs, Millicent."

"And leave you and Raffles here?"

"You can take Raffles with you," I said. "The main thing is I want you to get them all in one room."

"Which room?"

"The library," I said. "That's where it all started. That's where it should end."

TWENTY-FIVE

They were all in the library.

I don't know how she managed it, but somehow she'd rounded them all up. They perched on chairs and sofas, stood propped against walls and bookshelves, or huddled in twos and threes to talk, probably wondering why she'd summoned them all there.

Which could have been my opening line. "I suppose you're wondering why she summoned you all here," I might very well have said.

But I didn't. I just walked across the threshold and took note of their reactions.

And they damn well reacted. Their eyes widened, their jaws dropped, and a few of them went a shade or two paler. Miss Dinmont's hands tightened their grip on the arms of her wheelchair, Mrs. Colibri clutched at a bookcase for support, and Colonel Blount-Buller's upper lip lost a little of its stiffness. There was a fair amount of gasping, but no one actually said anything, until Lettice Littlefield cried out, "Bernie! Is it really you?"

"In the flesh," I said, and pinched myself. "See? You're not dreaming, and I'm not a ghost."

"But you were—"

"Down at the bottom of the gully, creased with a kris," I said. "Except I wasn't, not really. And one reason I burst in on you like this was to see which dog didn't bark."

That got some stares of incomprehension. "*The Hound of the Baskervilles*," I explained. "What Holmes found significant was that the dog didn't bark. Well, if somebody didn't twitch or gape or go pale at my appearance, it meant he wasn't surprised. And who would be unsurprised to find me still alive? The person who knew I wasn't dead. And who would know that better than the man who didn't kill me?"

"Well said," the colonel allowed, and a couple of heads nodded their approval of my logic.

Then Leona Savage said, "I didn't kill you."

"Huh? No, of course you didn't, and—"

"I didn't kill you," she insisted, "but I was surprised to see you here, because I saw what I took to be you at the bottom of the gully and consequently thought you were dead. I'm not the man who didn't kill you, but I'm certainly one of the persons who didn't kill you, and I was surprised nonetheless. It's a good thing I didn't have a heart attack."

"An excellent thing," I agreed, "and I'm sorry to have shocked you, but—"

"In fact," she pressed on, "nobody here killed you, because you're still very much alive. So I don't see—"

"Oh, for Christ's sake, Leona," Greg Savage said. "You always do that."

"I always do what?"

"That," he said, with feeling if not with precision. "You know what he means, or you ought to. Somebody in this room is a killer. He killed Rathburn and Orris and the cook, and most recently he killed Gordon Wolpert. And the rest of us all assumed he'd killed Rhodenbarr here as well. But the killer, whoever he is, knew he hadn't killed Rhodenbarr."

"Because it's the sort of thing a person would remember," Bettina Colibri said softly.

"And consequently he wouldn't be surprised," I said. "But I got a look at all your faces, and you all looked surprised."

"I knew it," Cissie Eglantine said, her countenance transformed. "We're innocent, each and every one of us. It was some nasty old tramp after all."

Nigel sighed, and I don't suppose he was the only one.

"It's not that simple," I said. "For one thing, even if the killer knew I was alive, he wouldn't necessarily expect me to turn up as abruptly as I did. Carolyn knew I was alive, because I'd told her what I was planning. But I got a look at her face a minute ago, and she looked almost as surprised as the rest of you."

"Well, you startled me, Bern."

"I startled everybody," I said. "That's fair enough, because I was startled myself when I found out about Gordon Wolpert a few minutes ago. And I'm afraid I'm not done startling you."

Miss Dinmont said she hoped there wasn't going to be more in the way of excitement. Dakin Littlefield rolled his eyes and muttered something unintelligible to his bride. Muttering seemed to be the order of the day, until Carolyn called out, "Quiet, everybody! He knows who did it. Don't you, Bern?"

Did I? I wanted to hedge, to equivocate, to waffle.

"Yes," I said firmly. "I know who did it."

There was a long silence. Then Nigel said, "I say," and I realized they were all staring at me.

"Sorry," I said. "It just seemed so decisive, putting it that way. You know what's been wrong with this whole bloody business from the start? It's too English."

"Too English?"

"Too polite, too soft-spoken, too cozy for words. Of course Cissie keeps wanting the murderer to turn out to be a passing tramp. The alternative is to believe one of us did the dirty deed, and we're all such jolly decent people it's quite inconceivable. And I've been investigating the murders in the same decent earnest English manner, first trying to play Poirot and then turning amateur sleuth, asking dopey questions and looking for motives and probing alibis as if that's going to tell me anything."

"And it's not?"

"No, because this isn't a cozy little English murder case at all. It's tough and hardboiled, and it's not going to be solved by pussyfooting around like Miss Jane Marple or Lord Peter Wimsey. This is Philip Marlowe's kind of caper."

"Philip Marlowe?" the colonel said. "Don't believe I know the name."

"He was Raymond Chandler's detective," I said, "and he knew about mean streets, and that's what we've got here in this house once you peel the veneer away. We may be miles away from any streets, mean or otherwise, but it all amounts to the same thing, doesn't it?"

"I don't know, Bern," Carolyn said. "Look at the murder weapons—a camel and a pillow to start with, and sugar in a gas tank and a dagger with a wavy blade. In Philip Marlowe's cases they mostly just shot each other, didn't they?"

"Yes, but—"

"And he'd get hit over the head and fall down a flight of stairs. Nobody's been shot, and nobody fell down a flight of stairs unless you count the library steps. The way things are going, I wouldn't be surprised if the next person to die gets murdered with tropical fish, and you know what Chandler had to say about that."

"That's all peripheral," I said. "When you get to what really happened, it's straightforward and it's brutal. And there's not a single tropical fish in it."

"Jonathan Rathburn," I said. "He came here by himself, took up residence in Young George's Room, and began behaving like a man with something on his mind. He scribbled away in a notebook and sat around writing letters that nobody ever saw. And he stared at people. Someone mentioned noticing him staring oddly at Leona Savage, but it wasn't because they were long-lost lovers or twins separated at birth. Rathburn stared probingly at just about everybody, at one time or another."

"I just assumed he was interested in people," Cissie Eglantine said.

"There was another guest who was interested in people, too," I said. "Gordon Wolpert. He was very different from Rathburn, tweedy and mousy where Rathburn was brooding and flamboyant. But he too came here alone, and he was a keen observer of his fellow guests, and he liked a bit of gossip, too."

"That's true," Miss Hardesty recalled. "He had a lot

of questions about everybody, and he'd make dry comments."

"Pleasant enough fellow, though," the colonel put in. "Seemed a decent chap."

"But he was a picky eater," I said. "Isn't that so, Mr. Quilp?"

"He picked at his food," Rufus Quilp agreed. "Pushed it around on his plate."

I looked to Molly Cobbett for confirmation. "He never ate much," she said. "He would always say the food was good, but his plate would be half full when I brought it back to the kitchen. It bothered Cook some."

"It bothered me," Quilp said. "I never trust a picky eater."

"Well, the man's dead," Greg Savage said, "so I think we can forgive him his lack of appetite. Maybe he was just watching his weight."

"But he was slender," Leona said.

"Well, honey, maybe that's how he stayed slender. By resisting the temptation to eat like a horse."

"He wasn't resisting temptation," Quilp insisted. "He wasn't tempted. The man simply did not care about food."

"Maybe there's something intrinsically suspicious about a lack of appetite," I said, "and maybe there isn't. I couldn't tell you one way or the other. What got my attention wasn't that Gordon Wolpert would never qualify for the Clean Plate Club. I was more interested in the fact that he lied about it."

"What do you mean, Bern?"

"You were there," I told Carolyn. "I think it was the first conversation we had with him. Wolpert said he'd extended his stay at Cuttleford House and might extend it again, because the food was so good. He even patted his stomach and made some remark about his waistline."

"Maybe he was anorexic," Millicent suggested. "I saw a program about that. These girls were starving themselves, but they thought they were fat."

"Somehow," I said, "I don't think he fits the profile. Anorexia's pretty scarce in middle-aged males. No, I think there's a basic principle involved. I don't know if you've noticed, but whenever a politician answers a question that you haven't asked, he's lying. Gordon Wolpert was doing essentially the same thing. He was staying on longer than he'd planned at Cuttleford House, and he was offering an explanation when none was required. And the explanation was untrue—the food wasn't what was keeping him here. That meant something else was, and it was something he wanted to conceal."

"Brilliant," Dakin Littlefield said dryly. "Only it's a shame you didn't ask him for an explanation before somebody tied a knot in his neck."

"You're absolutely right," I told him. "I did what amateur sleuths always do—I waited until I could be absolutely certain. I suppose it has to be that way in the books, or otherwise they'd end on page seventy-eight. What I should have done was shoulder my way in and ask impertinent questions. But I didn't, and somebody strangled him."

The colonel cleared his throat. "So it was Wolpert who aroused your suspicions," he said.

"Right," I said. "I knew someone was sitting right here in this room with Jonathan Rathburn. I was on my way to bed and they were in here."

"You never mentioned that," Nigel said.

"No, I didn't."

"And you saw them in here?" Lettice said. "Well, don't keep us in suspense, Bernie. Who was it?"

"The lights were out," I said, "and it was pitch dark inside, so I didn't see anybody. I could hear that there was a conversation going on, but it was too low-pitched to identify the speakers, and of course I didn't want to eavesdrop."

"I wouldn't have been able to resist," Lettice admitted. "Didn't you hear even a tiny bit, Bernie?"

"Not a word, and I didn't hang around long. I was tired, and I'd had that wee dram of the Drumnadrochit. Besides, I was being well-bred and English, and it wouldn't have been the proper thing to do. But it's a pity I didn't listen a little more closely, or just waltz right in and turn on a light. I might have prevented a murder."

"Or watched it take place," Miss Dinmont said with a little gasp. "If you'd walked in just as the murderer was swinging the camel—"

She broke off, all atremble at the horror of the idea.

"It would have been awkward," I agreed, "but it never happened, and what did happen here at Cuttleford House this weekend has been awkward enough. What did we start out with? A perfectly delightful English country house—"

"It's nice of you to say so," Cissie murmured.

"—with a full complement of congenial if slightly dotty guests."

This brought a *harrumph* from the colonel.

"Two men seemed out of place," I went on. "Rathburn, with his penetrating stares and his furious bouts of scribbling, and Wolpert, at once praising the food and pushing it around on his plate. A picky eater, as Mr. Quilp has labeled him, and not to be trusted. My first thought was that one of them killed the other."

"Mr. Wolpert killed Mr. Rathburn," Cissie said.

"Well, it could hardly have been the other way around," her husband pointed out.

"That was my thought," I said, "but I couldn't be sure. I knew how Rathburn was killed—the camel and the pillow—and I knew why, but—"

"Why?" Carolyn demanded.

"To keep him quiet," I said. "He came here looking for somebody and he knew something, and he was a threat to somebody with a secret. I figured Wolpert had a secret, or why would he be disguising his reason for lingering here? So it seemed logical to guess that Rathburn had stumbled on the secret, or ferreted it out, and Wolpert killed him to keep his secret safe."

"You know," Dakin Littlefield said, "I never thought I'd hear myself say this, but I've got to hand it to you. It sounds to me as though you've got it cracked. Wolpert's the killer."

"But Wolpert's been killed himself," Leona Savage objected.

"But was it murder?"

"What else could it have been?"

"Suicide," Littlefield said. "Are you with me in this, Rhodenbarr? Wolpert kills Rathburn to keep his mouth shut—and incidentally, did you happen to find out what secret Rathburn had picked up on? I assume there was more to it than Wolpert's lack of appetite."

"I assume so too," I said, "and I thought I might find a hint in Rathburn's room. After all, he spent all his waking hours writing notes and letters. But either he found a great hiding place for them or the killer scooped them up before I got there."

"So the secret died with Rathburn," Littlefield said. "Well, what difference does it make, anyway? Rathburn knew something and Wolpert wanted to keep it dark, so he killed the fellow. In the ordinary course of things he'd have checked out the next morning and gone on home, but the bridge was out and he couldn't get away. Eventually remorse overtook him, and he probably realized he'd be caught sooner or later. Who knows what goes on inside a man's mind?"

"Who indeed?"

"So he did himself in," he said. "Took the easy way out and did the Dutch act."

"But there were marks on his neck," somebody pointed out. "A sign that he'd been strangled."

"Or tried to hang himself," Littlefield said. "You know how people who slash their wrists have hesitation marks, little cuts they make while they're getting up their nerve? It seems to me you'd have the same thing if you were trying to work up the courage to hang yourself. Say you stood on a chair with a rope around your neck, and before you kicked the chair away you bent your knees, just to get an idea of what it was going to feel like. The noose tightens, you realize this isn't gonna be much fun, so you decide it's simpler to live. But by that time you've already got rope burns on your neck, or strangulation marks, or whatever you want to call it."

"Then what killed him?" Carolyn wanted to know. "He wound up parked on the lawn chair next to Rathburn and the cook. How did he get there and what did he die of?"

"He still wanted to kill himself," Littlefield said, "even

after he lost his nerve with the rope trick. He went out back and sat down in the chair next to the man he killed."

"If memory serves," the colonel said, "the cook was in the middle chair, with Wolpert and Rathburn on either side."

"What difference does it make? He probably killed her, too. Or she died of depression because he didn't finish his dinner, and he felt responsible for depriving the rest of us of decent meals. Whatever it was, he pulled a blanket over himself and died."

"Of what?"

"Search me," Littlefield said. "My guess is he had a snootful before he tried to hang himself. He probably had a couple more pops by the time he went out and sat next to the other two stiffs. Wouldn't have been a stretch for him to doze off and die of exposure."

"It happens all the time," I agreed.

"Or maybe he took poison. Wasn't he the one who knew all about which mushrooms would kill you? I don't think he ran around gathering mushrooms under the snow, but he probably knew a few other things you could take if you wanted to go to sleep and never wake up. He probably used poison to kill the cook, and he had a dose left and took it himself." He shrugged. "When you come right down to it, what difference does it make? He killed a man and he's dead himself now, and if we could just find a way out of here we could all go home."

"Wouldn't that be nice," I said.

"Damn right it would," Littlefield said, "and I'm about ready to take a shot at it. The sun's up and the snow's not falling, so I think it's time Lettice and I hit the road. Not that it hasn't been fun, but—"

"Orris!"

It was Earlene Cobbett who cried out the lad's name, and by the tone and volume you'd have thought he'd risen from the dead and lurched into the library. The whole room went dead silent as we all stared at Earlene, who had the grace to blush behind her freckles.

"For God's sake," Littlefield said, "give it a rest, will you? It's pretty obvious your cousin was boinking you, and I guess you wound up with a cake in the oven, but all that wailing just gets on people's nerves. It's not going to bring him back, and he probably wouldn't marry you anyway, but the kid'll have his father's name all the same. That's the advantage of incest, plus it cuts down on small talk." Another cry, this one wordless, issued from Earlene. "Hey, c'mon," Littlefield said. "Can't you do something, Eglantine? Fire her and send her home, say."

If Littlefield was trying to win friends, he was going about it the wrong way. The men frowned their disapproval, while the women glared murderously at him. He looked around, shrugged. "Bunch of bleeding hearts," he said. "I give up. Scream your guts out, honey. Live a little."

"All Earlene is trying to say," I said, "is that we mustn't forget Orris. Isn't that right, Earlene?" She nodded furiously. "And her point is a good one. Because there are a few elements your theory doesn't cover, Littlefield."

"Like what? The kid in the gully? Hey, he wasn't too swift. The bridge went and he went with it. It's a shame, but what's it got to do with Wolpert killing Rathburn?"

"Why did the bridge go?"

"According to you, somebody sabotaged it. Cut part of the way through the ropes."

"Why would somebody do that?"

"I don't know," he said. "To kill Orris? It seems like a dumb way to go about it. Look, Rhodenbarr, I know it's tempting to see foul play everywhere you look, but don't you think it was possible those ropes just snapped of old age or something? Maybe they were ready to go for a while now, and the kid just had some bad luck."

"So Wolpert killed Rathburn and the cook and then took his own life," I said. "And Orris's death was accidental."

"Have you got a problem with that? Because I have to tell you it sounds reasonable to me."

"Well," I said, "I might have a slight problem with it."

"Oh?"

"Here's how it looks to me," I said. "As Cuttleford House settled in for a long winter weekend, there were two men in residence with a hidden agenda. The snow began falling. And, late in the evening, two more guests arrived to complete the party."

"The Littlefields," Nigel said.

"Lettice and Dakin," I said, "pressing onward in spite of the worst winter storm in memory. The two of you were the last people to cross the bridge."

"Lucky us," Littlefield said.

"A couple of hours later," I went on, "Rathburn was dead, bludgeoned and smothered."

"By Wolpert."

I let it pass. "A few hours after that, Molly discovered the body and raised the alarm, uttering the well-known Cobbett scream. We all came on the run, and when Nigel tried to call the police, the phone was dead."

"Because somebody cut the wires."

"We didn't establish that until later," I said. "It wasn't

until after Orris's death that Nigel walked around the house and determined that the phone wires had been cut. So it's not inconceivable that the storm had knocked out the phones, and the wires weren't cut until later. But it's far-fetched, and it would seem more likely that the phone wires had already been cut by the time Jonathan Rathburn's body was discovered."

That made sense to everyone.

"The next thing that happened," I said, "was that the snowblower wouldn't work. It was presumably sabotaged, possibly with sugar in the gas tank. And the *next* thing that happened was the collapse of the bridge, spilling Orris into the gully and taking his life."

There was a small cry from Earlene, ignored by all.

"Someone severed the phone wires," I said. "Someone sugared the snowblower. Someone cut the bridge supports. And until we know who did each of those things, we haven't solved the puzzle."

"Wolpert," Littlefield said.

"Gordon Wolpert?"

"Why not? He's the villain here. If he was desperate enough to beat a guy's brains out with a bronze camel, I don't suppose he'd draw the line at yanking out a couple of telephone wires."

"But when would he do it?" I wondered. "And why?"

"Why cut the wires? There's a no-brainer. To keep the cops from being called."

"So that they couldn't investigate," I said.

"Makes sense, doesn't it?"

"Does it?" I frowned. "Maybe. Let's let it go for a moment. What about the snowblower? Why sabotage it?"

"So that What's-his-face couldn't clear the path and the driveway."

"Why would he want to prevent that?"

"Same answer. To keep the cops from coming."

"But why would they even try to come?"

He rolled his eyes. "You know, Rhodenbarr," he said, "you made more sense when you were dead in the gully. The cops'd come because there was a dead man in the library."

"But the phones were out, so how would they know about Rathburn?"

"For all he knew," Littlefield said, "somebody here had a cell phone. I'll grant you the snowblower bit was kind of lame, especially if he'd already knocked out the bridge. But maybe Wolpert was the kind of bird who'd wear a belt and suspenders. He wasn't taking any chances."

"Let's look at it from another angle," I suggested. "Cutting the phone wires would keep the cops away. Wrecking the bridge and the snowblower would keep us here."

"Right," Littlefield agreed, "but it's not working anymore, because Lettice and I are about ready to get out of here."

"Well, stick around for a minute," I said. "Long enough to explain why the killer would want to keep all of us from leaving."

He opened his mouth to say something, then closed it, then shrugged. "I don't know," he said. "So?"

"So it's interesting," I said. "Here he's murdered a man and he's arranged things so that the cops can't be called right away. And then at the same time he's cut off his own escape route. We can't leave, and neither can he."

I let the silence hang in the air. Miss Dinmont was the first to break it. "He had us all trapped. And he could take his time and kill us off one by one. First Orris, then the cook, then Mr. Wolpert and Mr. Rhodenbarr—"

"But Mr. Rhodenbarr's alive," Miss Hardesty pointed out. "And Mr. Wolpert was the killer himself."

"That's true," Miss Dinmont said, her voice a little calmer now. "It's all very confusing, isn't it?"

"Very," I told her. "And I was thinking along the same lines as you, Miss Dinmont."

"You were?"

"I was. And it's all because I thought this was an English-country-house kind of murder. But it's not."

"It's not?"

"Mean streets," Carolyn said.

I nodded. "I thought a desperate fiendish killer was going to work his way through the guest register, knocking us off one by one. But what we've got in actual fact is a man who killed one person and wants to get away with it. That's why he did what he could to make it look like an accident, arranging Rathburn's body at the foot of the library steps. No one would suspect the man had actually been murdered, and if by some miracle the cops found anything incriminating, well, he'd be hundreds of miles away by then. And, to make sure he'd have a head start on them, he tore out the phone wires."

Littlefield sighed theatrically. "Isn't that what I said, Rhodenbarr?"

"Not quite. You said the killer also sabotaged the bridge and the snowblower. But he didn't."

"Oh?" said the colonel. "How can that be?"

"I guess the bridge was an accident after all," Greg Savage said, "and I hope your insurance coverage is up to date, Nigel. As far as the snowblower is concerned, well, I guess the thing just conked out by itself. You know how some cars won't start on really cold days? Maybe it was like that."

"Snowblowers are supposed to perform on cold days," I said, "since they're essentially useless on warm ones. No, I'm willing to bet there was sugar in that gas tank, and I know damn well the bridge supports were cut. But not by the killer."

"Then who—"

"Someone who didn't want the killer to get away. Someone who'd been keeping an eye on Rathburn because he sensed an opportunity for profit. If he could isolate Cuttleford House, with nobody coming or going, he might do himself some good."

"I don't see why Wolpert couldn't have done that," Dakin Littlefield said. "It's true he tried to make Rathburn's murder look like an accident, but you proved it wasn't. So he realized somebody would try to get out and call the cops, and he went and cut the ropes supporting the bridge."

I shook my head. "No footprints."

"No footprints?"

"Going to and from the bridge. It was deep and crisp and even out there until Orris slogged through it. You and Lettice got here late last night, Littlefield, and it looked for all the world as though no one had been on the path to or from the bridge since the two of you."

"That's true," Nigel Eglantine said. "That was deep virgin snow that Orris had to walk through, poor lad. I remember noticing the depth of it when he set out, and there were no recent footprints to be seen."

"Footprints in the snow," Littlefield said, and shook his head.

"Late the night before last," I said, "Rathburn was murdered. The murderer—let's call him A—"

"Why not call him Wolpert?"

"Humor me," I said. "Anyway, A killed Rathburn, made it look like an accident, ducked out to rip out the phone wires, and then went upstairs to sleep the sleep of the unjust. Enter B."

"B?"

"Our clever little observer. Did he slip into the library and discover Rathburn's corpse? Possibly, but I don't think so. I think he cut the bridge ropes *before* A murdered Rathburn."

"Why would he do that?" Leona Savage wondered.

"Because, even before A murdered Rathburn, B realized the stage was set. All the players had arrived at Cuttleford House. Once Lettice and Dakin Littlefield had made it across the bridge, it was time for the bridge to come down."

Littlefield had been leaning against a bookcase. Now he snapped to attention. "Wait a minute," he said. "What the hell did our arrival have to do with B and the bridge?"

"Once you were here," I said, "he wanted to make sure you stayed."

"Well, it worked," he said. "I've been wanting to haul ass since the moment I got to this godforsaken hellhole."

"Oh, dear," Cissie Eglantine said. "We try so to make Cuttleford House a pleasant place for all our guests."

"There, there," Nigel said, and patted her hand.

"But he called it a godforsaken hellhole," she protested. "It's not, is it?"

"Of course not," the colonel assured her. "Would I spend half the year in a hellhole? The man's upset, Cecilia."

"I know the food's not all it might be," Cissie said, "because of what happened to Cook, and the snow's made things difficult for everyone, and what with poor Orris gone—"

The inevitable cry came from Earlene Cobbett.

"Excuse me," Rufus Quilp said. The fat man was sitting in an overstuffed armchair, and I'd thought he'd been dozing. But he hadn't missed a thing. "This is getting interesting," he said. "A killed Mr. Rathburn. B dropped the bridge in the gully, either shortly before or shortly after Mr. Rathburn's murder. If after, he may not have known it had taken place."

"That's correct."

"And if before, did he know it was likely to take place? Did B expect A would murder Rathburn?"

"Probably not. He knew the Littlefields had arrived, and he didn't want anyone else coming or going."

Littlefield sighed, exasperated, but Rufus Quilp persevered. "So he slipped outside," he said, "and cut the bridge supports. And, I suppose, made assurance doubly sure by sugaring the snowblower."

"No," I said. "He didn't do that, and why should he? It wouldn't prevent anyone from coming or going. Anyone else could do as Orris did, and indeed what B had done himself to reach the bridge. It might be slow going, especially as the snow continued to fall, but it wouldn't be impassable for any of us. Except Miss Dinmont, of course. You'd need a clear path for a wheelchair."

This upset Miss Dinmont, who required immediate reassurance that the snowblower had not been sabotaged as a deliberate attempt to inconvenience or imperil her. When Miss Dinmont calmed down, Mrs. Colibri wanted to know who'd sugared the snowblower.

"Because it seems entirely gratuitous," she said. "What effect did it have? It simply inconvenienced us."

"It inconvenienced Orris," I said. "The person who poured the sugar in the engine—let's call her C—"

"Her, Bern?"

"Well, him or her," I said. "I thought I'd give the male pronoun a rest. C didn't have the slightest idea that A was going to kill Rathburn, or that B was planning to bring down the bridge. All C knew was that it was snowing to beat the band, and that it would be a good joke on young Orris Cobbett if his beloved snowblower could be rendered *hors de combat*. It was his job to keep the path clear of snow, and the snowblower made that task an easy one, whereas it involved a lot of heavy lifting if you had to do it the old-fashioned way, with a snow shovel."

"All my fault!" cried C. "I swear I never meant for nuffin bad to happen to him! Never! I *loved* him, an' now he be dead, and it be all my fault!"

TWENTY-SIX

It was Earlene Cobbett, of course, and I'll spare you the fits and starts in which she told her story, along with the exclamation points that! accented! virtually! every! word! of it. She had not meant to injure Orris, nor had she intended any lasting harm to the inoffensive snowblower. As she understood it, a cup of sugar in its gas tank would just stop it from running, and eventually someone would have to drain it and supply it with clean gas, at which time it would be as good as new.

And Orris would be as good as new, too. She was a bit peeved with him, less for his having managed to impregnate her than for the attentions he'd been paying to her cousin Molly. It wasn't the worst thing in the world, for after all boys will be boys, and at least it was all in the family, and not as if he'd been misbehaving with a guest, or some stranger. But he still deserved to be taught a lesson, and an hour or so of snow shoveling did not seem inappropriate.

"You didn't do any harm," I told Earlene, "except to the

snowblower, and in a couple of weeks it'd be useless anyhow. It could probably do with a good overhaul between now and next winter."

"Need a new engine now," the colonel murmured.

"As far as Orris is concerned," I went on, "if anything, you gave him a few extra minutes of life. If the snowmobile had started up right away, he'd have cleared the path in a few minutes' time, and that means he'd have wound up in the gully that much sooner. I know you miss him, Earlene—"

"I loved him!"

"—and he's gone, and nothing can bring him back, but there's no use crying over spilled milk, and at least you don't have to worry that you were the one who kicked the pail over." The metaphor stopped her tears, anyway; she stood there blinking, trying to figure out what the hell I was talking about.

"Well, so much for C," Greg Savage said. "It's upsetting for the poor girl, but she didn't have anything to do with what happened to Orris, or any of the rest of it, either. So we're back to A and B. B cut the bridge supports shortly before or shortly after A murdered poor Rathburn."

"Matters would be greatly simplified," the colonel announced, "if B would identify himself." An eloquent silence greeted this remark, and he broke it himself by elaborating. "After all," he said, "while B's action had the awful luck of causing an accident, it's not in the same category as murder. B just wanted to keep us all here."

"A fate worse than death," Littlefield muttered.

Cissie gave him a look, and Rufus Quilp piped up with the observation that cutting the ropes was hardly an innocent prank. "He didn't just disable the bridge," he reminded us. "He booby-trapped it, cutting partway through the ropes so that the bridge would collapse as soon as someone set foot on it. If he merely wanted to isolate us here, why not cut all the way through the ropes?"

"He was trying to murder someone," Miss Hardesty said. "But he couldn't have meant to kill Orris. And if he had someone else in mind, how could he know that person would be the next one to try to cross the bridge?"

"He couldn't," I said.

"My goodness," Mrs. Colibri said. "Do you mean to say that he didn't even care which one of us he killed?"

"No," I said. "I mean to say he wasn't trying to kill anybody."

"But Mr. Quilp just said—"

"I know what Mr. Quilp just said, and his point is well taken. Here's what I think, although I admit I can't prove it. I think B slashed all the way through the cables. He didn't set any traps, booby or otherwise. He cut the ropes and dumped the bridge in the gully."

They looked at me. Leona Savage said, "Then when Orris gave up on the snowblower and walked to the bridge—"

"It was already out."

"And he kept walking?"

"It bothered me," I said, "that nobody actually heard the bridge fall. Greg, you and Millicent were outside when Orris had his accident. You both heard him cry out. But did you hear the bridge crash into the gully?"

"I might have," he said. "I don't remember."

"All I remember," Millicent said, "is Orris screaming."

You'd have thought this would bring some sort of outcry from Earlene Cobbett, but it didn't.

"It's not as clear-cut as the dog that didn't bark," I told them, "and there's no way to run an experiment, but I'd have to guess that the bridge made a lot of noise when it fell. But if it fell during the night, when most of us were sleeping and all of us were inside the house with the windows shut, and the snow was coming down thick and fast, well, I'd say it would have fallen as silently as Bishop Berkeley's tree."

Millicent looked baffled by the reference. "It was a tree that fell in the forest," her mother told her, "and it didn't make a sound because there was no human ear there to hear it."

"But it would still make a sound," Millicent said. "Anyway, Orris made a sound, and both my ears were there to hear it. Bernie, if the bridge was out already, why didn't Orris turn around and come back to the house?"

"Ah," I said. "That's a delicate point."

"But I'm sure you have the answer," Littlefield said dryly.

"I didn't know Orris terribly well," I said, "but my sense of him was that his SATs weren't quite high enough to get him into Harvard."

"He was a hard worker," Nigel said, "and a stouthearted lad."

"A good man in a tight spot," the colonel put in.

"But not, uh, terribly quick in an intellectual sense."

"I think we get the point," Littlefield said. "Old Orris was dumb as the rocks he landed on. Where are you going with this, Rhodenbarr? You saying he didn't notice the bridge was missing until he was standing in the middle of the air?"

"He was very likely snowblind," I said in Orris's defense.

"He was frustrated, too, from trying to get the snowblower to work, and worn out from slogging through deep snow. And how many times had Orris walked that path and crossed that bridge? Hundreds, surely. It was automatic for him. He didn't have to think about it."

"He must have been even dumber than I thought," Littlefield said. "Even now, after lying in the snow all night, I'll bet his body temperature's still ten points higher than his IQ."

"It was a mistake anyone could have made," I said, with more conviction than I felt. "But the point is that B wasn't trying to kill Orris or anyone else. He slashed the ropes clear through."

"All the more reason why he should identify himself," said the colonel, returning to his earlier argument. "He's not a murderer, and his testimony could help us."

"That's true," I said, "but we're not going to hear it."

"Why not? All he needs to do is speak up. After all, he's right here in this room."

That brought it home. They looked at each other, trying to guess which one of them had slashed the ropes and unwittingly sent Orris to the bottom of Cuttlebone Creek. I let them dart questioning glances back and forth.

Then I said, "No."

"No?"

"No, he's not in the room."

"But—"

"B's in a lawn chair," I said.

The colonel stared. "You're saying he's dead."

"I'm afraid so."

"There are three dead bodies in lawn chairs, Rhodenbarr. Unless you're saying—"

"No," I said, "we haven't lost anybody else. Three bodies, and one of them's B."

"The cook? *She* slashed the ropes supporting the bridge, and killed herself out of remorse at having caused Orris's death?"

"I suppose now and then somebody commits suicide out of remorse," I said, "but it sounds as though we've got an epidemic of it here. I'm sure the cook had a kitchen knife that could have sliced right through those ropes, but the only way she tried to keep everybody here was by cooking wonderful meals. She wasn't B."

"Then it must have been Mr. Rathburn," Mrs. Colibri said. "You said the ropes might have been cut before the murder, so I suppose Mr. Rathburn might have cut them. He must have gone outside, and then when he came back Mr. Wolpert was waiting for him in the library."

"Perfect," Littlefield said. "All the perpetrators are dead and there's nobody here but us chickens. Can we go home now?"

I said, "It wasn't Rathburn."

"That leaves Wolpert," Rufus Quilp said, folding his hands on his stomach. "But how can he be B when he's already A? He can't be both letters, can he?"

"There's twenty-six letters in the alphabet," Millicent said. "Enough for everybody to have two."

"But Wolpert only gets one," I said. "He's B, because he was the one who cut the bridge supports to seal off Cuttleford House. He'd been keeping an eye on things for days, waiting to see how the hand played out, and once everybody was here he wanted to make sure nobody left. But he didn't kill anybody. He didn't murder Jonathan Rathburn and he didn't kill himself."

"Then who did, Bern?"

"Someone who's right in this room now," I said, "and maybe he'd like to accept Colonel Blount-Buller's invitation and identify himself. No? Well, in that case I'll identify him. It's Dakin Littlefield."

TWENTY-SEVEN

"That's it," Littlefield said. "Lettice, grab your coat. We're out of here."

"I don't think so."

"You don't, eh, Rhodenbarr? Well, what do I care what you think? I don't know who picked you to be the head wallaby in this kangaroo court, but I don't have to listen to any more of it. The cook's dead, our room's drafty, and I'm not having a good time. And I don't particularly appreciate being tagged as a murderer. The only crime I've ever committed was ignoring a couple of overdue parking tickets. Oh, and I jaywalked a few times, and years ago I tore off that little tag on the mattress that you're not supposed to remove, though I've never been able to figure out why. But aside from that—"

"What about the bearer bonds?"

That stopped him. "I don't know what you're talking about," he managed, sounding about as convincing as if he'd said he never inhaled.

"You've got an envelope full of them in your suitcase,"

I said. "I didn't have time to count them carefully, but the total runs to a few million dollars. It's a nice little nest egg to start married life."

Lettice looked horror-struck. "Bearer bonds," she said. "What bearer bonds? Where did they come from?"

She may have meant the question for her husband, but I answered when he didn't. "From your employer," I said. "I'm afraid that's why Dakin came along looking to sweep you off your feet. You provided him with access to the back rooms of the brokerage house you worked for, and it didn't take him long to find something to steal."

"But that's crazy," she said. "I know what bonds you're talking about. They were in the safe in Mr. Sternhagen's office. If they turn up missing right after I go away on my honeymoon, I'm the first person the police would look for." She turned to her husband. "How could you do it?" she asked him. "What made you think you could get away with it?"

"You were planning a honeymoon in Aruba," I said. "Isn't that what you told me?"

"Yes, but—"

"I think you were supposed to have an accident in Aruba," I told her. "A mishap while swimming or boating, say. And your bereaved husband, traveling under a different name and carrying a different passport, would have returned to the States alone, perhaps stopping off in the Caymans to deposit funds in an offshore account. The authorities would be looking for you, all right, but you'd be dead and your husband would have ceased to exist."

"That's absolutely crazy," Littlefield said. "You know how I feel about you, Lettice."

"Do I?"

"Of course you do. The bonds were to give us a good start in our life together, and—"

"A good start! Eight million dollars is more than a good start."

"Call it a start and a retirement fund all in one," he said. "It would be a cinch for us to change identities in Aruba and go someplace together where they'd never find us. And it'll still be easy, once we get out of here."

"When were you planning on telling her, Littlefield?"

"When we got to Aruba." He turned to her. "I wanted to make it easy for you to act natural on the plane. As soon as we got there, I was planning to tell you everything."

"But you didn't go to Aruba," I said. "You let her talk you into coming here."

"Yeah," he said, "and don't ask me why. There's people knocking each other off left and right, and I'm the one who winds up getting accused of murder."

"You didn't want to come here when I first mentioned it," Lettice remembered, "and then you decided you liked the idea."

"I saw how much it meant to you."

"It didn't mean that much to me. I thought it would be a lark, that's all. And I said since we already had reservations in Aruba maybe we should go, and you said—"

"Jesus," he said, "I just wanted to make you happy."

"You thought you could hide out better here than you could in Aruba," I cut in. "Especially if you didn't bother to cancel the reservations. By the time the authorities figured out that you never boarded the plane, you'd have had a chance to cover your tracks pretty thoroughly. You'd stay here a few days until the trail got cold, and then you'd head on out. It wasn't a bad idea, but you picked the wrong place to come to."

"We all did," he said with feeling. "Why anyone would want to stay at this pesthole is beyond me."

There was a cry from Cissie Eglantine, hardly the sort of utterance one had come to expect from Earlene, but expressive all the same.

"I liked the place just fine myself," I said, "until people started dropping like flies. But the minute you got here, everything went haywire."

"Why?" the colonel wondered. "I'm not surprised this chap's a thief. I thought him a bad hat and supposed he lived off women. He has that air about him."

"Thanks a lot," Littlefield said.

"But what was the connection between him and the other two, Rathburn and Wolpert? Why should his arrival put the match to the powder keg?"

"They must have all three been in on it," Miss Dinmont said. "Conspiring together, thick as thieves."

"That's crap," Littlefield said. "I never met either of those birds before in my life."

The colonel cleared his throat. "And we're to take your word for that, eh, sir?"

"I'll take his word," I said. "Whatever his plans might have been for after he left Cuttleford House, Littlefield came here planning nothing more than a quiet honeymoon weekend. But he walked right into the kind of coincidence that's evidently damn near inescapable in English country houses."

I glanced at Lettice. "Coming here was Mrs. Littlefield's idea. She'd heard that there had been a late cancellation. She called, and she learned that there had indeed been a party who'd called to cancel, and she got the room."

"So?"

"But I hadn't canceled," I said.

"You?"

"There was a point where I thought I would have to cancel," I said, "but things worked out after all. I mentioned something to somebody, and word got to Mrs. Littlefield through the grapevine. You know how things get around."

I hurried on, before it occurred to them to wonder how a bit of news could find its way from my lips to Lettice's ears. "Here's the point—someone else did call up to cancel, just in time for the Littlefields to get his room."

"Cousin Beatrice's Room," Cissie said. "And a gentleman did call. I don't know why I can't remember his name."

"Pettisham."

"That's it," she said. "I remember he had an accent, and I thought that was odd, because the name is very English, isn't it? Or at least it sounds English, although I don't know that I've ever actually known anyone named Pettisham. Petty, certainly, and Pettibone, but not Pettisham."

"Pettibone's definitely an English name, isn't it?"

"Oh, I would say so," Nigel told me. "An old name, too. I'd guess there was a Pettibone came over with the Conqueror."

"That would figure," I said, "because the name's an anglicization of the French. It combines two French words, *petit* and *bon.*"

"Small and good," Mrs. Colibri translated. "Do you suppose the implication is that good things come in small packages?"

I glanced at Carolyn, who beamed at the very notion. "Pettisham's been anglicized, too," I said, "although I don't know that there were any Pettishams among William's troops at Hastings."

"It would be possible to find out," the colonel offered.

I told him I didn't think we had to go back that far. "My guess is that it's a much more recent name," I said, "and that the two words it combines are *petit* and *champ*."

"Small champion," Carolyn said.

"Small plot of land," Mrs. Colibri corrected. "Or, you know, like a field or meadow."

"Sounds like the name of a smallholder or yeoman," the colonel said. "And thus not terribly likely to have been one of the Conqueror's Norman knights."

"That's some coincidence," Littlefield said. "Not only did we call for a reservation, but the guy who canceled didn't cross the Channel with the bastard king of England. What do you figure the odds would be on something like that?"

"The coincidence," I said, "is that you both had the same last name."

"What's that supposed to mean?"

"Pettisham," I said. "*Petit champ.* Small plot of land. Little field."

"Jesus," he said.

"The first time I met Gordon Wolpert, he got to talking about malt whisky. There were a lot of distilleries, he told me, although he'd always supposed it was a small field. That was the phrase he picked, though it didn't fit the conversation that well, and he bore down on it, too, to stress it. Then he went on and used the phrase 'a petty sham,' and looked disappointed when I failed to react to it. When Pettisham called and canceled his booking, Mrs. Eglantine got the chart of room assignments and crossed out his name. A few hours later she wrote 'Littlefield' in the same space."

"Who was Pettisham?" Millicent wanted to know.

"Cissie says he sounded foreign," I said, "and he was certainly mixed up in some sort of foreign intrigue. I don't know whether he was actually an agent of a foreign power, and I couldn't say whether he was buying or selling, and whether the transaction involved secrets or valuables. The two men who could tell us are both dead."

"Rathburn and Wolpert," Carolyn said.

"That's right. They were both waiting for him to turn up. Rathburn was keeping an eye on everybody and I guess Wolpert was keeping an eye on Rathburn. And then Dakin Littlefield arrived, with a glamorous companion and an arrogant manner and a guilty secret, and they both took action. Wolpert wasn't sure how he was going to handle things, but he knew he didn't want anyone getting away before he made his move. So he cut the ropes and dumped the bridge in the gully."

"And Rathburn?"

"Made an approach to Littlefield. He was always scribbling away, so my guess would be he wrote out a note and passed it to you in the hallway."

"He slipped it under the bedroom door," Lettice said.

"I never saw any note," her husband said.

"Don't you remember? There was a folded sheet of yellow paper under our door when we went to the room. You picked it up and read it, and when I asked you what it was you said it was nothing."

"Oh, that. Well, it *was* nothing. I couldn't make head or tail out of it. Looking back, I guess this guy did have me mixed up with somebody else. I just thought he was a crank, or he stuck his little love note under the wrong door. So I crumpled it up and forgot about it."

"You turned pale," Lettice said.

"Because you thought he knew something," I put in. "You had eight million dollars' worth of negotiable bonds in your possession, and just when you thought you were free and clear somebody slips you a cryptic note demanding a secret meeting in the middle of the night. You couldn't say anything to your wife, and you couldn't just ignore the note. You had to meet him."

"Not to harm him," Littlefield said. "Just to find out what he knew, and to tell him he was barking up the wrong tree. The room was pitch dark when I got there. I figured it was empty. I started to switch on a light and a voice told me to leave it dark."

"And?"

"And I wound up sitting in a chair next to his. I guess there was something Pettisham was supposed to turn over to him, but all I could make out at the time was that he wanted something from me, and I figured that meant the bonds. I wasn't about to give them up to some joker I couldn't even see. But I never meant to kill him."

"Why else would you brain him with the camel?"

"I didn't know it was a camel."

"With a hump like that? What did you think it was, the hunchback of Notre Dame?"

"I didn't even see it," he said. "For Christ's sake, it was darker than the inside of a cow. I just grabbed the first thing I touched and clocked him with it."

"If you'd grabbed the pillow instead of the camel," I said, "poor Rathburn would be alive today. How's that for rotten luck?"

"I just wanted to stun him," Littlefield said. "You know, to knock him out. I figured I could tie him up and stick him in a closet where nobody'd find him until we had a chance to get out of here."

"And then you smothered him with the pillow."

"There was some blood on his face. I used the pillow to sponge it off."

"Very considerate of you."

"And I guess I held it there too long. Or maybe he was already dead from the blow to the head. Or maybe—"

"Yes?"

"You want to know what I think, Rhodenbarr? I bet he had a heart attack *before* I ever touched him with the camel. See, that would explain how I hit him on the back of the head, even though I was aiming at his forehead. He must have been pitching forward, and I hit him after he'd croaked."

I looked at my watch. I had to admit the heart-attack notion showed a resourceful imagination, but if he could even try on a line like that it was a waste of time letting him talk. Right now, though, wasting time wasn't a bad idea.

"What about the pinpoint hemorrhages?" the colonel demanded, wasting some time himself. "Don't they prove the man was smothered?"

"I wouldn't know about that," Littlefield said. "I'm not a doctor, but then neither is anybody else in the room. Maybe there's more than one way to get those pinpoint hemorrhages."

"Entirely possible," I agreed. "Maybe they're a natural consequence of the synergistic effect of getting crowned with a camel seconds after you've died of a heart attack. What about Wolpert?"

"Wolpert?"

"The second man you killed."

"Didn't I already explain how that was suicide? First time around I thought it was Rathburn's death he was feeling guilty about—"

"But it couldn't have been, because you're the one who killed Rathburn."

"Well, I was there when he died. I'll admit that much, although I still think it was a heart attack that finished him. What Wolpert was feeling guilty about was cutting the bridge ropes so that the boy genius did his Wile E. Coyote impression and tried to walk on air."

"And he tried to hang himself, then wandered outside and died of shock and exposure."

"You got it. Makes sense, doesn't it?"

"I'll tell you what happened," I said. "Gordon Wolpert never had any doubt what happened to Rathburn. He kept it to himself and bided his time before he made his pitch to you. What did he want? The same thing Rathburn was after?"

"If he was planning anything, he never followed through with it. There were a couple of times I noticed him giving me the eye, as if he wanted to tell me something, but he never got around to it. And then the next thing I knew he was out there on the third lawn chair this morning, dead as a doornail."

I looked at my watch again. Where were they when you wanted them?

"I saw you," Millicent Savage said suddenly.

"Huh?"

"Talking to Mr. Wolpert," the little darling insisted. "And you said something about meeting him later. I heard you say it."

"That's crap," he said, disgusted. "There was nobody within earshot." He realized what he'd said, then made a face and shrugged and gave up. "Oh, the hell with it," he said. "I could spin it out a little more, but what's the point? I thought we could work something out, like you'd all go along with it for a share of the bonds, but there's too many of you and somebody'd be sure to hold out. Anyway, why share? I don't have to share."

And he pulled out a gun.

Don't ask me what kind of gun it was. Guns make me nervous—people keep them in drawers so that they can shoot burglars with them, and I'm opposed to that—so I've never taken the trouble to learn anything much about them. I could tell that this one was an automatic, not a revolver, and that was about all I could tell. I could also tell that it was big (though probably not as big as it looked) and that it was pointed at me.

"Nobody move," Littlefield said.

Nobody did.

"You're right," he said. "I killed them both, and I don't know why you had to make a federal case out of it, because they both asked for it. Rathburn thought I was somebody else, and I couldn't manage to stall the son of a bitch. I didn't mean to kill him, not at first, but then when I switched a light on and saw him lying there I got a look at the library steps and saw how easy it would be to make it look like an accident. But that would only work if he was dead, so I picked up the pillow and put him out of my misery."

"And Wolpert?"

"He knew I'd killed Rathburn. I don't think he even

knew what it was Rathburn wanted from the guy who never showed up, but he saw an opportunity to do himself some good by putting the squeeze on me. I tried fencing with him, but the little bastard was pretty slick. Before I knew it he'd managed to worm out of me that I had a briefcase full of stolen bonds, and he was all set to cut himself in."

"Until you cut him out instead."

"I lost my temper," he said. "That's the same thing that happened with Rathburn, when you come right down to it."

"But you didn't grab a camel this time around."

"What I grabbed was his necktie," he said. "Grabbed one end of it in each hand and pulled until his face got purple. I couldn't figure out what to do with him, so I took him outside and parked him on a lawn chair and threw a sheet over him. I didn't figure anyone would notice."

"You didn't figure anyone would notice?"

"Well, maybe I wasn't thinking too clearly. It was late and I'd had a hell of a day, plus I'd helped myself to a couple of glasses of that Drum stuff. And I didn't write it down in the book, either, Nigel. I'm afraid your honor system doesn't work too well with guys like me." He gestured sharply with the gun. "Hold it right there, Colonel. That's as close as you get if you don't want a bullet."

I glanced at my watch again. Keep him talking, I thought. "Speaking of bullets," I said, "I'm surprised you brought a gun along on your honeymoon. Your wife probably thought you were just glad to see her."

"Funny," he said. "The gun belonged to Wolpert. I took it off him when I dragged his body outside. He never got the chance to use it, but I'm in a different position."

"You're not wearing a necktie."

"And I've got the gun in my fist already, and it's got a full clip and a live round in the chamber. It's a thirteen-shot clip, so you can do the math yourselves. If anybody makes a move I start shooting. I'll shoot the men first, and if I run out of bullets toward the end I'll finish the rest of you by hand. I never planned on killing anybody, but I already killed two people and if I have to knock off the rest of you I'll do it. What the hell are you looking at, Lettice?"

"My God," she said, aghast. "I *married* you!"

"And we both know why," he said, sneering. "You thought you were getting a rich husband, because I always had plenty of money to throw around. Well, this is how I get it. I steal it."

"Are you going to kill me, too, Dakin?"

"I'm not going to kill anybody unless I have to," he said. "What I want to do is figure out a way to get out of here with the bonds, and with enough lead time so that I'm in the clear before anybody can call the cops. The phone lines are out, so you can't call anybody, but if I walk down to where I can ford the stream, somebody else can do the same thing after me, and it wouldn't take you long to get to a phone that works."

He paused, thinking it through, and I listened and heard something in the silence. At first I could just barely make it out, but then it got a little louder.

"I'll need a hostage," he said. "If I've got somebody with me, you'll have to stay back, won't you?"

"I'll be your hostage," the colonel said.

"You? Jesus, that's just what I need is a fat old blimp with a stiff upper lip to drag around over hill and dale. If you didn't drop dead from the exertion you'd be looking for a way to get the jump on me. No, the kid'll be my hostage."

"You son of a bitch," Greg Savage said. He took a step forward, and Littlefield swung the gun in his direction.

"Not so fast," he said. "I'm taking her with me, whether I have to shoot you first or not. Listen to me, people. If you all cooperate, everybody gets out of this alive. All you have to do . . . What's that noise?"

"Noise?" I said.

"Dammit, Rhodenbarr—"

"You mean that pocketa-pocketa-pocketa? Sounds like a helicopter to me."

"A helicopter."

"And it sounds as though it's coming right here. I wonder who it could be."

"How did—"

"It seems to be landing on the front lawn," I said. "Maybe it's Mr. Pettisham, full of apologies for having been delayed. Maybe it's Ed McMahon, Littlefield, to tell you you've won the Publishers Clearing House sweepstakes. You'll be a rich man even if you have to give the bonds back. My God, man, it's your lucky day."

He just stared at me. He didn't say a word, and neither did anybody else. We were still silent when the front door opened and a group of men trooped through the hall and found their way to the library.

Their leader, the only one not wearing a uniform, was a big fellow in a gorgeous gray suit that looked as though it had been custom-tailored for someone else.

"Well, here we all are," he said, casting his eyes around the room. "It's Mrs. Rhodenbarr's son Bernard, and it looks like you went and rounded up the usual suspects. You got the right to remain silent, all of youse, but I wouldn't advise it, because the sooner we get this sorted out the sooner we can all get home. And the sooner the better as far as I'm concerned, because I never seen so much snow in my life."

"My God," Carolyn said, "it's Ray Kirschmann, and I'm actually glad to see him. I never thought I'd live to see the day."

But she had, and she'd live to see others, which was more than you could say for Dakin Littlefield. He gave a little cry of abject despair, then stuck the business end of the gun in his cruel mouth and pulled the trigger.

The big problem with automatics, or so they tell me, is that they're apt to jam. This one didn't.

TWENTY-EIGHT

Four days later I was perched on a stool behind the counter at Barnegat Books, unwrapping a killer sandwich from the Russian deli around the corner. They use a particularly crinkly waxed paper, except I don't suppose it's actually waxed, I suppose it must be some sort of miracle polymer laminate designed to wreak havoc with generations yet unborn. Whatever it is, it's noisier than the D train, and crumpling it never fails to get Raffles's attention. He perked up, I feinted left and threw to the right, and he refused to be faked out, pouncing like a champion.

"I thought the layoff might hurt him," I told Carolyn, "but he's not the least bit rusty. I'll tell you, though, he's glad to be back."

"He's not the only one, Bern."

"You said it. I suppose the country makes a nice change, but I'm a city boy at heart. I'd rather be on a bench in Bryant Park with life going on all around me. Give me the subway at rush hour, a couple of fire engines with their sirens wide open . . ."

"I know what you mean, Bern. The simple pleasures."

"Well, you know what Sydney Smith said about the country. He said he thought of it as a sort of a healthy grave."

"All that fresh air, Bern. If you're not used to it . . ."

"Exactly. It was starting to get to me. But all I really needed was a couple of days at home and I'm my old self again. Working in the bookstore, playing with my cat."

"Same here. Washing dogs all day, then going home and watching my cats wash themselves." She grinned. "And going out at night for a few pops and the chance of an adventure."

"An adventure?"

"Last night," she said, "I got a heavy dose of spring fever, because that's what it is, spring, even if they haven't got the word yet up in the Berkshires. So I went for a walk, and where did I wind up but the Cubby Hole?"

"What a surprise."

"Well, I got smart feet, Bern. They took me there all by themselves, and—" She broke it off at the tinkle of tiny bells over the door, announcing a visitor. "Later, Bern," she said. "It'll keep. Look who's here."

I looked up, and there she was, the Widow Littlefield. I hadn't expected her to be wearing black, and she wasn't, looking quite spiffy instead in a dove-gray suit with a nipped-in waist. Her blouse was white, and her bow tie, floppy and feminine, was the bright red of arterial blood.

"Bernie," she said. "It's so nice to see you. And there's your sweet little cat." She caught sight of Carolyn and her face darkened. "Perhaps this isn't a good time."

"It's a perfectly fine time," I said. "You're looking well, Lettice."

"Thank you, Bernie."

"You remember Carolyn."

"Your wife," she said. "Except she's not your wife. It's very confusing. When you called, I thought you might want to come over to my apartment. Or that you'd invite me over to yours."

"I thought it would be nice to meet here."

"So you said. But I didn't expect there would be three of us."

"Four," I said, "if you count the cat. And I can't guarantee there won't be more. You might find this hard to believe, but every once in a while I actually have a customer walk in here."

"How nice for you."

"But that probably won't happen," I said, "and until it does we can talk freely. I didn't get much chance to talk to you after your husband ate his gun."

She shuddered. "What an unpleasant expression," she said. "And I wish you wouldn't call him my husband."

"You're the one who married him," I said. "I suppose you've got grounds for an annulment, but he saved you the hassle of getting one, the same as he saved the state the cost of a trial. You're single again, and you're in the clear as far as the cops are concerned. How about Mr. Sternhagen? Is he letting you come back to work?"

"He insisted I take the week off," she said, "but of course he wants me back."

"I guess he was happy enough just to get his bonds back."

"He got them back before he even knew they were gone, Bernie. And he realized that I was as much Dakin's victim as he was. It was indiscreet of me to give Dakin an opportunity to have a copy of my key made, but Mr. Sternhagen knows I'll never let anything like that happen again."

"I guess it must seem like a horrible dream," I said.

"It does."

"But your eyes are open now, and it's all over."

"That's right, Bernie. It's just a good thing the police got there when they did. I still can't understand how they managed it."

"They used a helicopter," I said.

"I know that."

"So the road conditions didn't matter," I said, "and the unplowed driveway didn't stop them, or the lack of a bridge across the gully. They just flew right over everything."

"I understand all that part. How did they know to come in the first place? And how did they know they would need a helicopter? And the man in charge—"

"Ray Kirschmann."

"He was a New York police officer, and he seemed to know you."

"I noticed that," I said. "Curious, isn't it?"

"But how did he . . ."

"Bernie called him," Carolyn said. "After he faked his own death by lowering a dummy into the gully, he walked downstream until he found a place where he could wade across."

"No wading required," I said. "Cuttlebone Creek was frozen solid. The only wading I had to do was through snow, and I don't think you call it wading when it's snow. It's either trudging or slogging, and it seems to me I did a fair amount of both."

"Then he doubled back on the other side of the gully," she went on, "until he got to the parking lot."

"The parking lot?"

"Right on the other side of the bridge, where everybody left their cars. He figured somebody would have a cell phone, and he opened car doors until he found one."

"Didn't people lock their cars? I'm positive Dakin locked ours."

"I guess I got lucky," I said. I didn't tell her that a locked car is not the most challenging obstacle you can place in a burglar's path. "I found a phone, and I was going to call nine-one-one but I couldn't figure out what to tell them. So I called Ray Kirschmann, and don't ask me what I told him. Don't ask him, either, because I woke him up in the middle of the night and he couldn't make sense of what I was saying. But he got the important part right."

"And arrived in the nick of time," Carolyn said.

I crumpled a piece of paper and threw it for Raffles. "Ray didn't have any jurisdiction up there," I went on, "but he got in touch with the state troopers, and they tried to reach Cuttleford House and confirmed that the phones were out. So they broke out a helicopter and brought Ray along for the ride. And the rest you know, because you were there for it."

"Yes."

"So I suppose you're wondering why I summoned you here," I said. "Today, I mean. This afternoon."

"I thought you just wanted to see me, Bernie."

"Well, it's always a pleasure, Lettice. But there was something I wanted to talk about."

"Oh? What would that be?"

"It would be the bridge," I said. "The one that spanned Cuttlebone Creek, until it didn't anymore."

"What about it, Bernie?"

"You remember how the bridge wound up in the gully, don't you?"

She nodded. "Gordon Wolpert slashed the ropes."

"Right. And the bridge went tumbling into the gully, silent as Berkeley's tree. And then the next morning Orris walked right off the edge, not even noticing that the bridge was missing."

"I remember," she said. "You explained it all in the library, before Dakin pulled the gun."

"I keep picturing Orris," I said. "Stepping right off into space like that. It's a pretty funny image, wouldn't you say?"

"Funny? The man was killed."

"I know, but it's right smack on the border of tragedy and farce, isn't it? And how could he do a thing like that? I mean, if he'd been running, say. Pursued by a bear, that sort of thing. But he was just walking, making his way through the snow, and all of a sudden there wasn't any snow, or any ground beneath his feet, either. He must have been surprised."

"I'm sure he was. Bernie, do we have to talk about—"

"Too surprised to scream, you'd almost think, but he managed to get a scream out. Can you imagine walking off a cliff like that, Lettice? In broad daylight?"

"You explained that he could have been snowblind, Bernie."

"True."

"And that he was intellectually challenged."

"Also true. The nearest thing to dead between the ears, you might say. Still, he had the inbred cunning of the Cobbetts, didn't he? You wouldn't think he'd try to walk through the air. You want to know what I think, Lettice?"

"What?"

"I think he stepped on the bridge and started walking across, and the ropes had been cut partway through, and they snapped, and *that's* how he fell."

"But nobody heard the bridge fall."

"Ah," I said. "Nobody heard it in the middle of the night, either. Maybe there's not that much noise involved. Maybe the shout Orris gave drowned it out, or merged with it so that no one noticed it. Remember, there was snow covering everything. That could muffle sounds. No, I think the bridge fell into the gully the very same time Orris did."

"That's what you thought originally," Carolyn said. "Remember, Bern? When you first told everybody the ropes had been cut?"

"That's right," I said. "That's how it looked to me, just from a quick examination of the ends of the rope. On one of them, it was easy to see where some of the fibers had been cut cleanly, and others looked as though they'd been stretched until they tore."

"I don't understand," Lettice said. "What difference does it make? Maybe Wolpert didn't want to risk making a lot of noise, so he just stopped cutting before the ropes parted. Or maybe what you said in the library was right, and Orris was in too much of a hurry to look where he was putting his feet. Either way he's dead, and either way Wolpert was responsible."

"You're probably right," I admitted. "Wolpert's answering to a higher authority, so it's academic whether he was purposely setting a lethal trap or just trying to keep anybody from getting across the bridge. And I don't suppose there's any real point in trying to salvage Orris's reputation for quick thinking."

I picked up a sheet of paper, but Raffles looked too comfortable. I didn't have the heart to disturb him, nor did I want to risk throwing the crumpled paper and having him ignore it. I always feel like a jerk when that happens.

"So I'll just let it go," I continued. "The police have it all wrapped up, and they're happy, so why confuse them?" I looked at the guileless face above the blood-red bow tie. "But I wouldn't want you to think you got away with it," I said.

"I don't understand," she said.

"You know," I said, "I'd have been willing to bet those would be the words out of your mouth, and what nonsense. Of course you understand."

"But . . ."

There's three dots instead of a dash after that *but* because I didn't chime in and interrupt. I just let the word hang in the air, wondering if it would wind up falling into the gully.

Then I said, "You cut the ropes, Lettice. You and Dakin were the last people over the bridge. He got into the house before you did. You either lagged behind or pretended to drop something and went back for it, but it gave you time to get a knife out of your purse and start sawing through the ropes supporting the bridge."

"Why would I do a thing like that?"

"I was hoping you could tell me."

"It's ridiculous," she said. "I'd be setting a trap for a person I'd never even met. You and I have been . . . *close*, Bernie. How could you possibly think me capable of such a thing?"

"You weren't setting a trap."

"But you just said—"

"If you'd had your way," I said, "you'd have sliced right through those ropes in a New York minute. But minutes take a lot longer up in the faux-English countryside. And you didn't have the right tools for the job."

Carolyn asked me what I meant. Lettice just stared at me.

I pointed at her purse. "If I took that bag away from you and dumped it out on the countertop," I said, "I bet I'd find a cute little penknife with a blade shorter than your pinky. It's a useful little accessory, handy for slitting an envelope or paring a fingernail or cutting a piece of thread. And you can even cut through a stout rope with the thing, but it's not easy. You have to sort of saw your way through, and it takes time."

She was silent for a moment, her arm pressing her handbag protectively against her side. Then she said, "Lots of women have knives in their bags."

"I know. Some of them carry Mace these days, and some tote guns around with them. Small guns, though, not like the cannon Dakin took off Wolpert's corpse. Little ladylike guns, same as yours is a little ladylike knife."

"If I had a knife like that," she said, "it wouldn't prove anything."

"It might if there were rope fibers in the casing. And if they matched the ropes on Cuttleford Bridge."

She looked long and hard at me, then lowered her eyes. After a moment she said, "I never meant for anyone to get killed. I hope you believe me, Bernie."

"I do."

" 'I do.' That's what I said, standing up next to Dakin in

front of the city clerk. That's what started the whole thing."

"What happened, Lettice?"

"I don't know," she said. "Somehow I knew I'd made a mistake. I knew it days before the ceremony, Bernie. I suppose it was intuition, little hints I picked up. I knew I shouldn't marry him."

"But you did."

"I almost got married a few years ago," she said, "to a perfectly nice young man, and I got cold feet and backed out at the last minute. So I thought I was just doing the same thing all over again, and I told myself I had to go through with it this time. I was afraid to go to Aruba, Bernie. I think I knew something would happen to me there."

"And that's why you talked him into coming to Cuttleford House instead."

"That's right. And then driving up I thought, well, I can leave first thing in the morning. I can grab the car keys when he's not looking and get out of there. And when we walked across the bridge . . ."

"Yes?"

"I thought, well, if we're snowed in for the weekend, and if I can't get away, then maybe I'll get over this case of the jitters and settle down and be a wife. But I wasn't sure if it would snow enough to keep me there. And I thought, well, if something happened to the bridge—"

"You'd be forced to stay."

"That's right. And I thought I would just cut the ropes, just like that, but they were thick and tough, and the cold didn't make it any easier. I had to give up because Dakin was coming back up the path to see what had happened to me, and if he saw me sawing away at the ropes—"

"He might have wondered."

"God only knows what he would have thought. I was going to go outside later and finish the job. In fact, I did come downstairs after I, uh—"

"Consummated your marriage."

"Yes. I was going to finish what I'd started, but I was also all flustered because you had turned up at Cuttleford House after all, you and uh—"

"Carolyn," Carolyn said.

"Yes. And I looked around until I found you, Bernie, and then I uh—"

"Finished what you'd started."

"So to speak, yes. And then I thought of going outside again, but I was so warm and cozy, and pretty sleepy, too, and the snow was still coming down out there. And I found myself wondering why I'd wanted to disable the bridge in the first place. I didn't have to seal off my escape route to make it through the weekend. Married life wasn't going to be so bad."

"Married life," I said.

"Well, I don't suppose I was likely to be the traditional wife, Bernie, baking cookies and mending socks."

"No," I said, "I suppose not."

"I never thought anybody would get killed. To tell you the truth, I thought it would take a chain saw to get through those ropes. I didn't realize I'd weakened them enough so that the bridge would give way if anybody set foot on it."

"And then Orris fell to his death."

"Yes. And I knew it was my fault."

"But you didn't say anything."

"No, of course not," she said. "What about you, Bernie?"

"What about me?"

"Are you going to say anything?"

"I just did."

"To anybody else, I mean. You didn't say anything to the police. I guess you hadn't figured it out by then."

"Sure I had. I knew Wolpert would have slashed right through those ropes, and so would anybody else who'd gone out there for that express purpose. There were plenty of tools that would have done the job. The kitchen was full of long sharp knives, and if you didn't want to go that far there were loads of exotic edged weapons on the walls, like the kris I wound up using to ruin my parka. So I figured the sabotage was a spur-of-the-moment thing, and that's when it came to me. Little Lettice, sawing away with a teeny-weeny penknife. Well, it turned out to be mightier than the sword, didn't it?"

"What are you going to do, Bernie?"

"Me? Sell books until six o'clock or so, then go home."

"You know what I mean. What are you going to do about me? Are you going to tell anybody?"

I shook my head.

"You're not?"

"I told you. That's enough."

"Why?"

"Why tell you?"

"Yes, why? When you called, Bernie, I thought I'd wind up coming over to your place, and you'd put on your Mel Tormé record and we'd enjoy ourselves in front of your phony Mondrian. But that's not going to happen."

"Somehow I guessed as much."

"It's never going to happen, Bernie. You ruined it forever. Why? That's what I want to know."

"Well," I said.

"Never mind," she said. "Don't tell me. I don't really want to know. You won't be seeing me again, Bernie. Goodbye."

TWENTY-NINE

"She may not want to know," Carolyn said, "but I do. What was that all about, Bern? Why'd you call her and make her come down here? And why schedule things so you got to play the scene in front of me? Not that I'm complaining, I wouldn't have missed it for the world, but . . ."

"But why did I do it that way."

"Right."

I thought about it and took a bite of my sandwich. It had gone untouched since Lettice walked in, and an interlude like that can give you an appetite. I chewed and swallowed and drank some cream soda, and I said, "Raymond Chandler."

"Huh?"

"It was a Raymond Chandler case," I said. "Once I realized that, I went out and took action, instead of trying to put the pieces together like some English gentleman assembling a jigsaw puzzle in his drawing room. That's why I did what I did that night while you were sleeping."

"When did Philip Marlowe fake his own death and stab

a dummy with a wavy knife, Bern? I must have missed that book."

"Well, you know what I mean. And I certainly had Marlowe and Chandler in mind when I wrapped it all up in the library. The way I confronted Dakin Littlefield? Pure Philip Marlowe."

"If you say so, Bern."

I drank the last of the cream soda. "Maybe you can't see it," I said. "But the business just now with Lettice, that was Marlowe."

"It was?"

"Uh-huh. I couldn't let her think she got away with it."

"You didn't want to play the sap for her," she said. "But that's not Philip Marlowe, is it? It's more like Sam Spade."

"He wouldn't play the sap for Bridget O'Shaughnessy," I said, "but this wasn't a matter of playing the sap. This was getting at the truth, no matter what it did to human relationships."

"And the truth was that she cut the ropes."

I nodded. "And there was no point bringing it up at the time, because it would just have confused the issue. I suppose she was guilty of something, whether it was malicious mischief or negligent homicide, because if she hadn't whittled away at the ropes Orris wouldn't have been killed. But how could you prove any of that anyway?"

"So you waited and brought it up now."

"Right."

"Why, Bern? Because you wanted an excuse to see her again?"

I shook my head. "Because I didn't want to see her again. She tried to cut down a bridge. Well, I wanted to burn mine.

You heard what she said, how she expected to wind up at my place listening to Mel Tormé. I wanted to make sure that didn't happen."

"Because you weren't interested."

"Because I was," I said. "And I always would be, and there could never be any future in a relationship with someone like Lettice, or much of a present, either. So I wanted to fix things so that I'd never see her again. Now I can't call her and she'll never call me, and that's the way it should be."

She pursed her lips and let out a soundless whistle. "I think you did the right thing," she said. "And I have to tell you, Bern, I'm impressed."

"Thanks," I said, "but don't give me too much credit. I just asked myself what Philip Marlowe would have done, and then I went ahead and did it."

"Raymond Chandler."

It was an hour later, and I'd actually sold something in the interim, a nice set of Daniel Defoe. The customer was a lanky fellow who owned a batch of launderettes. He'd almost bought the set two weeks before, but I'd felt obliged to point out that it was missing a volume. Conscience may not make cowards of us all, but it can spoil a lot of sales.

He came back and carried the books to the counter. "I thought about it," he said, "and it struck me that a complete set would cost a good deal more."

"No question."

"And if I ever locate the missing volume, I can probably pick it up for a couple of bucks, and then I'd be way ahead of the game."

"You would indeed."

"So I'll have something to look for, and I'll enjoy that. And if I never complete the set, well, who cares? They'll look fine on the shelf the way they are, and as far as reading them is concerned, hey, who am I kidding? I had to read *Moll Flanders* in college, and I read the Cliff's Notes instead. Aside from the Classic Comic of *Robinson Crusoe*, that's as far as I ever got with Defoe." He patted the stack of books. "I intend to have a go at these," he said, "but I'll wait until I've read all seven volumes before I start pissing and moaning because the eighth volume is missing."

So I bagged the books and took his money, feeling for all the world like virtue rewarded, and a little later the door opened again, and a familiar voice said, "Raymond Chandler." And I looked up and it was Carolyn.

"The book," she said. "The reason we went to Cuttleford House in the first place."

"*The Big Sleep*."

"Right. We saw it on the shelf, and it was still there after Jonathan Rathburn was murdered, and then a little later it was missing. What happened to it?"

"I took it."

"You took it?"

"For safekeeping," I said. "And so I'd have something to read."

"Something to read?"

"In Rathburn's room. I knew I was going to hole up there, and I didn't know what I'd find on the bookshelves, so I stowed *The Big Sleep* in the top drawer of his dresser. It's a good thing I brought it, too. The only books in there were Victorian romance novels by women with hyphens in their names."

"And you actually read the book?"

"What's so remarkable about that? Chandler's still a good read."

"I guess it wasn't the Hammett copy, huh?"

"What makes you so sure?"

"Well, you wouldn't actually read it if it was, would you? A book worth so much money?"

I opened a drawer, withdrew a book, opened the cover. "Nowadays," I said, "most authors use the title page for a simple signature, or the half-title page for a full inscription. But Chandler didn't do this sort of thing often enough to care about the proper form. Here's what he wrote on the flyleaf: 'To Dashiell Hammett, who put homicide in the mean streets where it belongs. I trust you'll give this little volume a place on the shelf next to your own. With appreciation and friendship, Raymond Chandler.' "

"Wow! Talk about literary history. Can I see, Bern? That's what it says, all right. But what's this?"

"Can you make it out?"

"It's a real scrawl, isn't it? Did Chandler write this, too? It doesn't look like his handwriting."

"It's not."

" 'What a pretentious bore. Let him take his book and shove it up his prissy hero's ass. Come to think of it, they'd probably both enjoy it.' It's not signed, Bern."

"No, it's not."

"Don't tell me, Bern. Is it . . ."

"It's Hammett's handwriting," I said. "More of a scrawl than usual, but that's how he wrote when he was drunk, and he must have been pretty far gone to write something like that. He certainly didn't like the book enough to take it home with him, and I guess somebody stuck it on a shelf."

"Raymond Chandler's first book," she said, "in nice condition, with an intact dust jacket. Inscribed by the author to Dashiell Hammett, and counter-inscribed by Hammett. And what an inscription!"

"It's something, all right."

"I guess it must be the ultimate association copy in American literature."

"Well, if you found a copy of *Tamerlane* inscribed by Poe to the young Abraham Lincoln, it'd probably put this volume in the shade. Barring that, I guess it's way up there."

"What's it worth, Bern?"

"I don't know," I said. "A fortune, but how big a fortune? I couldn't even guess. You'd need to hold an auction to answer the question. It would depend on who showed up and just how badly they wanted it."

"Wow."

"But it doesn't matter," I said. "I can't sell it."

She stared at me.

"Lots of things didn't come to light up at Cuttleford House," I said. "We never did find out what became of the real Mr. Pettisham, or what Rathburn and Wolpert were hoping to get from him. And I kept Lettice's secret, and there were probably other people keeping other secrets. But one thing that did come out was my two occupations. Millicent Savage had already told everybody that I was a burglar—"

"Because you'd made the mistake of telling her."

"Well, yes. But now Ray told them, too, and they had to believe it. Besides, that explained how I'd been able to get into various rooms and unearth various facts. But it also came out that I was a bookseller."

"So?"

"So after the dust had settled and before you and I could head for home, Nigel Eglantine took me aside. Ever since they bought the place he'd known they ought to do something about the books. He'd hesitated approaching a dealer because he didn't know who would prove trustworthy. But he could tell I was an honest chap—"

"Hadn't he just learned you were a burglar?"

"I guess he figured I must be an honest burglar. Anyway, he wanted to know what I'd charge to go through the entire library, pull the books that were worth selling and the junk that ought to be disposed of, and arrange the remainder into some semblance of order. I told him I'd spotted a fair number of collectible books on his shelves, and that I'd broker them for a split of the net receipts. And while I was at it I'd clear out the obsolete travel guides and world almanacs, the *Reader's Digest* condensed books, the theme cookbooks from the Junior League of Chillicothe, Ohio. All the junk you can't unload at a yard sale. When I was done he'd have a nice piece of change, an orderly library, and a lot less clutter."

"And you'd have a few days in the country and a fair return on your time."

"It'll take more than a few days," I said. "I'll have to close the store for at least a week, and probably two. But I'll do it in August, when it'll be so hot here in town I'll be able to talk myself into going to the country. And yes, I'll be well paid for my time. He's got a lot of books there, and some of them'll bring decent money."

She frowned, thinking it through. "But what about *The Big Sleep*? He never knew it was there, and it's not there anymore. Can't you just consign it at Christie's or Sotheby's without saying where it came from?"

I shook my head. "With something like this," I said,

"provenance is everything. What really authenticates the handwriting is the passage from Lester Harding Ross's memoir that indicates the meeting of the two men took place, and that there was a book signed and presented. If I want to get top dollar for the book, I have to be able to say where it came from. Even if I don't say a word, anyone who walks the cat back is going to wind up at Cuttleford House, and once the book is connected to Cuttleford House I'm on the spot."

Raffles put his forepaws out in front of him and stretched, humping his back to show what he thought of the prospect of being walked back to Cuttleford House.

"So when you go there in August you take it along in your suitcase," Carolyn said, "and you discover it there. You'd have to split the money with Nigel and Cissie, but your share still would be a decent sum, wouldn't it?"

"I suppose so."

"And you'd make a name for yourself. You'd be the man who discovered the Hammett copy of *The Big Sleep*."

"Yeah."

"What's the matter, Bern?"

"I'd be the man who let the world know that one great American writer scribbled an inscription full of fawning praise for another great American writer, who didn't care enough about the book to take it home with him. Instead he scrawled a nasty little addendum to the inscription and left the book behind. Oh, I'd make a name for myself, all right. I'd be the man who smeared muck on two of his favorite writers."

"They're the ones who smeared the muck, Bern."

"Well, I don't have to be the one who points it out to the

world." I sighed. "I could make a few dollars," I said. "I could sell the book privately and hope that word of the sale never found its way back to Cuttleford House. I could smuggle it back in the way I smuggled it out, make a big show of discovering it, and cut myself in for a percentage of what it would bring. But you know what I'm going to do?"

"If you tell me you're going to burn it," she said, "I swear I'm going to scream louder than Earlene Cobbett."

"Burn it? Are you out of your mind?"

"No, but—"

"I'm going to keep it," I said. "For God's sake, Carolyn, this is the book Chandler took along to give to George Harmon Coxe. He wound up giving it to Hammett instead, complete with flowery inscription, and Hammett . . . well, we know what he did with it."

"Right."

"I don't really think Edgar Allan Poe ever inscribed a copy of *Tamerlane and Other Poems* for a young Illinois lawyer, and even if he did I'm never going to have a chance to hold it in my hand, let alone own it. But I can own this book, Carolyn. No one will ever know it's mine, but I'll know."

"Like the Mondrian hanging in your apartment."

I nodded. "Exactly like the Mondrian," I said.

"Lettice thinks it's a fake, because how would you come to have a real Mondrian? You got it the old-fashioned way. You stole it."

"I really enjoy owning that painting," I said, "and the fact that it's stolen doesn't lessen the enjoyment a bit. So what if I can't ever sell it? And so what if I can't sell *The Big Sleep*? I'll get as much or more satisfaction out of sitting in my chair and looking up from my book at my painting. Then I'll have another small sip of Glen Drumnadrochit, and then I'll read some more Chandler and look some more at Mondrian."

"Where did the Drumnadrochit come from?"

"Scotland, originally. By way of Cuttleford House, because I stuck two bottles of it in my bag on my way out the door."

"That's a terrible thing to do, Bern. Two bottles?"

"Uh-huh. One's for you."

"Oh," she said, and thought about it. "Maybe it's not so terrible."

I was reading Raymond Chandler and sipping Glen Drumnadrochit when the phone rang.

"It's me," she said. "Bern, what about the cook?"

"The cook?"

"At Cuttleford House. Who killed her and why?"

"Beats me," I said.

"But—"

"According to Ray," I said, "they can't determine the cause of death, beyond saying it was cardiac arrest. In other words her heart stopped beating, and it's a rare case of death when that doesn't happen. They couldn't find any trace of poison, though it's hard to say how thorough a toxicological scan they did. It's possible she had a heart attack, or a brain aneurysm, or a stroke. On the other hand, when people are getting killed left and right, it's hard to believe that a death like hers could be completely accidental."

"She could have heard something on the radio," she said. "A news flash, and it shed some light on what was going on, and somebody knew that she knew, and killed her."

"It's possible."

"Or she could have witnessed something, or overheard something."

"She could have," I agreed.

"Or somebody else had it in for her," she said, "for reasons that had nothing to do with Rathburn or Wolpert or Dakin Littlefield. And whoever it was just seized the opportunity."

"Maybe that's how it happened."

"But which is it, Bern?"

I shrugged, even though she couldn't see it over the phone. "We'll never know," I said.

"But—"

"It's perfect," I said. "It's so Raymond Chandler. You know the story of when they were filming *The Big Sleep?* They were going over the script, and somebody wanted to know who killed the chauffeur. And nobody could figure it out, so somebody thought of calling Chandler, since after all he was the one who wrote the book. So they called him and asked him."

"And?"

"He said he didn't know. Isn't that great? Just because he wrote the book didn't mean he knew who killed the chauffeur. And we'll never know who killed the cook. Just like Raymond Chandler."

There was a long silence. "I don't know," she said at length. "The English mysteries may be a lot less realistic, what with people getting killed with tropical fish and all, but there's something awfully satisfying in the way it all works out in the end. If a cook dies, by the end of the book you always know who killed her."

"And it's generally the butler," I said, "whereas the real world is a lot less certain, and there are things you never do find out. I realize it's frustrating, but you can live with it, can't you?"

"What the hell," she said. "I guess I'll have to."

· A NOTE ON THE TYPE ·

The typeface used in this book is a version of Bodoni, based on the fonts cut by the Italian printer Giambattista Bodoni (1740–1813) at the turn of the nineteenth century. Early in his career his work was conventional (though he was always forward-looking and was an admirer of the work of John Baskerville), but as a product of his time, Bodoni believed that type design ought to be rational. Late in life he produced the revolutionary fonts named for him, the first of the so-called "moderns," characterized by high contrast between thin and thick strokes and "unbracketed" (untapered), thin, right-angled serifs. For the first time, type left behind both the chisel and the quill, so *modern* is an appropriate term: Once typography was free of its roots in engraving and calligraphy (and despite the disapproval of the likes of William Morris), an explosion of variation in letter forms started, one that has continued ever since.

Bernie Rhodenbarr also appears in the following
No Exit Press paperbacks:
Burglars Can't Be Choosers (£4.99)
The Burglar in the Closet (£4.99)
The Burglar Who Liked to Quote Kipling (£5.99)
The Burglar Who Studied Spinoza (£4.99)
The Burglar Who Painted Like Mondrian (£5.99)
The Burglar Who Traded Ted Williams (£5.99)
The Burglar Who Thought He Was Bogart (£5.99)

For readers of this book only, we have a special offer.
Choose any three of the above titles for just £10.00 inc P&P
(UK only), a saving of at least £5 and you will also receive
a copy of the leading crime fiction magazine - CrimeTime
(worth £2.50) - absolutely FREE.

Cheques, P.O. payable to Oldcastle Books Ltd.
Mastercard & Visa Accepted.
No Exit Press (Lib pb), 18 Coleswood Rd, Harpenden,
Herts, AL5 1EQ.